One Night

at the

Jacaranda

One Night at the Jacaranda

Carol Cooper

Text copyright © 2013 Carol Cooper

The right of Carol Cooper to be identified as the author of this Work has been asserted by her in accordance with sections 77 and 78 of the Copyright, Designs and Patents Act 1988.

All characters and events in this work, other than those clearly in the public domain, are entirely fictitious. Any resemblance to any persons, living or dead, is purely coincidental.

All rights reserved.

ISBN-13: 978-1492803423

Chapter One

Sanjay

Bloody bollocks. Why didn't he have a girlfriend? Or even a wife? He'd never wanted to get married, have kids, that whole routine. Still, it would have done the trick.

Sanjay put on Nirvana and whacked up the volume. Time was when he and his mates, especially Ben, would put on a CD before they did anything, whether it was gelling their hair, yakking on the phone or pretending to tidy their rooms.

Nowadays music was no longer a reflex. Sanjay had to consciously choose the right CD for his mood. This evening Nirvana were perfect. They so often were. He found two socks that matched, then shoved his shoes on.

Why, bloody why? For about the thousandth time, he blamed himself for not having had someone, anyone, since Laure. If he hadn't been on his own, it might have all been OK. Or maybe if he'd worked somewhere that did medical checks, like

Marks & Spencer or the Army, instead of that excuse for a charity that he was actually with.

OK, so there were a couple of flaws here. For one thing, Sanjay loved working for Kids First. For another, the Army hadn't been great for Ben's health.

Now that was another thing that made him livid. He flung the cupboard door open, denting the wall with the knob.

Tie. Which one? While Cobain dirged on about a heart-shaped box, Sanjay considered his options. Knitted nasties that his dad insisted were dead trendy or would come back in fashion (they never were and never would). Hideous polyester numbers that even the sales guy in Topman wouldn't have worn. Silk ties that cost too much and still looked ordinary. And the black tie for funerals. Thanks for that little reminder.

Nah. Fuck the tie. Tonight was hardly a bloody job interview, was it? He'd just wear the shirt and look casual. Trying too hard was a bad look.

Sanjay examined himself in the mirror to see if the open neck would expose the scar above his collarbone. But really, was anyone going to check him out that closely?

In the hall, he discovered that Dainty had thrown up again. Bollocks! He wiped it up with paper towels, reflecting on the fact that cats never regurgitated fur-balls onto the floor or crapped on the bed unless the owner was in a frantic hurry.

God, it smelled vile. Just like cat food did when it came out of the tin. If he could have his life over, he would cook his cat fresh fish and liver. He wouldn't name her Dainty either.

There was some more sick on the corner of the Ikea rug. He tore off another hank of paper towel. Bollocks, bollocks, bollocks. This was his new favourite word, and no wonder.

Before leaving, he gave Dainty a kiss in the middle of the tabby patch on her head. "Bye, Daint. Wish me luck."

Dainty, now on the sofa looking grumpy, did not even feign a response. Grabbing his keys and mobile, Sanjay turned off Nirvana and left the flat, locking the deadbolt behind him.

Perhaps he should have read magazines, he thought as he clattered down the stairs, like *GQ* and *Men's Health*, or whichever ones had features on checking your goolies and not leaving your health to chance. But he hadn't, because he wasn't the worrying checking type. He'd always figured life was for living. It was also, he now knew, for dying.

What an ace chat-up line that was going to be.

On the bus, he ignored an old bat angling for his seat and mulled over the last 10 months or so. They said this cancer was treatable, but only if it was picked up early, at a stage when removing the testicle would do the trick. He didn't really mind having a false one. Not that anyone had seen it lately except his oncologist.

But he did mind the spread of cells through his lymph system. They had infiltrated up to his neck, for fuck's sake! Before he was diagnosed, he never thought about where cancers spread, or how they got there. Now he struggled to think of much else.

As the bus approached Marylebone Road, doubts crept in. What was he actually looking for? A nursemaid, a passionate fling, or just a shag? Any of those would do. At least it would prove he was still alive.

Karen

Karen piled lentil bake onto her son's plate. "You don't have to like it. It's for eating, not falling in love with." She regretted it as soon as she'd said it, but too late.

"Ha-ha!" trilled Charlotte. "Damon is in lu-urve."

Damon scowled at his big sister. "You're a moron." This earned him a poke in the side of his Manchester United shirt from Charlotte when she thought their mum hadn't noticed.

"What's a moron?" asked Edward who was only four.

Ashley, a whole year older than Edward and thus infinitely wiser, explained. "Duh! It means a real thicko."

Edward went back to arranging lentils in a pretty pattern around the edge of his plate.

Karen ran her fingers through her hair. It was hardly a nourishing meal if nobody actually ate it. "When you've all finished, bring your plates over so Charlotte and I can put them in the dishwasher." At

10, Charlotte was the oldest and least likely to break anything.

"Do I put them in the dishwasher with the lentils still on?"

Karen made a face they called the Mum Sigh. "Now Charlotte, you know the answer."

On the counter, Karen's mobile chirruped. "Oh, hi, Rose. We're just finishing supper."

When she heard Rose's suggestion, Karen went into the hall. "No, I do not! Speed-dating sounds vile. Yes, I realise it's been a while." In truth there had been no dates since Thomas had moved out six months ago. She lowered her voice. "Of course I miss sex."

"Time you did something about it" said Rose, who reasonably pointed out that eligible men were hardly going to beat a path to Karen's door. And no, the meter reader didn't count.

"And what would I wear?"

Rose reminded her she always looked amazing. "The world needs a chance to see you."

"Well, I don't know. When is it anyway?"

"Tomorrow. Me and the Tupperware club signed you up. And don't argue. I'll babysit."

Yes, she did miss sex. A lot.

The best years for sex were before children, but the best time for sex was anytime.

She had been cleaning the bath. No point getting dressed first, so there she was, attacking the gunge around the taps once and for all.

As the water was running, Karen felt him before she heard him. A whisper of a touch as Thomas caressed her inner thighs. That always did it for her.

He dropped his bathrobe on the floor. Now she had Cillit Bang in one hand and something far more interesting in the other. She whimpered with pleasure at his hardness.

She didn't need to look up. His bare feet were planted on the floor behind hers. He worked her for mere seconds before she felt the want overwhelm her. The bath cleaner clattered into the bath. Lime scale could wait.

Grabbing the edge of the tub, Karen spread her legs wide. She was so wet she could hear it. He barely needed guiding in. Just one delectable sliding movement, then that bolt home. She moaned as he hit the top spot.

Thomas' need was equally urgent. The bathmat moved rhythmically beneath their feet.

Oh. My. God. She had to grip the bath tighter to make sure she didn't sag onto the floor. She could only see him if she glanced in the mirror on the right-hand wall. She looked again.

Like porn, only better.

She cried out as the heat rose and engulfed her. He became harder for a few moments before she felt him fill her with warmth that would soon ooze out and drip down her leg. She loved that almost as much as her own climax.

Karen blow-dried her hair and chose a dress she'd adored for nearly 10 years. It wasn't what you wore as much as how you wore it. In a glossy at a jumble sale, there was once an advert that said *Just wear a smile and a Jantzen.* She hadn't a clue what a Jantzen was. Might have been a designer jacket or another word for orgasm. Whatever. Confidence could hide any deficiency.

Since the most pressing deficiency was financial, all her clothes were finds. Accessories were another story. While you could get away with a £4.99 dress from Oxfam, you had to have good shoes, and those babies cost serious money.

The other problem was her body. After feeding four babies, anyone would fail the pencil test, but whole pencil-cases could have nestled under Karen's boobs. If she found someone suitable, she'd have to pray for a power cut.

As promised, Rose arrived right on time. "You look really lovely, Karen."

"Thanks. I hope the children behave."

"They will" said Rose.

This was unlikely. They often said kids behaved better for other people than for their parents, but hers played up even more, a fact Rose had obligingly forgotten. Why wouldn't they act up? No baby-sitter would put them on the naughty step or ban TV for a week.

Karen put her shoes on by the front door. "Ooh, nice" said Rose.

They were Karen's favourites, green with little bows. Even in the sale two years ago the price-tag had caused palpitations. She dreaded to think how many lentil bakes she could have made for the cost of those little beauties. "Thanks, Rose. Wish me luck."

Laure

Although Laure had only been in from work 20 minutes, the heap on her bed was impressive. Underneath the jeans, silky tops, skirts of all shapes and lengths, and tights in various shades lay a well-thumbed copy of *Flirt Your Way into His Heart*. Laure had consigned most of its advice to memory and tonight she would put it into practice. First, the right amount of eye contact. Then active listening and some mirroring. If he put his arm on the table, she'd put hers there too. She might match him drink for drink as well, though she drew the line at spreading her legs wide and scratching her crotch.

But she couldn't decide what to wear. Red dress? Too obvious. Blue shift? Men liked blue, but it didn't do much for her. What about the Joseph blazer? On balance, no. Black was better for a trip to court than an evening out. She settled on a charcoal velvet skirt, a muted grey Armani top, and red suede heels.

There was still one important issue to resolve. Laure's occupation intimated men, and the Flirt Coach of the Year didn't cover that topic in her books.

This time, she told herself as she smoothed on tinted moisturiser, she might use her real name, but say she was a secretary. No, a hairdresser. Hopefully this was not going to be a repeat of the Great Bloke Crisis of 2011, or those of quite a few previous years as well.

And tonight, she warned herself, she wouldn't go home with anyone. Though it wasn't clear to her why, first-night sex had blighted a lot of previous relationships. Nonetheless she was wearing the briefest La Perla knickers she could still walk in. Just in case.

Finding someone was a challenge. Online profiles meant drastic re-invention. In real life, she was Laure Dimmock, lawyer aged 38. In Dateland, it was another story.

But then dating sites were populated by guys who posed with pot-bellies and sandals and lied through their teeth. Obviously they all claimed to have GSOH, which meant they laughed like drains at their own jokes.

Many said they loved curling up by the fire with someone special. In her entire life, Laure had only met one man who lit fires. Her great-uncle. Internet daters often claimed to be tactile and sexy. That was plain creepy. The more discursive entries were equally cringe-making: *I'm into all kinds of sports, and keen to find a partner who wants to explore our physical passion in all its forms.* Why didn't they just write *deviant* and be done with it?

In her dream world, Laure would randomly meet a hot guy while out shopping. He'd have eyes like molten chocolate and a French name like Yves. They'd swap phone numbers and then - well, the rest was in soft-focus.

In reality, the only time she'd spotted anyone attractive at the supermarket, she'd up-ended her handbag. Instead of helping her collect coins and tampons off the floor while begging for her number, the guy had turned away and carried on studying tea prices.

Clearly she had to leave her comfort zone and apply herself to dating with the same diligence she'd used when studying for her LLB. They said sport was a great way to meet people. But there were reasons why that wasn't going to help Laure, not counting the fact that she couldn't play tennis. Her feet looked huge in trainers, and her honey-coloured hair frizzed up when she perspired.

Sailing clubs had entailed hours of drinking, only to spend most of the weekend frozen, wet and nursing a head injury from the boom or whatever it was called attacking her without warning. From time to time Laure considered getting a dog, because people always stopped to talk. But the poor mutt would have got lonely during the day. Laure knew what loneliness was like.

Laure curled her lashes to make her eyes brighter and younger, then dabbed a new Clinique cream to disguise a hint of darkness and a few more wrinkles than were welcome. From her chin she plucked two stray hairs that had grown overnight, thanks to the Lebanese genes that she'd got from her mother. All the aunts were notable for their hairy chins.

Sighing, she plugged in the straighteners. Finding a date wasn't really the problem. It was hanging onto him. This time, she would be more careful. The last boyfriend had not reacted well when she said they'd have to get a move on if they wanted kids. Actually she wasn't sure what his reaction had been. She hadn't heard from him since.

Well, you lived and learned. As she slicked on lip gloss, she looked into the mirror and repeated aloud her mantra: *I am not desperate. I am calm, I am serene, I am a sex goddess.*

Geoff

"So I thought I would go wheat-free."

Geoff could have written a book called *The Last Patient*, he reflected, tilting the consulting-room chair back as far as it would go, which wasn't far as he had a cheaper model than his partners. Sometimes patients booked the latest slot so they could be seen after work, but mostly it was because they knew there was nobody after them.

Then they said 'This won't take a minute.' True. It took more like an hour. Or, in the middle of a long list of symptoms, they'd come out with 'Well, at least I'm not keeping anyone waiting.' That was how he'd missed his son's nativity play.

Obviously the main obstacle to writing was lack of time. What with the clinics, paperwork, meetings and a trainee to look after, his week was full. He could have done with more time to see Davey.

By the time Geoff got to the Jacaranda tonight, there would only be the dregs left. At medical school he'd always been first in the queue for pretty girls, as well as prizes like the Finucane medal. Gone were those days. He had erectile dysfunction now. Not yet 40 and on the scrap-heap of sex. What kind of a doctor was he if he couldn't sort out his own ED?

With a jolt, Geoff realized Mrs Thing was still talking about her irritable bowel. She passed rabbit pellets one day, but the next it was like a length of toothpaste. "I don't think the wheat-free helped much. Do you think I should cut out milk?"

Geoff made a non-committal noise while Mrs Thing continued. His trouble with names would have been all right had he stayed in hospital medicine. There, it was OK to be distant and distracted, *de rigueur* to talk about 'the aneurysm in bed three' to colleagues, and to peer over your glasses absent-mindedly on ward rounds and imply, if not actually say, 'Which one are you?' It meant your mind was on higher things like, say, cystic lesions of the pancreas or vaccines for dengue fever. But in the cosy, cuddly, touchy-feely world of general practice, it did not do at all.

Now Mrs Thing was filling in the details. "At work last week, I used the toilet three times, and every time it came out just like a smoothie. But this weekend just gone, it was fine. I only did a toilet once, but it was, you know, nice. Really nice."

Geoff had been a doctor for 15 years, but he still failed to see how a bowel movement could be described as 'nice', let alone 'really nice'. He hoped to God the women at speed-dating didn't witter on about their bowels.

Michael

Michael installed himself at his immaculately shiny kitchen table with an apple and a block of mature cheddar. As he'd cut the apple into 16 pieces, he allowed himself 16 small cubes of cheese to go with it. They helped the apple down. If it weren't for the fact that apples were healthier, he'd have done without the Granny Smith and just put away a slab of cheddar.

There'd be little to eat at the venue, though there'd be drinks. Expensive ones.

Now Michael had inadvertently eaten two pieces of cheese in a row, so he forced two pieces of apple down to make up for it, wincing at the sharpness. Obviously you had to meet women face to face. On the internet, you could waste a lot of time emailing then setting up a meeting, and you didn't have to be a chartered accountant as he was to realise it was inefficient.

You might plan what to say to the fit blonde from North London who claimed to be a top property consultant, only to find out when you met that she lived in Milton Keynes and manned the phone in some estate agent's, and that her photo was 20 years old to cover up for the fact that she wasn't fit anymore. Some of the women had the drawback of having never been fit, ever. They posted a friend's photo instead.

Presentation mattered. As with books, the cover could tell you if it was likely to be a goer. But he also had his protocol to perfect. *What job do you do? Where do you live? How did you vote at the last election? What do you like reading?* His list ranged from Dostoevsky through Gabriel Garcia Marquez to the latest offerings, including some of the better titles from the publisher he worked for.

He'd made several copies of the list, because what was the point of asking questions if you didn't record every answer? He would put ticks or crosses next to each question. This would help him get exactly what he wanted. He rubbed himself hard in anticipation.

Harriet

Harriet sat by the mosque, examining it critically in the fading light. How she hated that mosque. But the minaret was OK. She tilted her head. Yes, it was practically straight. Or as straight as possible in the circumstances.

Maybe Simon wouldn't notice. After all, he'd barely used it as an alarm clock since he'd bought it on a business trip to Oman. It was 100% plastic and bright turquoise. Only once had Simon ever woken to its thunderously loud *Allah-hu Akbar*. Harriet was always the one to rouse him in the morning, with his favourite cup containing Lapsang Souchong made the way he wanted, which meant with a teapot because he insisted that made it taste superior.

She hadn't meant to break his tacky clock, but her sleeve had caught on the needle-sharp minaret, which was how it had ended up on the floor.

Good stuff, Superglue.

It was time to go. Harriet had meant to arrive early to soak up the atmosphere, chat to people and pick up juicy quotes. Now it looked like she was barely going to make the start. Apart from waiting for glue to dry, she'd also had to apply make-up to look the part, take phone calls from subs with queries (all lame), and find a bag that was big enough without looking suspicious. It had to be the tote bag, with a chiffon scarf covering the Dictaphone.

A digital machine would have been nice, but money was tight. Harriet packed a couple of blank tapes, as an assignment sometimes took twice as long as expected and turned out to be three times as interesting. She wasn't about to make that mistake.

People always assumed you wore a wire to record conversations. Well, maybe on TV they did, but that was prohibitively expensive, so freelances like her used a handheld of some sort. Finally Harriet tested the machine.

Damn. New batteries needed. She took two out of Simon's mosque clock, saying *Allah-hu Akbar* to it by way of thanks.

When she'd started out, she'd intended to become a household name, but now, 16 years on, she was still a lowly freelance. Once, she'd had dreams of a swish penthouse of her own. Well, Simon had put a roof over her head and lent her money as well. They'd been together a long time. He wasn't a bad man, and she owed him. She winced as she recalled quite how much.

It was galling to ring a PR agency and, when she gave her name, to be asked 'From which company?' It proved, if proof were needed, that nobody had ever heard of her. She used to reply 'I work for myself.' Nowadays she'd say 'I'm from Bullshit Media. Shall I spell it for you?'

She arranged her scarf in the tote-bag. Tonight's feature was part of a series called *The Seven Ages of Dating*. At first the commissioning editor of *RightHere!*, a short but terrifying Glaswegian, had asked Harriet to do a really fun piece on women who traded their baby for a Hermes handbag. When Harriet's jaw dropped, the editor assured her there were zillions of women out there that would feel unconditional love for a Birkin, especially since it wouldn't poop and cry all night, and it certainly wouldn't tell them it hated them in 12 years time.

Harriet knew what 'really fun' pieces involved. After making hundreds of phone calls and pestering everyone on Facebook and Twitter, she'd still end up without any case studies willing to give their real names and photos, let alone women young, slim and blonde enough. Editors always claimed to know their demographic through and through, but Harriet doubted if any of the readers were the smart sassy under-40s that *RightHere!* claimed they were. The magazine could probably keep 99% of its readers happy with knitting patterns and offers on cod liver oil.

Instead Harriet had asked "Could it be a Mulberry bag?"

The editor gave her a withering look. "Are ye daft? Nobody would do that."

Thank God Harriet had wangled *The Seven Ages of Dating* instead. Before leaving the house, she scribbled a note for Simon, saying she'd be back around 11, and propped it up by the kettle. Not that he looked at anything she wrote these days. If he did bother, he'd probably complain he couldn't decipher her impossible scrawl.

Chapter Two

The Jacaranda had the longest zinc bar in Marylebone. Occupying the lower two floors of a Georgian building, the restaurant was surrounded by upmarket grocers, specialist bookshops, funky gadget stores, designer boutiques and a couple of charity shops which took in a lot of designer cast-offs. Despite there being more cafés, patisseries and restaurants than anyone could possibly need, they were always full of customers lured by the aroma of warm bread and freshly ground coffee. Marylebone was very much the place to be, especially if you had nothing very much to do.

Using the outside stairwell, Harriet went straight down to the bar on the lower ground floor. Inside, the walls were wood-panelled, and the famous bar would have caught her eye even without the pink fluorescent sign above it that said, elegantly yet superfluously, *BAR*.

A young woman in a flapper dress and pearls busied herself ticking names off a list. "Welcome" she beamed.

"Thank you. Is this 20s night?" Harriet asked.

"Oh no, we always dress up" replied the man next to her. His slicked down hair was a perfect match for his gleaming dinner jacket. "Great to see you here. We hope you have a fantastic time." He smiled at Harriet as he held out a badge.

Harriet pinned on 5 HARRIET.

Around the room, the small tables were of assorted sizes, and few of the chairs matched. The overall impression was eclectic, haphazard and inviting. Surely you were bound to have a great time in a place where the management was laid back and unfussy.

According to flyers on the tables, at weekends the Jacaranda played host to retro bands like Suzie Came to Dinner, or Vincent & The Grenadines. Quiz evenings and comedy acts were Tuesdays and Wednesdays. But this was Monday, when the laughter seemed a little uneasy and the atmosphere held a tinge of desperation. Tonight was Date Me Quick night.

Harriet got out her notebook. At this stage she was gathering info and turning phrases in her head. *Who put the *ming* in *mingle*,* she scribbled in her notebook. She hadn't yet worked out her angle for *The Seven Ages of Dating*, but she would soon.

At the bar some of the speed-daters chatted animatedly, doing a spot of tentative bonding while sizing up the opposition.

The men she could talk to later, during the course of the evening. The women had to be interviewed now. She doubted her Dictaphone functioned in this noise so it had to be short-hand. If anyone showed interest in her scribbling, she always said it was a shopping list. Nobody ever questioned why you'd write your lists in T-line.

Over there was a gypsy-type woman, all dolled up. She gave Harriet a glance before returning to a thin man with an outsized Adam's apple.

Harriet aimed to know exactly what people hoped for from the evening, and how long each of them had been single. It was easy to get people talking. A good opener was 'Have you been speed-dating before?' Everyone was asking that anyway, and they couldn't all be journos. Nervous people loved to unburden themselves. The brazen cheek of a question like 'How old are you?' or 'How much do you earn?' sometimes helped. It was her job to make them say something printable.

Harriet smiled at a woman in a strange lacy dress. It paid homage to Alexander McQueen, even if it didn't quite work with the striped blouse underneath. "Hey" Harriet said. "You look nice and relaxed."

"Just knackered really" said the woman, whose lapel badge said 1 KAREN.

Harriet took in her green shoes. "Love the heels, Karen. Are they L K Bennett?"

Sanjay

Still out of puff, Sanjay paused to pick cat hairs off his jacket. He wasn't sure if he was breathless from sprinting for the bus, or if it was metastatic spread of his disease. That was the trouble with the Big C. Every little thing that happened, every slight itch or ache, could be the onward march of those vicious cancer cells. Even under the microscope the swirl of cells looked as mean as snake-eyes. Sanjay didn't have a microscope, but he had Google.

"Hi, how are you?" someone asked him as he walked toward the bar. She was wearing a bright scarf draped around her shoulders, the kind of scarf that didn't really cover anything, just made you wonder what was beneath.

"Fine, thanks." Only family actually wanted to know how you were.

"I guess I will see you later" she promised as she flicked her hair and slid away.

Sanjay got a mineral water from the bar and sipped it slowly until his breathing eased. Anything stronger might have knocked him out. Some said the analogy between cancer and a guerrilla force was an overworked cliché, but, in Sanjay's experience, it was entirely apt. He'd discovered that no doctor, however smart, could deal with the sneaky onslaught of disease. His cancer was a Taliban Tumour. When was the time to retreat, he had no idea, but he knew that you couldn't predict when or where the next strike would be, or the form it might take. And you couldn't win, no matter how advanced your weapons.

Dorottya

Dorottya tossed her long black hair over one shoulder and lapped up the attention she always got, especially when she wore bright red lipstick and a Romany-style scarf. She had removed her wedding band, although she doubted if any man would have noticed had she left it on. Men were such idiots, she told herself while bestowing a dazzling smile on the congregated males.

This she had suspected from a young age. Her theory had been confirmed on leaving her home town of Szeged and going to work for her first family in England. Then, her hair had not been so glossy or so black, nor had her teeth been so white, but modern science could do a lot for mousey girls with stained incisors. English lessons helped, though progress was less about pronunciation and more about fluency in body language. By her third au pair job, she had reinvented herself as a femme fatale, albeit one with impeccable references when it came to looking after young children, helping them play creatively, cooking nourishing meals and keeping house. This last au pair posting was a huge success. So successful that she had been promoted to stepmother.

"Can I get you a drink?" asked a short man whose eyes were too close together.

As usual the women were much better turned out, thought Dorottya. She giggled strategically and replied "I'll have pink champagne."

"Bubbly, eh? Just like you." He stood so close that she felt his breath as he handed her the glass.

"Thank you." He was repulsive and there was no way she was going to hook up with him, as the English expression went. But she still lowered her eyelashes as she took a sip.

He wasn't much good at thinking things through, because you could end up buying lots of expensive drinks on a night like this without seeing a return for your outlay. And he obviously hadn't been speed-dating before, unlike Dorottya. She sighed. One was forced to find a little fun from time to time.

Michael

Michael had all his notes to help him. He looked up briefly when someone said "Hi, you look well prepared."

Of course he was. Everything was ready. At work, they sometimes said you couldn't reduce the sum total of literary endeavours to a simple plus or minus figure on a balance sheet. But they were wrong. Books were commodities, same as everything else. No exceptions.

Michael shuffled through his duplicated sheets and tried to contain his rising excitement.

Dan

Dan studied the crowd as he sipped his third lager and fine-tuned his story. No wrong moves tonight. Slovenia was a good choice. No, a fucking great choice. Nobody ever went there. Well, they hadn't before he went through the portals of HMP.

Besides, nobody would catch him out. Nobody ever did. OK, they had once. Obviously. But no need to go there.

Course, he could always go on the pull locally. But the last time he'd done that, he'd needed the sexual health clinic.

Well, he had the all-clear again. And he was going to get himself some.

Really he didn't look too bad, if he said so himself. Apart from that one tooth. Thanks, Maxy. Now one thing to avoid was shagging a cop, or a probation officer or something. Shouldn't be hard. He'd developed a nose for them.

That woman with the notepad. Couldn't figure her out. She was asking a load of questions. Whatever her game was, he wasn't going to tick her on his scorecard.

Bottom line was, all you needed for speed-dating was an email address and a debit card. Then, on the night, clean clothes and clean breath. Jeans and a white shirt. Perfect outfit, especially with his nice new belt. Nicked, natch. That was the trouble with being banged up. No matter how honest you were when you went in, stuff happened in clink.

He kept telling himself he was still the same Dan. But he'd changed. And the world had changed bigtime, which made it hard when you'd been away so long. That was why the Slovenia story was a winner.

Gulping down the rest of his lager, Dan suppressed a burp. He was a little scared. Not shit-scared. But scared nonetheless.

"OK, everyone," bellowed the young geezer in the penguin suit. "Welcome to tonight's Date Me Quick event." He asked them all to listen up to a few final instructions. They should put in ticks and crosses as the night progressed, because it was going to be busy and confusing. "Right then, you ladies are going to stay at your tables, and you gentlemen are going to move around clockwise. When I toot on this, it means your three minutes are up."

He demonstrated on a party tooter. "Please make sure you move on promptly. It's only fair. And you don't want to be removed from your chair by the next guy, especially if he's bigger than you." A ripple of nervous laughter went around the room. "One more thing, folks. I shouldn't have to say this, but don't talk about sex. Three minutes into a date isn't enough to get you to that stage. Got your scorecards and biros ready? Let's get dating!"

Chapter Three

Harriet

"I've got psoriasis" said number 16.

"OK" said Harriet.

You couldn't see it, he explained when Harriet peered at him. It was on his belly, chest and back. The worst place was his navel.

Feigning interest, Harriet asked her questions, wondering all the while what made people click. "So who's your type?" she asked him.

"I don't really have a type."

Harriet guessed it would be someone who didn't mind skin flakes everywhere.

Otherwise it was going pretty well, she thought. At this rate, she'd soon know all about them, their jobs, their families, their dirty secrets, the lot. Every journo knew that grubby details made great copy.

'*Ungle*, Hurriet, *ungle*.' The editor's words did a Scottish reel in Harriet's head. But she wasn't worried. There'd be loads of material from which to tease out the perfect *ungle*.

She'd change her tape soon. A trip to the Ladies would do it. Obviously, being here was a bit of cheat, but she wasn't the only one who was attached. There was that dark-haired woman, for a start. Anyway, making Simon jealous wouldn't hurt at all.

Her last date before the break looked confident without being flashy. Unlike the men who'd turned up straight from the office looking tired, 2 DAN wore jeans and a crisp white shirt, open-necked. Harriet clocked his pricey belt and prepared to uncover his story.

Dan

Christ! The fucking woman with her fucking notepad. She wasn't writing now. But she was asking a shit-load of questions. Like 'Whereabouts in Slovenia?' Her eyes shone with enthusiasm. What kind of enthusiasm, he couldn't tell. He just knew it was the wrong sort.

"I was working in a tiny village. You probably wouldn't know it unless you'd travelled around the country a bit."

"I've never been to Slovenia."

That was a relief. "But you should. It's a beautiful country."

"So what's the name of your tiny village?"

"Kika." Smooth recovery, that. Kika was no fucking village. It was his first dog, the one they'd had before his dad legged it.

"Tell me about it."

"Not much to tell. Mainly farms. Couple of shops. Oh, and a school. Education is taken very seriously in Slovenia."

"Is there a church?"

"Sure, there's a church. And a place that fixes tyres. Everywhere's got those. Because the roads are so bad, you see." Nice touch, he told himself. Pat on the back. If you didn't pat yourself on the back, nobody else was going to. The most basic life lesson ever.

"What were you doing there?"

"I was helping with some construction work."

"Really? And did you get to see much of the country?"

"A bit. It's pretty, especially the north of the country." Nope, nothing wrong with the Slovenia story. It sounded just right. Nobody ever asked him what he was doing these days because they were so impressed by his little travelogue.

"So what's your job now?"

OK, almost nobody. "Well, basically I collect, categorise and deal in classic computer games. They're very popular." Pure fucking genius, he told himself. Nobody who was that brilliant should have ever ended up behind bars. "Vintage computer games are so in right now." Better be. They were the only kind he knew.

She wasn't taken in by this diversion. "Do you work for a small company? Or a large one?"

Christ! She must be a copper or a lawyer. Whatever, she was exactly the type of woman to be avoided. "Well, it's a newish company, not that big."

"I might know it. What's it called?"

That hooter didn't come a moment too soon.

The next one was nice. Sexy too. Dead easy to imagine her without clothes. Until, that is, she told him about her six kids. Maybe she only had four. Whatever. His eyes glazed over when women went on about kids. It wasn't the stretch-marks that put him off, the tits hanging down to the knees, or even the looseness in all the places that should be tight. Kids meant love, money, heartache. In their way, every bit as dangerous as cops and lawyers.

Had it not been for all her kids, he would have ticked her and scribbled *Not bad*. At this stage there were two important tests. One: did they hint at settling down? Unfortunately some of them seemed to have planned their wedding already.

Two: could he imagine them horizontal or, better, bent over his dining table? His bedsit didn't actually have a dining table, but the last few years had taught him a fuck of a lot about visualizing.

Next one was a corker. Hint of Latino or something. He could definitely give her one. Preferably several. Down, boy, he told himself as he installed himself opposite her.

She smiled, showing a row of pure white teeth. Her name was Laure, which she explained was the French version of Laura.

"And what brings you here, Laure?" Apart from making his heart race, of course. But he wasn't about to make her barf with cheesy lines.

"Same as you, I guess."

"You're trying to meet women, right?" One of the best life lessons of all: make 'em laugh. If they opened their mouths, they'd soon open their legs too.

She duly laughed and shook her lovely head. Instantly, this helped him imagine her in several different positions. Not that he or his pecker needed encouragement.

"Then what brought you here would be the number 10 bus."

"Actually I took the tube." How the hell had she made that sound erotic?

"I've been living abroad so I'm not even sure where the 10 bus goes anyway."

"Me neither. I never take the bus." She had a brilliant smile.

"What do you do?" he asked, leaning closer across her table.

Perhaps it was his imagination but she was leaning in too. "I'm a hair stylist."

"I used to know about hair. In the past. As you see, such knowledge would be wasted now." He ran a hand across his bald head.

She laughed obligingly. In the last few years he hadn't heard many people laugh with him. Against him, sure. Mostly Maxy, obviously.

He and Laure chatted about stuff. Dan could remember how to flirt even if it wasn't a skill you honed inside. Educationally jail hadn't been a total waste, though, because you did learn a lot. Like how to use a pigeon as a, well, carrier. Basically your supplier had to sort out a dead pigeon. Not so dead that it was going to fall apart, because he had to hide the stash inside. Then stitch it up again. Then lob it over the wall into the yard. None of the screws ever seemed to wonder what the fuck was happening to the life expectancy of pigeons. That was because they got their cut.

Guys also got drugs via their visitors' mouths. Nobody found it strange when you sucked the face off the girlfriend you hadn't seen for a month. But Dan hadn't really fancied snogging his visitors, especially not his mate Colin.

Now Laure was looking right at him in an unsettling sort of way. While twiddling a lock of hair, no less. "Your hair's really lovely" he said.

"Thank you" she replied as she fiddled with her hair some more. He had a pretty good idea what that meant.

The organizers advised against talking about sex during speed-dating. But they couldn't stop you thinking about it. In his experience, nothing could.

That hooter went far too soon. And now it was his turn to talk to some legless bint who was about to roll off her perch. What was the point? May as well take a fag break. Fuck it! He hadn't even smoked when he went into prison. Now look what had become of him.

Sanjay

Bollocks. Sanjay didn't feel so great now. They had said the treatment might cause sweats, and they weren't wrong. He was light-headed too, probably another one of the side-effects. On the other hand it could have just been the weirdness of the evening.

He asked questions, and got answers that meant nothing. Three minutes later he'd begin again. He scrawled in the margin, mopped his brow and plonked himself at the next table.

"Hey, relax. It's not a hospital appointment" said a woman called 1 KAREN.

"Ha. I've had a few of those lately."

"I'm sorry."

"That's OK."

"I don't know what to say."

"Don't worry about it." Nobody ever knew what to say.

She did her best to change the subject. "Have you got kids?"

He couldn't remember what else they talked about. Probably films. Between them was a kind of curtain that you could feel but not see. Soldiers who'd come back from Iraq and Afghan said civvies never understood. Sanjay got that.

"Good luck" said Karen when the hooter went, and kissed him on the cheek.

The contact was brief, warm, soft. It only made things worse, because it reminded him of sex. Great sex that could be gentle but didn't have to be. Sex that raised your core temperature by several degrees and made you feel instantly better, not cold and rubbish like a one-night stand. Not that sex was really ever far from his thoughts. Death and sex. Of course they were linked. The French even called orgasm the little death, *la petite mort*.

Now he was at the next table and realized he hadn't put any ticks or comments on his scorecard for a while. The evening was shaping up into a desperate muddle. Was everyone else this confused?

"Hi" she said. "I'm Harriet."

She was a copy-editor, and she asked a lot of questions. He fingered his Adam's apple, but there was no tie there. It just felt like an interrogation by his CEO.

Have you tried internet dating? How long have you been on your own? were normal questions, though some were off the wall like *How quickly do you decide if it's a tick or a cross?* But perhaps it meant she was interested.

And she liked cats. That was good. He smiled at her a lot.

He wasn't smiling when he sat at the next table. Bollocking bollocks, he said under his breath. Of all the speed-dating joints in all the world, he thought, she has to walk into mine.

Chapter Four

Laure

"Bollocks, Laure. I didn't know you were back, let alone free and single and looking for love."

"Well, there you go. Nobody knows everything."

"When did you get back?"

There was no point pretending with Sanjay, or carrying on with flirting techniques, sitting close, lips slightly parted, surreptitiously dabbing vaginal mucus inside the wrists to maximize the pheromone effect. "Eight months."

"That long? And how was it? You never said." Sanjay grinned, showing teeth as always, except something about him had changed.

"The Hague was good. Great experience. And good for the CV."

"I thought you'd get in touch when you got back" continued Sanjay.

"Well, you know. Can't turn the clock back and all that."

Now he was frowning. "The clock wouldn't need to be turned back if - "

She interrupted with a sigh. "Please. Don't start on about that."

Mercifully he didn't tell her he missed her, or give her some meaningless crap about staying friends. But she would have liked him to say something to kill the awkward silence.

"Anyway, how are things?" she asked.

"They're bollocks. Absolute bloody bollocks."

"Same old Sanjay then. But you look different. Maybe your hair?"

"I've got cancer. It fell out with the chemo but it's growing back."

She tried not to gasp. "Shit. I'm really sorry. But you're getting treatment, right?"

"Yeah, but it's spread."

"Oh God. Where?"

"Left testicle. Then lymph glands near the stomach. Then into my neck."

"Shit" she said again.

"It's kind of lethal." Then he explained.

She had no idea what to say, so she went for "Have you still got the cat?" She supposed it was really 'our cat', but there was no way she could bring herself to say that.

"Of course. She's lovely, when she's not throwing up."

"I thought she'd grow out of that. Did you change her name?"

"Nope."

"Hey." Someone was tapping him on the shoulder. "Time's up."

"Sorry" he said, scraping back his chair and turning away without saying goodbye.

Laure barely listened to the next guy but she automatically did the leaning in, the mirroring, the touching of her hair. The questions were getting idiotic. *Marmite – love it or hate? If you were a car, what car would you be? What was the last book you read?*

This guy actually had a sheaf of papers in front of him. He spent more time looking at them than at her. Really she needn't have bothered.

Michael

That 4 LAURE wasn't taking his questions seriously. What was the point of her? Then there was a woman who asked more questions than he did. She didn't even write anything down! But the fit black-haired woman, Dorottya, was another story. And she was interested. The proof was that she gave him her card, just like that.

Now he was talking to a housewife, 1 KAREN on her badge. She had read none of the books he reeled off, so he tried asking for whom she'd voted.

"The Greens."

He consulted his list. He had left off the Greens. "OK. Which do you prefer, *Star Wars* or *Lord of the Rings*?"

"I don't mind. Whichever keeps the kids quiet."

"And if you were to read a biog, which would you go for – Nick Clegg or Joe Biden?"

When she replied "Mickey Mouse", he knew the woman was crazy. May as well take a toilet break. He rose and headed for the gents.

Once in the cubicle, he locked the door. He only wanted to pee, but as he held his cock he began to think of Dorottya, and it instantly grew bigger and firmer. Now it was as hard as a cricket bat. It would have been good had her hand been there instead of his.

There was only one thing for it. He clenched his buttocks and pumped like a piston gone frantic. Closing his eyes, he saw her lying in front of him, craving him. His movements became more violent as he thought about shooting all over her face.

As it was, it got onto the wall and the cistern handle. It was amazing how much there was this time. He felt overwhelming relief.

Karen

A breather at last, thought Karen as she kicked off her green LK Bennett shoes under the table. It was easier to smile when your legs weren't killing you. A woman in her mid-thirties was no match for four kids, especially when she had to go in goal. Good thing she could stay seated tonight while the men moved around.

Stretching out her feet relieved the ache, but it didn't ease her confusion. How many had she talked to? At half-time she checked the score-card with the ticks, crosses and question marks.

As of now, question marks dominated. All the 'dates' were three minutes of non-descript chat that barely progressed beyond questions like *What do you do? Have you been speed-dating before? Have you got kids? Do you smoke? If you were a car, what make would you be?* She wasn't going to admit that her identity had merged with a clapped out Toyota RAV-4 that doubled as an outsized wheelie bin.

"Hi! I'm Gary!" said one man, jabbing maniacally at his lapel with his finger. That was just about the most interesting thing he said.

It still made a change from the Tupperware Club. That was what the local mums called the evenings they spent together moaning about the price of school blazers or discussing how to get grass stains out of their kids' gym kit. There was no Tupperware, but there was always wine.

One sad case spent their three minutes telling her about his work rota. She could barely stifle yawns as he described his shifts at the warehouse, detailing his hours on each day of the week. That, he explained, was why he never met any interesting women.

Karen nodded. "Sure."

OK, she wasn't going to meet Prince Charming here. But Prince Charming didn't exist. And, if he did, he wouldn't need to go speed-dating.

It was a challenge to remember which date was which, but the nicest man so far had a badge that said 1 GEOFF. She asked him what his job was.

"Research."

"You experiment on animals?" This was not a good sign.

"Of course not! Only on humans."

It was the kind of thing her children would say. "You're kidding, right?"

He smiled. "Of course I'm kidding. Actually I use computers. They feel less pain, I'm told."

Geoff

He had to get his act together about his work. Obviously, he wasn't going to admit he was a GP. That would be like inviting the entire room to bore him to death with their headaches, ingrowing toenails and aching knees, as well as all the benefits of alternative medicine, none of which had ever been demonstrated in scientific trials.

And what the hell had possessed him to ask that woman about her four children? It made him want to tell her about his son, and talking about Davey made him go gooey like every other absent father on the planet. He would have preferred to come across as suave, sexy and sophisticated, the James Bond of general practice. Not that he'd ever been on a hit-list, unless you counted the patient who sent him letters on scented notepaper to say he was a lovely young man and she wished she was 60 years younger.

He liked 1 KAREN - those badge numbers helped, in case there were more Karens - but kids were hardly sexy conversation fodder.

The speed-dates were a bit like consultations, only shorter. And you didn't take anyone's clothes off even if you wanted to. Of course the names and details were a hopeless jumble, like the time he'd skidded in the snow as an undergraduate, sending all the papers in his bicycle basket flying into the gutter.

As an aide-memoire, Geoff tried to focus on some distinguishing feature about each woman. Now this new one had a huge number of moles. Dysplastic naevus syndrome. Made her a sitting duck for skin cancer, unfortunately. One prominent mole sat perched in her cleavage. It was tempting to reach out and examine it more closely. He acknowledged that dysplastic naevus syndrome might not be the only motive.

After her came a real stunner. The badge said 4 LAURA or something. She had two faint dusty-looking moles on her left cheekbone. Not at all pathological. It gave her face a hint of asymmetry, but if anything that made it even lovelier. There was a touch of the exotic about her. Maybe she was part Greek? Italian? Even Turkish? He didn't ask for fear of offending.

The striking thing was the effort she was making. People-pleaser, perhaps.

One nice thing about 1 KAREN was her easy manner. She wasn't wacky or uptight. He surreptitiously ticked her name as soon as possible, lest he forgot.

Luckily the organizers had put the women's numbers on the table as well as on their badges.

It meant you could find the next date without peering at her breast to figure out which number she was. That kind of thing could result in serious trouble.

The Hungarian woman might have liked it, though. She had a throaty and frequent laugh. When she moved in close, he smelled the cigarettes on her breath, and felt her long hair brushing against his wrist. He was sure her accent got thicker as she whispered in his ear "What is your star sign, *dahlink*?"

He had no idea, which didn't impress her at all. She still blew him a kiss as he left, but she didn't press a card into his hand as she had done with the previous man.

The next woman launched into a zillion relentless questions. Had he been to university? Did he like animals, and if so which ones? Where did he shop for food?

He shrugged. Anywhere that sold ready-meals and alcohol.

"So what bracket would you say your income is in?"

"Well, I wouldn't, because I hardly know you." In truth his income was pretty good, even after forking out alimony. Quality of life was another matter. It was easy to be miserable on 120K a year when you could only see your son for a few hours every two weeks. But there was no reason for the woman with the big handbag to know any of this.

"OK. So - "

"Sorry, must make a phone call" he said as he got up. He didn't really need to make a phone call, but he really, really didn't need another gold-digger.

Chapter Five

Harriet

"How was the losers' evening?" Simon asked from the bed. He was sitting up reading with his half-rim glasses while listening to Radio Four. God, she was allergic to Radio Four. Radio Three was even more likely to bring her out in hives, but at least Simon had the decency to listen to work-related stuff when she was out of ear-shot.

Harriet put down her tote bag outside the bedroom, making a mental note not to leave it there overnight. "It was all right, actually."

"Hm. Let's hope it wasn't another of your commissions that never see the light of day." He reminded her of the time she'd bought four issues of *What Holiday?* only to find her feature on canals had been dropped.

"My name may not always appear in print, but it's on the cheque just the same." Harriet knew she sounded petulant. "Anyway, tonight I got what I needed." Best not tell him she was disappointed. She'd hung around afterwards, hoping to catch some action, but if any of them had copped off that evening she'd missed it.

Simon put down his music magazine. "Like what?"

"Lots of info. So I'll go through my notes and tapes, and put it all together."

He pushed his glasses to the top of his head and stared at her. Harriet felt an icy blast of disapproval even before he pointed out "You just said it again."

"Said what again?"

"So. You said 'So'."

"So? So your point is?" She tried not to raise her voice. Already he was giving her a special face to remind her he was infinitely superior. At what point had he stopped being just a music critic and branched out into criticising everything?

"Just don't miss your deadline this time."

Long ago, he would read her pieces with interest. Back then she'd also jot down the humorous things he said, sometimes weaving them into her pieces. Until she realized they weren't witty epigrams but actually snide comments at someone else's expense.

They ended up having sex because he wanted it. She was curious to know if it was as good as it used to be, which was stupid, because that was impossible. It never would be again.

Years ago, Harriet would go with him on the foreign jaunts he made to discover new music and find old instruments. These were trips when they couldn't wait to get back to their hotel room, lift, wherever. She would sit waiting for him in some dusty café under a wide-brimmed hat, pretending to write as she sipped an over-priced Fanta. In reality she was rewinding the last tape of their love-making in all its knee-trembling, pelvic-clenching glory, complete with the after-burn in her lower belly that would last hours but was totally worth it.

Tonight, she also hoped that sex might put him in a good mood. But all that was a lot to ask of a simple and, to be honest, wholly perfunctory fuck. She moved her hips for a couple of minutes, building up to a crescendo when she half-heartedly faked a climax. It did at least make him roll off and fall asleep. Even Simon found it hard being supercilious during slow-wave sleep.

Harriet got up to brush her teeth. Two and a half years. That was all. No love could last beyond two and a half years. It was a scientific fact. She had read it somewhere. That was because the phenomenon called love was just a hormone storm. It took two and a half years to pass. Afterwards there might be calm, acceptance, affection, or maybe indifference. Then again, sometimes it left massive damage. Like Hurricane Katrina.

Once, Harriet had loved Simon so much that she'd have done anything for him, including the one thing she had found most difficult in the world. But that was then. She'd been with Simon for eight years now, so their relationship was well past its sell-by date. It felt like borrowed time, if she was honest, but it was painful to be that honest. How couples managed to raise children, she'd never understand.

If a stable relationship was the best environment for kids, then why was monogamy so damned difficult?

She climbed back into bed next to Simon's sprawling form, but slept poorly. It was hard to make yourself comfortable when you weren't sure you wanted to touch your bed-fellow.

Even though she had it on tape, Harriet replayed the evening in her mind.

"So what do you do?" she had asked him, half expecting to hear that he worked in a dark-room and never saw daylight.

He had grinned, showing dimples. "I make money."

"Lots of it?"

"Quite a lot. But I don't make it for myself. I'm a fundraiser for a charity. We do stuff with inner-city kids" 4 SANJAY had offered, almost apologetic.

"So let me guess – you can't sting their parents for dosh?"

"Exactly. It's hard getting money from anyone for these kids. Everyone thinks they're wasters who carry knives and deal crack. I guess some are, but there you go. And what do you do?"

This evening, as on many other assignments, she claimed to be a copy-editor. She explained that her job involved beating and pummelling other people's writing into shape. "God, some authors react to the removal of a comma as if you'd slaughtered their babies. Writers are such a neurotic bunch." That was a sweet touch, if she said so herself. "So, tell me Sanjay, have you ever been married?"

"No."

"OK. So you haven't got a girlfriend at the moment?"

"Wouldn't be here if I did."

"So when did you last have a girlfriend?"

His dimples had gone.

Harriet ran through the usual batch of questions. When the Dictaphone clicked, she felt rather than heard it, and put her hand down into the bag instinctively. "Will you excuse me a minute? I need to wash my hands."

She changed the tape as quickly as she could. The first thing Sanjay asked when she returned was "Do you like cats?"

That was unexpected. "Very much, but I don't have one at the moment." She remembered Simon's arrival in her life, and his horror at the cat fur that, he claimed, filled the air in the flat, sucking all the oxygen out of it and poisoning his lungs. To think she'd actually given her beloved Pushkin away. Even all those years later, there was still a cat-shaped hole in the middle of her chest. "And you?"

"I've got a cat" he was saying. "She's got a kink in her tail and – "

"Excuse me, mate" said a man leaning over their table. "But that hooter went ages ago."

"Sorry, didn't hear it" he said.

Neither had Harriet. "So I guess you've got to go then."

"Yeah. See you later" said Sanjay as he got up.

Everyone said 'See you later.' It wasn't like it meant anything. She was probably never going to see him again, though it was nice that he had a cat. Harriet thought momentarily not just of Simon, but of people like Mussolini and Napoleon, who had also hated cats. An idea for a feature? Already the intro whirled its way into Harriet's head.

Think cats are just good at purring, catching mice and scratching furniture? Think again. A feline friend could help you check out your boss, pick your friends, even choose a partner...

The next morning, Simon woke early and snorted repeatedly, as he often did first thing. He always claimed to be clearing his airways because his sinuses were blocked, but it sounded more judgmental than that.

After he'd gone to work, Harriet settled at the computer with a mug of coffee. Never tea, and certainly never Lapsang. She had a piece about bayonets to write, but first she logged onto Date Me Quick. Because she had to choose someone for her article, she placed a tick by 4 SANJAY, 1 GEOFF and a couple of others.

Maybe she should tick every single male?

No, that was over the top. She would stick to these and see what happened.

She wasn't sure of her angle yet, but the editor wouldn't want a straight feature on speed-dating. Unfortunately there seemed to be no pattern in how fast people made up their mind. Harriet had profiled them all: income, occupation, marital status.

Six were separated, not yet divorced, and at least two creeps were still married. But statistics did not a story make. And if she compared speed-dating with internet dating, it would mean extra work for no extra money.

The Seven Ages of Dating, she thought ruefully, could take a hundred years.

Harriet logged off the site and got on with phone calls. She returned some emails, deleted press releases about new products to stop feet smelling, and tried not to think about Date Me Quick.

Halfway through the day came the dreaded phone call from *RightHere!*

No, Harriet admitted, she hadn't quite nailed the angle yet.

To cut the editor short, sometimes she said her hands-free was playing up, or she used the time-honoured 'I'm driving' or 'You're breaking up.' Today she went for "Sorry, I have to rush off to visit my sister. She's just had a miscarriage."

Like she even had a sister.

And her deadline was looming for the piece on bayonet collectors. Harriet had to cobble it together somehow.

Stamps, coins, matches, sea-shells, button badges, first editions, rock memorabilia. Maybe you too collect some of these? Bert on Sesame Street treasures bottle-caps, while students all over the world hoard hub caps and traffic cones. However odd or hideous the article, you can bet someone somewhere on the globe considers it an object of desire.

Collecting and classifying things often start in childhood, but many adults amass huge collections of different objects. Few other species do this. It's likely to be

Likely to be what? Having no idea, Harriet let her brain wander. The minaret did not look at all wonky from here. Simon hadn't noticed the repair at all. Superglue was a wonderful invention. They should make some that worked on relationships.

Dan

On the bus home, Dan memorized the numbers of his favourite dates. He'd need them to enter his preferences on the Date Me Quick site. The info was on the score-card in his pocket. But wasn't it better to take what you had in your pocket and put it in your head? Then no man could take it from you. That was a quote. He couldn't remember who the fuck had said it, but clearly the geezer had never been in jail or he'd have stashed his stuff in a completely different part of his body.

He got off by the discount shoe shop where the window had more sale posters than shoes. Walked past the Golden Fry chip shop that had shut, possibly forever. Hard to tell. Turned right by the launderette that offered *Dry Cleaning, Fully Finished.* Now who the fuck would want partially finished dry cleaning?

Down by the betting shops he went. This wasn't the best part of London. But it was good being out and about. Looking at places. Things. Like the dodgy-looking locksmith. Probably did a roaring trade. He knew how it worked.

In the parade, the late-night food and booze shop had stacks of foreign-looking vegetables on display outside. Very trusting. And the mini-cab place at the end had the usual weedy yellow light out in front.

A light breeze swept around the corner as he crossed the street. It would have ruffled his hair had he still had any. As it was, it only ruffled sheets of free newspaper in the gutter.

He ignored the waster taking a leak in next door's front garden. No idea who it was. Cared even less.

Inside his front door, he kicked aside the heap of mail for residents who'd moved out months ago.

He wished the people downstairs would leave. But their rap music blared out as per usual. That's all he ever heard from them. That and the sound of shagging. He'd seen them only a couple of times. Fat white couple. Even fuck uglier than their fuck ugly music.

It was impossible to say how old these flats were. Well, bedsits really. With coat on coat of blistering paint. Patchwork of carpet remnants. Layers of woodchip. Years of abuse by a stream of lodgers that didn't give a toss. Of which he was one, it had to be said.

He went up to his room. Flipped on the 40 watt ceiling light. Shut the door. Placed the score-card on the bedside table.

Miraculously, it was still there next morning, right next to the coil of his good leather belt. He wasn't used to his stuff being in the same place a few hours on. But that, he figured when the morning brain-fog cleared, was because he was on his own.

In his bedsit.

Not a cell.

And Maxy was nowhere near.

Dan didn't have broadband, or even proper internet on his phone. Just a shitty cheapo connection. Meant he had to unplug the landline first. Not that anyone ever belled him on it. Nobody had the number anyway.

Today it was on a go-slow. A ciggie or two would have whiled away the time while the computer cranked itself up. But he was going to give them up.

He inspected his front teeth in the mirror. That plate wasn't exactly a turn on, was it? Maybe one day he could get a bridge. It would look better and feel better. Even sound better. It had behaved last night, but he lived in constant worry of the slurping noise that would start without warning and meant the fucking thing was working loose. And another thing. Last week alone the glue had cost him £8.50. Nearly 450 quid a year. He wondered how much a bridge would cost.

He smiled at the mirror. He used to be handsome. Now he wasn't so sure. And he was bald these days. But didn't women, in their perverse way, actually like slap-heads?

Finally. The fucking thing was up and running.

Skipping the intro to the site, he checked his memory against the score-card. 4 LAURE was lovely, but others were nice too. Now that he was finally out, he didn't plan on wasting any time. No more eggs in one basket. So, after he ticked 4, he also ticked 2 DOROTTYA, plus a couple of others that his score-card said were *not bad*. In the end, he ticked nearly all of them. Except the nosy bitch with her endless questions about Slovenia.

What else was he going to do today? Buy a paper, for a start. Dan read the *Guardian* now. A must for his long-term plans. Whenever he went into the shop, the newsagent dished out opinions as if he were a leader-writer. Yesterday he had told Dan why he thought footballers should be paid less, and how much Bank of England base rate should be. Dan had nodded. Thing was, you never knew who could teach you stuff.

Then Dan would look for work. At least, that was the idea. He would also wander around Kilburn. Go into a few shops. Generally get re-acquainted with the world. He was beginning to get his head round the fact that he was no longer in jug.

He got dressed, cemented his plate in with the last of the Fixodent, and went down into the street.

Something good was going to happen. He could feel it.

Michael

Michael's morning took a turn for the worse when he found five apples in the fridge and no cheese. Now he would have to make toast, which was if anything more complicated. It took vigilance to get the toast just right, and then care to apportion exactly the right amount of butter onto each slice. Too little and it was like chewing a sheet of sandpaper. Too much and it was a revolting paste. The butter had to be at the correct temperature too, or else you couldn't spread it properly.

He left the Venetian blinds shut. Perched on his leather chair in front of his shiny black desk, he turned on his Mac. Beside it was the Lenovo, the laptop he mostly used for porn.

There were a lot of data to sift through before making his decisions and entering his ticks, but that was OK since the office wouldn't expect him till 9.30 or 10. Publishing houses didn't exactly operate like Swiss chronometers.

Some of the editors were hard-nosed and hard-working, but there were plenty of ditzy young things who populated publicity as well as most of the lower echelons. The kind of stupid giggly woman who habitually rolled up late and hung over, having locked herself out of her flat in South Ken while wearing a satin dress with puff sleeves. Their mistakes were just as stupid. Only recently some complete unknown of an author, no doubt destined to sink without a trace taking his unearned advance with him, got shirty because there was a mistake on the back flap. Said blunder had been made by one of the giggling girlies, naturally, but the bottom line was that the jacket cost a bundle to reprint. Who the fuck did that amateur think he was? Lee Child?

Michael examined his score card, and then his rows and columns. Reluctantly he had to accept that all the info from last night wasn't that much help.

Still, looking at it dispassionately, which was the only way to look at anything, 4 LAURE was the main attraction. He ticked her right away because she was hot. He ticked 1 KAREN for no particular reason, and 2 DOROTTYA because she was panting for it.

None of this took long because he had the best Mac you could buy, and the fastest internet to go with it. It was the checking afterwards that needed time. After all, he didn't want to get this wrong. He didn't stop to consider that the women might not all tick him. His ticks were the ones that mattered. He checked them all though twice, and then one more time, just in case. Then he spent a few moments thinking about Dorottya.

Glancing at the clock, he saw he had 15 minutes left. He could either check the cricket results or knock one off before getting on the Central Line. He thought of Dorottya. It was no contest.

Geoff

Just as Geoff stepped into the shower the next morning, there was a call from a worried parent. The child needed to be seen before morning surgery. According to the mother, the boy had a rash and was burning up, so she was scared it might be meningitis.

Geoff dried himself. Kids were always burning up. It was a miracle any were still alive, given their tendency to self-combust.

The mum had probably just seen some overpaid, over-rated TV doc, who always told everyone to call out their GP, just in case. He could hear the telly in the background while the mother was on the phone. She explained that she couldn't bring Tyler to the surgery because she had the other two kids as well.

As he got into his hybrid Toyota, Geoff had a text from his ex saying she needed more money and *it wd hlp 2 hav it b4 u pik D up 4 w/e.* She didn't sign off but it was Sonya. She hadn't said it was a game of chess either, but Davey was clearly a pawn. Geoff hated that. It was bad for Davey, but had no idea what to do. A discussion with Sonya had not helped. On his way to the patient, he had many thoughts on the subject of Sonya, none of them charitable.

When he got to the patient's home, Burning Kid was playing happily. His temperature was normal, and his rash was due not to meningitis or blood poisoning but to a label on his new T-shirt which was chafing his neck. Geoff asked for a pair of scissors and made a ceremony of excising the label.

"Well, it's best to make sure, isn't it?" his mother offered.

Geoff knew what it was like to be worried about a sick kid. When Davey had first had asthma, he'd nearly ended up on a ventilator. But a GP still had to educate parents, so Geoff explained to Tyler's mum that children who were seriously ill didn't usually sit up and do jigsaws.

She looked at him through narrowed eyes as if she had just decided to hate every doctor on the planet.

Geoff ended up late for surgery. It wasn't till he'd seen some 20 patients, dashed off his letters and signed the repeat prescriptions that he found time for a pee. He took a sample back to his consulting-room, the hot specimen bottle concealed in his fist so none of the staff would see it.

He waited a full 30 seconds before checking the colour of the dipstick against the chart.

Still blue. So it wasn't diabetes. There must be another reason for his problem.

He logged onto Date Me Quick. Skipping the time-wasting intro, he went straight to his choices.

He ticked 1 KAREN right away, for being real. He also ticked 4 LAURE, for being beautiful, as well as 8, 16 and 21, whose names he couldn't recall but whose faces and numbers were crystal clear. Well, more like crystal that had been in the dishwasher a few times too many.

Sanjay

When Sanjay opened the door, Dainty met him in the hall. She chirruped as she snaked around his shins, pestering for food. That was the most beautiful sound in the world.

After tickling her neck and massaging her behind the ears, he turned on all the lights and scanned the flat quickly. It was dumb to pad around in darkness when your cat could chunder for England.

The floor looked clean, as did his duvet. Good. Sanjay kicked off his shoes and for a moment he felt OK. Tired, but actually OK. It had helped to spend a few hours not thinking about cancer.

Dainty deserved a treat. In her bowl there was Best De-Lite, barely touched. Sanjay emptied the bowl down the loo.

Back in the kitchen, he seemed to be out of Dainty's current favourite, organic cat food. She was such a middle-class cat. The stuff came in tiny foil sachets that cost about three times more than any other food. Still, it was worth it to hear her purring as she wolfed it down. Sanjay found a tin of Princes tuna instead and mashed the contents into the cat bowl.

There was a voicemail from his sister, asking if he wanted to help her flat-hunt, innit.

Innit was an affectation. Like him, Sita had been to an independent school, then she'd got a 2-1 at Oxford. He sighed. It was too bad her maturity didn't match her great intellect. Actually, any amount of maturity would have been good.

He selected a Nusrat Fateh Ali Khan CD and let the 60 watts per channel fill his living room with rhythmic ululating. Installing himself on the sofa with his laptop, he logged onto the Date Me Quick site and ticked 5 HARRIET. After a pause, he ticked

2 DOROTTYA. For sex, obviously. Then he ticked 1 KAREN. She was the one in Southwark. Or was she? Didn't matter. He ticked a couple more. Surely one of them would be OK with a fake goolie.

Sanjay was worn out now. The evening had been long, and Nusrat was hypnotic. He was also very dead.

Despite feeling drained, Sanjay let himself get distracted on Facebook. Occasionally he posted status updates, but mostly he stalked his little sis. Sita had posted 87 new pictures of herself. Maybe they'd been taken at a fancy dress party. It was hard to tell, because Sita went through phases of dressing like various celebs. Not that you could ever mistake her for any of them, unless they too were Asian and size 14.

One of the pictures showed her as an outsized Jessie J, mercifully before she shaved her head. Why anyone would want to look like Jessie J was totally beyond him.

He went to lie on the sofa, getting his back covered in cat hair. Soon his front was furry too, because Dainty came and sat on his chest, purring her appreciation and stinking of tuna. Pure stress relief, that cat.

Nusrat came to an end, but from here Sanjay could reach the stereo without disturbing Dainty. He changed the CD to Queen. *We Are the Champions* was energizing. The band also fulfilled a key criterion, which was that one or more of them was deceased. This was just one reason why he preferred Dusty Springfield to Duffy.

Sanjay's CD collection also included Joy Division, INXS, the Who, Hendrix, Johnny Cash, the Doors, James Brown and the Grateful Dead. The Beatles, of course. Went without saying. And the Red Hot Chili Peppers counted, because Hillel Slovak had died. Anyway, he really liked the Chilis. And Ian Dury and the Blockheads. Top bloke, Ian Dury, as well as extremely dead. Could you be any deader than having a movie made about your life?

Sanjay had the Manic Street Preachers as well, though they didn't quite fit the bill because there was a chance that Richey Edwards might still be alive. Still, the Manics sounded dead. That had to count.

He loved lying here stroking Dainty, making her purr like a boiling pot. What was going to happen to her when he died, he wondered. Could his crazy sister look after her?

When he went to bed that night, every limb ached as if piano wire had been threaded through his body and someone was pulling it tight. He couldn't recall when this had started, but these days it happened more and more.

He'd talk to Sita soon.

In the small hours, Dainty threw up on the duvet and Sanjay made up his mind. He was going to tick Laure. She was still special. So was the sex. Something stirred as he remembered. Did he want to go out with her again? He didn't know, but he did want to see her again.

Chapter Six

Karen

"Mummy?" Charlotte marched in with her pink slippers. "Mummy! Pay attention. Edward's wet the bed."

"How do you know?" Karen asked, though it was a stupid question because 10-year olds knew everything, especially Charlotte. With a weary sigh, Karen shut her laptop and heaved herself out of the chair.

As usual, Charlotte was right. Edward had soaked mattress, duvet, pillow and Mr Cow. He was cold, soggy, ammoniacal and fast asleep. Must have peed ages ago.

Karen changed the bottom sheet expertly without waking him. Then she hoiked his pyjama bottoms off and swapped them for a clean pair. He now had a Bob the Builder top and ancient Postman Pat bottoms.

Kneeling down to pick up the wet stuff was unexpectedly painful. "Bugger!" She extracted a Stickle Brick embedded in her knee. The health and safety mob should really get to grips with injuries from plastic toys instead of fretting about conkers and pooh-sticks.

Charlotte was leaning in the doorway. "Was that a swear word?"

"Yes. Yes, it was."

"What does bugger mean?"

"It's another word for Stickle Brick. Now go back to bed."

Once downstairs, Karen picked her way across the living-room and lay on the sofa. Should she go back to the site? Perhaps she hadn't ticked the right men, assuming there was such a thing. It would do no harm to log on and tick a few more now, would it? After all, it might be ages until the next time Rose could babysit.

Rose had been excited when Karen got home. "Well? How was it?"

She'd smiled. "It was fun, thanks. How were the kids?"

"They were fine. Did you meet a rich man?"

"No, and before you ask I didn't snog anyone either, but it was fun. Great to get out, talk to people who weren't all moaning about mobile phone masts and the price of chicken. Thanks so much for tonight. You're a star."

Rose looked thoroughly cheated by the lack of gossip. "No problem. Well, see you on the school run tomorrow."

"Sure." It wasn't clear where the word 'run' came from because everyone drove. It was more like the dodgems.

"OK. Well, good night."

"Thanks again, Rose. You're the greatest."

Karen shut the front door and appraised the view. Wooden bricks were sprinkled across the floor, which was par for the course. A school tie had been tied artistically around the lampshade. That would be Ashley. The TV remote control was in pieces. That would be Damon. One of the open books on the floor seemed to have a page bitten out of it. That would be Edward, who had yet to learn any better. There was a watering can by the TV, with a doll shoved head down inside it. That would be Charlotte, whose ideas on crime and punishment verged on sadism.

Sighing, Karen did what any mother would have done. She poured herself a gigantic glass of plonk, and sat there until Charlotte came in to tell her Edward had wet the bed.

After changing Edward and chasing Charlotte back to bed, she went online to make the most of the calm. Since Thomas' departure had left a gaping hole in her finances, she was looking for work. Thomas drifted, he charmed, he searched for the meaning of life, and inevitably he paid alimony shockingly late. It was just something she had to deal with. She wasn't going to go to court over it.

Karen needed a job more than she needed a man, though Rose maintained the exact opposite. In a previous life, Karen had been in human resources. But that was years ago, and only for the briefest moments when the kids really played up did she ever regret giving it up for her family.

The stumbling block was, what could she do now? She'd asked this aloud one day. Ashley had listened. Then he'd cuddled up on her lap and said charmingly "You can do anything, Mummy."

She'd kissed his sweet-smelling head.

Perhaps he was right. Maybe all she needed was a smile and a Jantzen.

She checked out www.greatnewjob.com and then another site with exclamation marks in every sentence. It promised fantastic money as a driving instructor. You could choose your own hours too! Then she turned to Date Me Quick and ticked 1, who was Geoff. A real man, thought Karen, probably not given to disappearing for weeks at a time to find himself.

Sanjay was number 4. She ticked him probably because he needed mothering, which was a poor reason, given that she had four children as it was. Number 2 was, she recalled, a banker. Not a great face, but he'd talked about holidaying in the Seychelles. Karen had never been to the Seychelles.

Then there was someone who said he was a Renault Megane. She wasn't totally sure he was number 18, but she ticked that box anyway. Or was he perhaps the one who'd said Elvis was his all-time fav? She was getting confused now, but it was too late. On this stupid site one could add, but couldn't un-tick.

Now she was losing momentum. Sipping her Valpolicella, she wondered who to add. Tricky.

Instead she put her head back and considered the day ahead: drag children out of bed, make breakfast, make packed lunches, remind Damon to use his inhaler if he hadn't lost it again, do the school run, look for work, tidy the house, go to the supermarket. Already she felt her muscles relax and her grip on the wine glass loosen.

Laure

Whenever Laure got in from an evening out, whether it was that night or some time the next day, she would normally remove her clothes and place them carefully onto the correct hangers. Then she'd try to work out where she'd gone wrong.

Tonight her mind kept going back to one person. He used to have *hair*, thought Laure. Lots of it, thick, glossy and so black that it shone blue. And a chubby face. He'd gone from chipmunk cheeks to skeleton features in just two years. How much longer did he have? It was an unbearable thought.

Resolutely not thinking about Sanjay, Laure flicked a fleck of make-up off her jacket. There was a tiny stain. It would have to be dry-cleaned. She added the jacket to the collection on the back of the door, destined for the Clothes Spa.

She contemplated her next move. Things needed to be planned, like a career. It was just that her career was a lot more successful than her love-life.

Opening her Mac, she ticked 1, 2, 3 and 6. Geoff, Dan, Michael, and someone whose name she had forgotten. She paused. Best not tick 11. She couldn't recall much about him, though he'd be The One if she wanted to learn more about reinforced concrete.

Another pause. Couldn't do any harm, could it? As an afterthought, she ticked 4 SANJAY.

An afterthought? Who was she kidding? Well, it was done now. What was ticked could not be un-ticked.

It was rubbish and recycling night in her road. Laure pulled on some jeans and found her manky old flip-flops. Gathering together newspapers, empty bottles, tins, and a bag of rubbish, she went out onto the landing and down in the lift. This wasn't the best time to think about Sanjay, but she did. Tears came welling up.

The Japanese woman from the flat below was outside at the bin too.

"Hello" muttered Laure without looking at her directly.

Smiling and bowing, the Japanese woman acknowledged her greeting. She was tiny and her rubbish bag was huge, no doubt heavy with the detritus that a family produces. Her hips were way too slim for sex, thought Laure, let alone for pushing out those glorious round-faced babies.

Laure sniffed back the tears. Now her nose was running. She rummaged in a pocket for tissues and blew it before she remembered that the Japanese thought nose-blowing was the height of bad manners. Quite why was a mystery. Surely Orientals too got broken hearts or the common cold?

She was still thinking of Sanjay when she went back up in the lift. He wanted her back. He'd as much as said so.

Did she want him?

Washing her hands after the bins, she knew she had to get him out of her head. On impulse, she left the flat. This time she caught a 414 to Edgware Road, the bus that she saw every single day but never used.

Starting at Crawford Place she wandered down, reading restaurant menus and peering in shop windows.

The jewellers had execrable taste. She'd have hated the gaudy display of gold necklaces and bracelets even without the animal pelts in the window, festooned over the glass shelves to no purpose, except ostentation.

Despite the hour, only banks were shut. It was still possible to use internet cafes, as well as buy mobile phones, electrical goods, medicines and saucepans. Grocery spilled out onto the pavement, with *batikha* even bigger than in Beirut.

'Life is like a *batikha*' aunt Victorine often said, spreading her hands apart to indicate its size. 'You can't tell what it's like until you break it open.' Profound in an auntie kind of way, thought Laure, because breaking open a watermelon took effort and made a big mess.

And a great-aunt from Beirut had a favourite saying which translated as 'One day honey, one day onions.' That too was very telling. It told you the Lebanese were big on food.

Apart from *batikha*, the grocers in Edgware Road were heaving with bananas, apricots, grapes, figs and vegetables like shiny aubergines, pearly white onions and wrinkly green things that she didn't know the name for. Fat bunches of sweet-smelling herbs lay scattered among them.

On one shoulder, a man carried a whole lamb, dead, skinned and no doubt *halal*, out of a shop. He was followed closely by another man with half a beast that could have come from Damien Hirst's studio.

The annual Saudi invasion had started. On the street were clusters of young men in T-shirts and jeans, and streams of women with pushchairs, most of them in a black *abaya*, some veiled so you could only see their eyes. How perverted to keep women hidden away. Laure gazed at their Fendi handbags and their retinues of children, ranging from babies in buggies to plump children of 10 or 12.

Older men sat outside cafés and juice bars, smoking *shisha*. Laure caught a heady whiff of sweet apple and raspberry smoke. The men stared hard at her, at other passers-by, at any passing Mercedes. They had nothing else to do.

Clusters of younger men huddled on corners, shouting into mobiles or talking urgently with their hands.

It was peculiar being there with all these Arabs, so different to herself and yet so similar. She ambled past *shawarma* merchants with their rotating pillars of lamb doner, past a sweet shop with its more delicate aroma of rose petals and almonds, past yet more restaurants, past the obligatory Starbucks.

Someone brushed against Laure's buttocks as she paused outside the newsagent. She didn't bother to turn around. The shop sold a range of Arabic newspapers, all a couple of days old. Although she just about knew the alphabet, she could barely read a word of the headlines. Shocking that she had never learned the language of her mother's family.

Laure wasn't Arab at all, she realized, and even less convinced that she wanted to be. Sure, there was their charm, generosity and hospitality. But Arabs also had insincerity, censorship, sexism, anti-Semitism, dictatorships. Not to mention God-awful lapses in taste, she remembered as she saw a furniture shop. The windows displayed bilious upholstery and Saddam Hussein-style tables and chairs.

Where did she belong? Either she was either culturally destitute, or rich beyond measure. Could be one or the other.

Her heart did a flip. Outside the sports café stood a slim man who looked just like Sanjay. As a reflex, she checked her outfit, and was horrified to see that she had come out in the worn flip-flops she only used for padding around the patio. That was so unlike her.

She followed him, though not too close. He went inside the café and headed straight for the counter. When he turned his head, she could see that it wasn't Sanjay. Of course it wasn't. The skin on the back of his neck might have been about the same colour, but this guy was clearly Arab. Another Gulfie, no doubt. To look inconspicuous, she examined the menu. That was when she realized that all the menus were the same in Edgware Road – every single dish, every single price.

Didn't matter which door you chose, or where you sat down to eat. In the end it was all the same, all the same big *batikha* making a big, big mess.

Dorottya

In her drawing-room, Dorottya looked past the flowers on the Osborne and Little curtains.

She let out a breath through pursed lips. He was mowing again. What was it with Englishmen and lawns? Roger was so obsessed with his precious expanse of grass that he had even designed a special mowing strip, as he called it, to make cutting easier and to prevent the children from wrecking the edges when they played cricket.

And another thing. Why had he decided to work from home? For years he'd had a perfectly good job in the City, which kept him from under her feet for the whole day, or even, if she was lucky, for days at a time. Now that he was self-employed, he irritated her much more. He was lucky she hadn't thrown one of his best plates at him.

Still, he had his garden to occupy him while she used her laptop. Dorottya logged onto the site and evaluated her options. Since she never had much privacy these days, it was important to know whom to tick. She knew it was *whom*, not *who*, thanks to the classes she had attended years ago in Paradise Road. Hungarians were far better linguists than the silly English.

"Ah, there you are, sweetie." Roger had appeared in the doorway without warning.

She snapped her notebook shut, breaking a nail. She would have to delete the history later, for sure. Last week he had spotted a credit card item listed as DMQ. When he queried it, she told him it was a shoe shop. He was visibly pleased that it had only been £30, which showed how stupid he was. What kind of man thinks you can get anything in a shoe shop for £30, except maybe a pair of laces?

"How is your lawn, *dahlink*?" As an accompaniment to calling him *dahlink*, a term she used whenever she wanted to charm anyone, she flashed her expensively veneered teeth. How bizarre that people from the UK went to Hungary for cosmetic dentistry when she had done the exact opposite.

"Coming along nicely. Don't forget the flower show this afternoon."

He loved plants with the same ferocity that he loved sex. She would use the same tactic. "But I've got a headache. I must lie down."

"It'll do you good to get out, sweetie. Fresh air and all that. Much better than sitting in a stuffy room hunched over a laptop all the time. I don't know why you spend so much time indoors. No wonder you have headaches."

"But you wanted me to study, *dahlink*." Fresh air was an idiot British idea. Hungarians never thought fresh air would help. They took patent medicines instead. If your brain needed a boost, you took a Cavinton tablet, not a walk in the country. "Roger *dahlink*, where did you put my Bensons?"

"You know I don't like you smoking. It's bad for the children."

Over the years there'd been lots of things that were bad for the children, like creeping into the au pair's room at night, but he had never shown much concern about that. "You can't tell me what to do. You're not my employer anymore."

"Can't I?" Now his face, normally smiling and a bit too pink, turned a touch nasty. Nobody would believe how ugly Roger was inside. People always thought he was a cuddly bear, a real *medve*. A *jegesmedve* at that, with his hair a premature white the exact shade of a polar bear at London Zoo. But he wasn't that nice, as anyone on the receiving end of his little games would soon know.

And he wasn't that daft. The English were particularly good at that deception. Like the Scarlet Pimpernel, who played the fool but was really smart.

"You're right, *dahlink*. I'm going to cut down" she said, rising from the sofa. And she would go to the stupid flower show with him at the stupid village church where everyone wore tweeds and a halo. Maybe if she showed enough enthusiasm for the displays she could dissuade him from carting her off to bed again before the children came home from school.

She put the notebook on the mahogany sideboard. In truth the idea of ticking any of the men from last night repelled her. It was enough to know she could still turn heads.

Chapter Seven

Michael

Michael turned off the skinflick on his Lenovo and logged onto the site at precisely 48 hours and 1 minute after the DMQ evening had started.

You have one or more matches!

Clumsy grammar. Still, what could one expect?

Click on the link below to find out more!

He clinked on the link to find that he had been matched with only one woman, 4 LAURE. Yet he had ticked three. Hadn't Dorottya been panting for it? The tease. He absolutely couldn't bear a tease.

Still, he had Dorottya's card with her number. He'd ring her. When they next met, she would no doubt realize her mistake. Surely 1 KAREN had encouraged him too? And she was a single mother, for God's sake! That meant she should be desperate. Not that anyone needed to be desperate to want him, obviously.

He banged his fist on the table, sending two apples rolling onto the floor. With his elevator heel he crunched one of them into the floor, making a mess of the pulp on the pale wood flooring. Didn't matter. The cleaning woman would be round later today.

The next step was to contact Laure. She was very sexy. Perhaps she hadn't taken his questions as seriously as he'd hoped, but what could one expect from a hairdresser? Unless he intended to waste the money he had invested in the evening, he'd have to make the most of her.

When he'd logged off, he did up his flies and went to the bin. It seemed a touch crass to leave everything to the cleaning woman.

Throughout the day he checked his iPhone, in case a late email arrived with another match. Maybe someone was away, or their internet wasn't working. When people had trouble with the internet, it was because they were either cretins or technophobes. Which was much the same thing anyway.

That morning there was a fearfully dull meeting but it wasn't wasted because he spent it composing an email. Talk turned to some new children's author they were all raving about. Even if this one could actually write, she'd probably never be another JK Rowling, Michael thought as he tapped at his iPhone under the table.

Hello there Laure.

Yes, that was nice and casual. Fleetingly he considered adding *I want to fuck your brains out* but that wasn't like him at all. He despised sentences ending in a preposition.

It seems as if we might have something in common.

It wasn't clear what, but they had at least ticked each other. He hoped to God she wasn't one of those women who liked traipsing around museums and art galleries. That would mean compiling a list of artists to discuss.

I enjoyed meeting you and I wonder if you'd like to pick up our all-too-brief conversation where we left it.

Not that he was sure where that was until he checked his spreadsheets.

Here's my mobile. Feel free to ring me anytime, or let me have your number and I'll give you a call.

Cheers

Michael

"Ah, Michael, you are with us after all. Before we disband, may we have your projections for the Farmer trilogy?"

Dan

Dan only had one match. The exquisite Laure. Fine by him, though it meant no scope for mistakes. Now what to write? He scanned the gloomy walls for inspiration and tried out various openers.

Hey, beautiful!

Hey, gorgeous!

Christ! The fucking internet crashed on him. He turned the modem off then back on again. Then he did the same to the computer. Then paced his bedsit to stop himself smoking. When he got the connection back, he tried again:

Hello Laure

You made a big impression on me.
Seemed a tad pathetic. Not the right effect at all.
Hello Laure
So pleased you ticked me too!
He shook his head. Worse than useless.
Hello Laure
I so enjoyed meeting you.
Nope. This needed to be light and upbeat. It was a good job he'd done a writing class in clink. Too bad he hadn't done a computer course as well. He took a deep breath. Tried again.
Hello Laure
Here I am sitting at work, looking out of my window at the glorious trees below. I'd love to meet up for a drink sometime soon if you're free. I think you live in Fulham. Am I right?

Hmm. Could he make the email more eye-catching? Someone like Laure would be getting plenty of mail, he was sure. He tried out a couple of smileys and a few emoticons before deeming them too juvenile. A winking yellow blob that waved its arms like a spastic and said *Hiya Sexy!* probably wouldn't help his cause. He experimented with various fonts. They were all the wrong side of metrosexual. In the end he changed the whole message to lower case.

hello laure
here i am sitting at work, looking out of my window at the glorious trees below. i'd love to meet up for a drink sometime soon if you're free i think you live in fulham. am i right?
ciao
dan

Much better.

He pressed *Send* before his PC decided to pull the plug on him again.

As it happened, the nearest tree was half a mile away. And instead of facing the window, his table was in front of a tattered black and white poster of New York. Found in thousands of student rooms and bedsits all over the world, the photo served only to emphasize the yawning gulf between his life and the vibrant throb of the city that never slept.

Geoff

As soon as the surgery was over, Geoff sprayed the room with air freshener. His last patient had been unacquainted with the simple properties of soap and water. Ah well, look on the bright side. Some days he had to use Glade after the first patient.

Now all he had left to do was compose an email, dig out someone's x-ray results, do an insurance medical form and write three referral letters and a complaint to the hospital. He began with the one to the hospital trust.

Thank you for intercepting my letter to a consultant colleague at your hospital, and for enlightening me on the management of eye symptoms. Ever since I qualified 15 years ago, I have in my deepest ignorance been sending patients with serious visual symptoms to an ophthalmic specialist for assessment. Until now, I was unaware that painless loss of sight in one eye required the expertise of a panel composed of a gaggle of nurses and a social worker.

My patient has not benefited from the additional three-week delay, and has now lost his sight in both eyes.

Glancing out of the window, Geoff noticed that the weeds were back in force in the narrow strip of ground along the path, and there were cigarette butts directly under the *No Smoking Anywhere in This Area* sign. There were also discarded leaflets explaining that antibiotics were unnecessary for viral infections. Fat lot of good that campaign had been. Now the leaflets lay on the path, adding to his feeling of impotence.

Geoff resisted pointing out all the grammatical mistakes in the hospital letter and simply finished:

My patient asked me if he should seek redress through the courts. Suffice it to say that I did not need to confer with a committee to give him my answer.

I await your constructive comments.

Geoff's rant might not restore anyone's sight or put life back into his own todger, but it made him feel much better. It was almost as satisfying as sex with his ex. Not, obviously, now that she was his ex, but back then when they had first met. They'd walk through the fields to Grantchester, stopping at a favourite spot along the way. It wasn't quite concealed from view, which made it even more of a turn-on. He'd lie on his back, watching her face through half-closed eyes. Behind her head there'd be glimpses of clouds cartwheeling in a Constable sky. Ah well. That was before he learned that if you had sex with Sonya you paid a hefty price.

When Geoff finally got back to his empty home that evening, he shoved a Tesco lasagne in the oven, sat down at his PC with a huge glass of Vinho Verde, logged in, discovered he had two matches, and began to compose emails.

Hello

It was great to meet you. Do you fancy

He nearly cut to the chase and typed *me?* but opted for *grabbing a bite to eat?*

Before sending his mails, he made each one more personal by adding Laure to one version, and Karen to the other one. Job done.

Just the little matter of his limp dick, then.

He ate in front of the TV. When he went to visit patients, he hated the telly being always on, but he understood it now. It was company of the least demanding kind.

He washed his plate and cutlery and left them to dry. It was too early for bed, too late to start doing anything new, so he refilled his glass and sat down again in the living room with its stack of unread journals. Daunting enough when they arrived in ones and twos, *en masse* they were positively repellent and were probably destined to stay forever in their plastic envelopes. Instead he turned on his new best friend again and watched something billed as comedy, only it wasn't funny. When he'd drained his glass, he opened another bottle. It wasn't helping his symptoms, but he didn't know what would.

This new place of his was still bare, with barely an imprint of him anywhere. He'd been in lots of houses like this. It was a void surrounded by walls. There was space to breathe, eat, sleep, wash, defecate. That was about it.

The part of the house he loved was the corner with framed photos of Davey on a table. Davey smiling in his swimming trunks on a freezing cold beach in Devon. Davey at the leaning tower of Pisa. Davey outside the school gates on his very first day at big school.

That morning, Davey had looked so small and vulnerable that Geoff feared he might never see him again. It was thoroughly silly, he knew even then, but he had taken the photo at 8.30am, just in case.

Geoff would have liked to store that day in a jar. Not just its near-miraculous moment at three when David came out of school with shining eyes, tie askew and the announcement that he liked fish fingers, but the whole of that day, with the funny feeling he had in his epigastrium on Davey's behalf. That memory jar could go alongside other jars of splendid days, to be inspected now and again as a reminder of how things had once been, and then put back for safe-keeping on the shelf of his life.

He'd have to distil some of the past, because no jar was large enough to take six years at medical school. There could be individual jars for graduation day, receiving the Finucane award, his first girlfriend, the holiday he and his ex-wife had taken to the south of France in his beat-up Polo. If he was in need of a fix, perhaps he could unscrew the lid and have a quick sniff. There was nothing like smell to bring back the past. As far as he could summon up from lectures gone by, that was because the olfactory pathways were closely connected with the hippocampus, where memory resided.

Every house had a scent, as he knew from visiting patients. It might be unwashed clothes in a pensioner's flat, or the pungent cleaning products some families used.

There were few smells in his own house, apart from new carpet with a hint of lasagne, fat-reduced, because he didn't have a death-wish even if he did have erectile dysfunction and his heart was breaking. By the table with the photos was a small collection of toys, a tiny fraction of the total that Davey owned, since most of them lived with him at his mother's. Here there were just a clutch of transformers, a couple of books, and some of the ubiquitous Lego.

Geoff sighed. Back in the day, he hadn't needed help. Losing morning erections was always significant. Every medic knew that. He ought to see his GP for some proper tests, not just a urine check for glucose, but meanwhile it would do no harm to prescribe himself a few Viagra. Just to tide him over till he got an appointment.

He examined the Lego car Davey had been making, following the instructions step by step despite his urgency in wanting to complete the model. One of the back wheels was losing its tyre. Geoff pushed the black rubber back on and put the car on the table. Sometimes, thought Geoff, you followed all the instructions and still the wheels fell off.

Chapter Eight

Laure

Your home was meant to reflect your personality. In that case, thought Laure, her psyche was in serious trouble. This Fulham flat should have looked beautiful but it didn't, because none of the furniture worked. Once dazzling at dinner parties in the Netherlands, the mirror-topped dining-table was too big for its current home, while her sofa was too short for the wall at the far end of the lounge. The coffee table with carved stone legs was plain awkward plonked in front of it. Even her favourite armchair, where she now sat, seemed out of place.

Soon after the move, she had had new drapes made to order. The fabric had great handle, as they called it, but all those metres of over-priced cloth still hadn't done the trick. The flat needed something more to make it harmonious. Feng Shui perhaps.

Right now she had more pressing matters on her mind. She stared at her Mac on her lap. Five matches. One of them Sanjay.

OK, she would think about Sanjay later.

Five matches. Very promising, but no need to get over-excited. She'd got excited countless times before, yet where had that got her? She was still alone now.

Five matches. And one of them Sanjay.

Leaving that aside for now, she had four remaining matches. This meant new opportunities to be seized, but gently, so they didn't notice they were being seized.

She frowned at the screen. She had no idea who one of them was, despite the holiday snap he'd sent. He promised to buy her dinner if she could work out the location. Just as generously, he allowed her three guesses. It was hard to see what his face was like with shades on, but the thing in the background was uncannily like the Eiffel Tower. Perhaps she had played dumber than was necessary for a hairdresser.

Turning to her other matches, she sent an anodyne email to Michael and Geoff, then took a bit more care over her message to Dan.

Hello Dan

Nice to know we both have the same impeccable taste.

Semantic point: was being a sad singleton of 38 the same as having impeccable taste?

How are you? I've been busy at work.

No. She was a hairdresser, for God's sake!

There's an interesting exhibit at the Royal Academy.

Probably of no interest to him or any other straight male. Certainly Sanjay had never wanted to go there.

There's a concert...

Nope.

Would you care to meet for a drink in the next couple of weeks?

But before she clicked send, an email arrived from him. Interesting. Well, she wasn't going to reply right away. That would be too keen.

It was five matches, if you included Sanjay. And he was still interested, wasn't he?

Sex had been astounding. It hadn't started that way. At first she had found Sanjay unadventurous, reserved and a bit too quick. After a few weeks it all began to click. The merest touch in the right place could set her alight in seconds. She told him nobody had ever satisfied her the way he did. He said nobody had made his bollocks hurt the way she did, which, as he explained, he meant in a good way. They had spent a whole weekend wearing out the bedsprings in a boutique hotel in the Cotswolds, and then in many other places besides.

But that was before. Before that Christmas. And before his cancer.

She had to email him before she could even think.

Dear Sanjay

I never thought I'd see you again, let alone at the Jacaranda. Now that fate has brought us face to face again, it seems logical to stay in touch.

I said I would always be there for you. In my defence, that would have been hard to do from The Hague. All the same, I'm ashamed that we failed to keep up the contact. I'm even sorrier that the last two years have been so unkind to you.

I would love to meet up again. I'd like to add that if you don't ever want to see me again, I'll understand, and will go away quietly.

She paused for thought. That bit wasn't necessarily true. And it was all terminally uncool. But surely she didn't have to play it cool with Sanjay anymore? She threw cool to the winds by signing off:

Love always
Laure

She clicked her Mac shut and put it back on the dining table. She couldn't even arrange furniture. What chance did she have of sorting out anything else?

Sanjay

Sanjay got in momentarily buoyed from his day's work, but once again exhaustion coshed him on the head as soon as he'd shut the door. He scratched Dainty behind the ears, gave her some Purina dry food, and had a little rest on the sofa. When Dainty came to nestle up next to him, she smelled musty. Poor kitty. She deserved better than being cooped up indoors.

She purred into his face and nudged him with her wet nose before deciding to curl herself up by his hip on the sofa. Sanjay reflected that his longest relationship ever had been with Dainty.

When he woke up, the flat was dark, his mouth was dry and he was disorientated. About two hours had gone by in dreamless sleep. But that was better, he told himself, than having another disturbing dream about Ben.

He rubbed his eyes and searched for his phone. Dainty had been sitting on it again. She protested with a long meow when he extracted it from under her warm belly. Bollocks! During his snooze, she had changed the input language to Afrikaans and taken some high res pics of her tummy fur.

Sanjay put Joy Division on his stereo and powered up his PC. Logging onto DMQ, he found he had three matches, 1 KAREN, 4 LAURE and 5 HARRIET. He was going to keep his emails simple and light. Brief too. Time and tide and all that.

Hi Karen

I really enjoyed meeting you. It would be nice to have a drink if you're free sometime, ideally for more than three minutes.

I'm sure you got lots of matches, so would it help to remind you that I'm the tall dark handsome one? Of course I also have a George Cross, a villa in Antigua and a Lear jet.

Cheers!

Sanjay

Changing only the greeting, he sent the same thing to Harriet. The Lear jet was one of his father's ambitious dreams for his son. A while back, Sanjay's father had expected him to be become nothing less than a Mittal, with all the trappings that meant you had arrived, or, in the case of the Lear jet, that you still had exciting places to go. Sanjay worked for a charity, which meant his parents had had to downsize their expectations. In the last year or so, they'd had to adjust them even further.

Now Ian Curtis was rending hearts on *Love Will Tear us Apart*. Of course it made him think of Laure. For a while, everything about their relationship, absolutely everything, had been brilliant. Until they hit that wall.

He decided not to email her yet. He didn't know what to say. It felt too late to reconnect. Time, tide, and all those bollocking things.

Karen

Charlotte was singing "Damon and Amy sitting in a tree, K-I-S-S-I-N-G". Damon's face was like thunder, which was the whole point of the exercise.

Ignoring them, Karen lifted the tuna bake out of the oven. Damon and Edward wrinkled their noses. Charlotte stopped teasing Damon long enough to pull a face.

Fortunately the bake tasted better than it smelled, so the kids deemed it edible, with a few modifications. Edward picked out every single pea and every single kernel of corn, and Damon extracted all the visible chunks of tuna and most of the invisible ones as well. Edward stopped playing with his food to ask "Mummy, what does sex mean?"

Charlotte and Damon sniggered. Karen felt only a tinge of guilt as she replied "It means what you say or write down if someone asks whether you are male or female. A male child is a boy, and a female child is a girl. See?"

Damon said he'd have preferred to have Robin van Persie as his mum, because he'd be able to go to more football matches, and also because he thought RVP wouldn't make tuna casserole. All told, it sounded like the striker would have made an ideal mother.

Charlotte announced that she was going vegetarian like her best friend Belinda.

"Does it mean you won't want to eat happy pig anymore?" Karen asked.

"Does vegetarian mean vegetables?" asked Edward. "Yuk."

"No happy pig" said Charlotte, flicking her hair. "Or free-range turkey either. You'll have to make nut roast for me on Christmas Day, Mummy."

Edward knocked his glass of water into his plate and wailed.

Mercifully Christmas was a long time from now, thought Karen as she mopped up the spill. She got Edward another helping of the bake, whereupon he stopped crying and busied himself by picking out the peas and corn all over again.

After supper, the kids watched some random video for the hundredth time, and Karen finally escaped to the Date Me Quick site.

Emails from both her matches! Geoff's mail made her smile. Grabbing a bite to eat sounded casual yet glamorous, the kind of thing that people who lived in loft apartments might do. In her world, bite-grabbing meant the kids were stealing one another's crisps.

Hi Geoff she replied.

Good to hear from you. How are the experiments going? I hope you're not ill-treating too many defenceless computers. Yes, it would be nice to get together. Have you a particular evening in mind?

Cheers.

Karen

The other one was from Sanjay. The bit about the Lear jet sounded upbeat, but she wouldn't reply just yet. He was vulnerable, and she had no idea what to say.

Karen dragged herself back to the reality that was bath-time, and yes, she explained as she did every evening, they needed baths every day.

"Why?" asked Ashley whose preferred clothing was mud.

Karen sighed. "Because you need to wash your bits and pits, that's why."

"Bits and pits! Bits and pits!" shrieked Edward as he flapped his arms and raced upstairs to be first.

Harriet

Best hurry up, thought Harriet, or else some other journo might have the same idea. And produce their copy a lot faster. Or the list of the 10 sexiest bars in London might change, leaving her with yet more research to do. No matter what venues currently topped the bill, in Harriet's opinion the best one of all would always be the Sanderson.

There's no shortage of trendy watering-holes in London, but what makes a truly fabulous bar? Your style guru checks out the clientele, the cocktails and the cool factor at 10 of the sexiest places to be.

Harriet left the latest of these sleek/sexy/trendy watering holes behind, wondering why they'd embraced such silly concepts. Who the hell had thought blue lighting was even remotely flattering to human features? And the seats were so low that nobody over the age of seven could possibly sit in comfort. What was more, their bar snacks looked like genitals, and tasted like.... well, hard to tell.

On her way home by tube, she once again pondered the two and a half year thing. First hormones, then habit, then maybe hatred? There was an article in there, surely.

The flat was quiet when she got in, a welcome contrast to the bars. When she turned on her laptop, it sounded like an espresso machine on speed. Not a good sign. She really couldn't afford another laptop just yet.

She turned it off then back on again. Logging onto Date Me Quick, she hoped Simon wouldn't be back from his concert for a bit.

One match! And there was a message from him already. She replied:

Dear Sanjay

It was a mad whirl of an evening, so your George Cross and your villa in Antigua must have slipped my mind. I do of course remember that you're tall, dark and impossibly handsome.

Have you made stacks more money since we met? Those disadvantaged kids need all the help they can get, if you have any spare cash in your pockets after refuelling your jet. As for myself, all I've been doing is trying to beat useless words into shape and meet irksome deadlines. But I have some time in the next week or two if you are free?

All the best

Harriet

PS How is your cat? You mentioned a kink in her tail.

For the sake of her feature, she hoped her mail would be enough to ensure they'd meet up again. She had been with Simon so long that she'd forgotten all the moves. Feeling inept made her incredibly sad.

As she was brushing her teeth, she heard Simon crashing into the flat, bringing stacks of work with him. He dumped a heavy bag on the floor, dropped his keys into the stone bowl in the hall, and slammed the front door. For a music critic, he really had no idea what a cacophony he made.

If she hurried, she could jump into bed and pretend to be sleeping before he reached the bedroom.

Chapter Nine

Laure

Laure smiled. A smile conveyed poise. It was also pleasing to others, or so she understood from everything she'd read on the subject of looking pleasing to others. When you smiled, you could be thinking happy thoughts, or you could be wondering, as Laure was now, what the hell horse-brasses were actually for. She was also guessing how long the carpet had been in this pub. Decades, judging from its hideous pattern, non-existent pile and the fact that it stuck to the feet and reeked of damp dogs.

"Well, I'm a lucky man, aren't I?" said Michael. "Tell me, what is the correct way to say your name?"

"It's Laure, as in *store*." She studied his face again. He was definitely not the one she'd meant to tick, and now she'd come all the way to this charming country pub. How soon was it OK to leave?

"Or *more*?" he suggested.

"Or *more*." Also as in *law*, but she wasn't about to drop clues. She explained that Laure was the French version of Laura. Unfortunately, he rather liked that.

"Shall we have a drink?" She was actually parched.

"Good idea, Laure." He made it sound as if she'd been brilliantly imaginative, but given the number of pump handles, spirit bottles and glasses at the bar it would have been hard to think of much else. Apart maybe from roasted nuts, or haddock and chips, served from 12-2, as per the specials blackboard.

Over their glasses of draught cider, Laure wondered who she had meant to tick, but couldn't figure it out. This time she didn't lean across or give him any encouragement. She found three coins and some broken crisps between the seat cushions while Michael talked about books.

When he stopped telling her how many copies some cricketer's biography had shifted, he said "You know, Laure, you were a bit cagey about giving out your phone number."

"Maybe I was. But women sometimes worry about being stalked."

"Was I stalking you, Laure? I had no idea."

"You weren't. I'm just explaining that my reticence reflects a wholly natural caution." Oops. A hairdresser wouldn't say that.

"Anyway, Laure, you've given me your number now."

She nodded and sipped her cider. "Yes, you've got it now." It was hard not to exchange numbers if you were going to meet, but he didn't need to know it was a cheapo pay-as-you-go used only for speed-dating.

"I think you said you'd never been married" he said.

Oh, good. He'd given up using her name in every single sentence. "That's right."

"No kids then, Laure? Not that it follows, ha ha."

"No. No kids." She was about to explain that she'd concentrated on her career, but remembered she was a hairdresser. Of course she wanted kids, before her ovaries gave up the ghost for good. She just wasn't about to leap into bed with anyone like Michael, not on the first date, not the next date, not ever. Now would be a good time to leave, but something deep inside stopped her. It was hunger. She'd rashly come out on an empty stomach.

"Shall we have a bite to eat, Laure?"

"Lovely" she said. "I'll have haddock and chips."

Sanjay

Sanjay opened the door of 32 Cornwall Gardens with his own key. Right away he knew his mum had been cooking for days.

"*Beta*!" she cried as she positively raced through from the kitchen. She hugged him, enveloping him in a haze of cumin, fenugreek and Calvin Klein Eternity. "Sita is here, look."

Sita occupied the biggest armchair in the through-lounge, a large leather blob that practically swallowed her sulking form. "Hey!" she said, looking up from a magazine. It was some mindless celeb drivel again, fodder for more of her wacky looks and even wackier diets. The looks never worked. Neither did the diets.

"Your father will be home soon, *beta*," Mum went on, trying not to show that she was examining him critically. She would latch onto the slightest hint of improvement since his last visit, while any change in the other direction always triggered hand-wringing. He hated to upset her, hence he was wearing a bright red flowery shirt. Hideous as it was, its luminous sheen made his skin look healthier. Also Mum had given it to him last Christmas.

"That's good. Haven't seen Dad for ages."

"You know, *beta*, your face is looking more round." She touched his cheeks with her roughened fingers. "Much better."

From her armchair Sita rolled her eyes.

Satisfied with Sanjay's mien, Mum went back to her kitchen and her noisy pots and pans.

Sita put down her glossy mag and looked at him. "How are you really, Sanjay?" Today she had blonde streaks and purple eyelashes. He hoped to bollocks they were fake.

He shrugged and plonked himself on the sofa. What was there to tell beloved little sister?

This huge room pleased him no end, with its two enormous Persian rugs of about the size of Persia. Only three pictures hung on the walls, and not one of them showed Ganesh, Shiva or any of that crowd. The walls were an off-white from Farrow & Ball, without a hint of textured wallpaper. Between the two outsized cream leather sofas stood a vintage floor-lamp. As a discreet and solitary nod to the family's roots, a sheesham wood table sat planted by the window, with just a vase of white flowers on it.

He hadn't always liked the decor. As a youngster, Sanjay had considered this room nothing less than shameful. He had longed for the chaos of his friends' homes, with their cluttered front rooms, turquoise gloss paint and flocked wallpaper or whatever they had got cheap. He had cringed when his mates came round. Adolescence had been agonizing. Why couldn't his parents have made an effort to fit in, just for his sake?

Nowadays he found the room tasteful, serene, and peaceful. Not that Sanjay himself felt at all serene and peaceful. He looked across at Sita. "Mum's making puri then" he said.

"Yeah" said Sita. "What you been up to, innit?"

"This and that."

"Sounds like a woman to me. Am I right, or am I right?"

"Not exactly."

Sita's purple-fringed eyes grew round. "Bro! Don't tell me you battin' for the other side now!"

"Course not. But there's nothing wrong with being gay."

She examined her shiny violet nails. "Gays are such a waste though. Like they're so cute, but they're so totally off limits."

Dad came home, bringing with him hugs all round and his latest stories from work. It was always trouble with suppliers, or else it was trouble with buyers. That happened a lot in import-export. Dad always swore at the end of a day's work, especially when he'd had to deal with people who had no head for business and really should have found alternative careers. This included pretty much everyone he knew.

As they stuffed their faces, Dad continued his rant. "That man does fucking bloody bugger all! If we all did like him, then wheels of business would come to complete bloody fucking stop, yar." He waved his fork around to make sure everyone got the gist.

Dad sounded really Indian when he was angry or excited. He also used a special voice that would have been great if telephones didn't exist. Sanjay thought the volume was even higher than normal, most likely to convince everyone that all was OK despite Sanjay's illness. It didn't fool him one bit.

As usual, Mum ignored Dad's tirade. She had a story of her own to tell, the one about her leg. It started with a nasty rash on her shin which she liked to exhibit to the relatives, as if they were a delegation of dermatologists. The accompanying soundtrack was a recital of her last few surgery attendances. "Every time I go to GP, he says 'how well you are doing, Mrs Shah'. And I tell him it is no good doing OK if you have bloody leg like this, hah. That is what I tell him."

Then she glanced at Sanjay and suddenly asked if anyone wanted more puri. They had already eaten more than they needed for a week because Mum operated on the principle that you never knew when or where your next meal was coming from.

"I'm totally stuffed, innit" said Sita.

Mum wasn't convinced but resigned herself to clearing the table. Dad, as befitted the modern British male that he aspired to be, went into the kitchen with her, balancing plates and shooing everyone else away from the sink.

That was when Sanjay told Sita about the date he'd had with Karen. "Well, just a coffee date" he added. He supposed it was good she already had kids. It wasn't so good that they were her specialist subject.

"But you like kids" Sita pointed out.

Sure, he liked kids, but he specialized in the kind that stole and lied, in short the kind that Karen would definitely not want her four little darlings to turn into.

Sita, for all her artful shallowness, understood this perfectly. "So was she, like, totally horrified?"

"Yes. Especially when I told her about the Fire Man."

"Fire Man? The kid that lights fires?"

"Yep, him. Anyway she couldn't see anything good about him at all."

Sanjay told Sita about the awkward silences, and the even more awkward conversation. Karen had wanted to know if he liked opera. He loathed opera. She then asked if he liked football. He didn't recall actually replying, but perhaps he'd accidentally made a head movement that could be taken for a nod, because from then on there was no stopping her. It was Man U this, and Man U that, or possibly

Man City – he forgot which. Apparently her son or daughter or someone was a big, big fan. She hadn't been to watch them because it was expensive to take the whole family to a game, but they had Sky Sports. Then she asked which team he supported, to which he had to say that it was none. During the whole date, Sanjay had felt he should be doing something else. Like visiting Ben.

Sita always got upset when Sanjay talked about Ben, so he stuck to telling her about his date.

"So is she like, shaggable?" Sita wanted to know.

He shrugged.

Sita looked gravely through her purple fringe. "Bro, everyone's shaggable."

"Including our parents?"

"OK, not them, obviously." There was a silence during which Sita was no doubt thinking about the time they had wandered in on Mum and Dad years ago. "Bet you scared her off or something. Oh God, you didn't show her a picture of Dainty on your BlackBerry, did you?" Sita waved a finger at him.

"Of course not! What do you take me for?" After a suitable pause, he added "Sita, will you do me a favour?"

"Just name it, bro."

He was meeting Laure soon but he wouldn't ask her that. "Will you look after Dainty after…. you know."

She shrieked. "What, with all that fur, and sick, and poop on the carpet, and the pee over the side of the tray because she won't crouch down properly?

And you know I live with Mum and Dad now, and Mum would go totally fucking mental with all the fur-balls, innit."

Sanjay stared at the floor and saw how impossible it would be. Dainty would claw that immaculate Shiraz rug in no time or else puke all over it, probably starting subtly so that it blended in with the pattern and caught everyone unawares until they walked barefoot. He shouldn't have asked.

"Of course I'll look after her, stupid! I was taking the piss. But you're not going to die, Sanjay. Dainty will die before you do."

"I hate you, Sita" he said, echoing what he used to say all the time as a child, but now meaning the exact opposite.

Laure

Laure couldn't see what Sanjay had against the Place to Eat, especially as Oxford Street was near his office. But there he was, wrinkling up his nose. It made his thin face look unnaturally dry and lined.

"Did you have to pick this place?" he asked.

She sighed inwardly. Not outwardly. That would hardly help her cause. She supposed she had thought of John Lewis because she used to come here with her mother. Then, it was always full of boys, probably because they too were being dragged out to buy school uniform before the start of term.

Although most of the boys were spotty, Laure would hitch her skirt up as far as she dared and make what she imagined were bedroom eyes. Not one of them had ever noticed.

Today Laure saw no school-children, just women struggling with shopping bags and baby-buggies. The babies were an unwelcome reminder. On the plus side, the cafeteria was noisy. She and Sanjay would need to sit close.

"I'm so very glad we met" said Laure, looking into his eyes.

Sanjay seemed perplexed. "We just got here."

"I meant years ago."

"Oh. Well, me too, of course."

He could have sounded a bit more enthusiastic, but maybe he wasn't feeling well. He'd been keen enough at the Jacaranda, hadn't he? She didn't dare remind him they'd had some good times. Instead she made what she hoped was an encouraging face.

Unfortunately he was looking out of the window and missed it. When he stopped staring moronically at cranes and buses, he said "So, how was *Den Haag*?"

"Good, but a tad confusing. The language is so strange."

"But you're good at languages."

"Well, it's difficult to follow when every other word sounds like a gurgling bidet. Some words like *danku* are easy, but others aren't that obvious." She was gabbling now, but couldn't stop. The words had gained momentum. "You might guess *danku* means thank you, but *bonje* means - "

"Do you want another Coke?" he said.

Not great to be interrupted, but at least it meant he wanted to carry on being here with her. When he got back with the Cokes, he said nothing so she continued. "When I first got to the Netherlands, I couldn't figure out where *Doorgaan Verkeer* was. Most of the road signs listed it, but if the place was that important, then how come I'd heard of Rotterdam and Utrecht, but had never heard of *Doorgaan Verkeer*?"

He shrugged. "I've no idea. Why didn't you check Google maps?"

"I don't know. Anyway, someone eventually told me it meant 'through traffic'."

He put down his Coke and wiped his mouth. "For a lawyer, you can be bloody thick."

This wasn't going quite the way Laure had in mind. All in all, she wasn't doing much better than with the schoolboys years ago. After a pause, she tried "I was so shocked to hear you'd been unwell."

"I'm still unwell, though obviously I've had worse days."

Laure tried to suppress the dryness in her throat with a gulp of Coke. She shouldn't even have been thinking it at a time like this, but she would have preferred Diet Coke. "I thought more and more cancers could be treated these days."

"Treated. Not cured, unless you catch them early. Overall, testicular cancer has a brilliant five-year survival if you diagnose it in time. But there are different kinds, and there are also different stages."

It was freaky how dispassionately he spoke, as if lecturing to medical students. She nodded sagely, feeling sick inside. Although he had already mentioned his cancer the other night, it was like being hit by a train all over again.

"Anyway, they asked me a while back if I wanted to wank some sperm."

"Wank?" She said it a little too loud. "Is that the word they used?" The people at the next table suddenly took enormous interest in their conversation.

"I said 'bank'. But banker, wanker - what's the difference?" Those other people nodded in hearty agreement. "Obviously, that's exactly how you bank sperm, then they take the sample and freeze it. What I don't know is what happens when the person dies and the sperm is still in the bank."

"I'm not sure either" said Laure carefully. This talk of sperm and death didn't seem quite the right way to his heart. And now the next table appeared to be pondering the sperm dilemma too. Laure wished the tables were further apart, or that those people would find something else to chat about. Shouldn't they be debating the virtues of different washing machines, or agonizing over a slice of chocolate fudge cake? But Laure didn't have much choice. It was now or never. She leaned towards him. "Sanjay, do you believe in recycling?"

"Well, obviously. If people don't recycle, then the environment's totally screwed."

"That's not what I meant."

Sanjay looked flummoxed.

Was she the only one who ever thought of recycling exes? This warranted a really deep breath. "I mean, do you think one can revisit the past? We had something really good, didn't we?"

"Oh. Well yes, we did. That's not in question."

"So what do you think?"

Finally he said "Laure, you know it went wrong for us. Now I feel the need to keep moving. If I don't go forward, I'm kind of dead already. If that makes sense."

Nausea gripped her chest as she forced herself to agree. There had once been a time when they were so in tune that they would say what the other one was thinking, like identical twins that documentaries always featured. Just as uncannily, Sanjay now kept saying the exact opposite of what she was thinking. "I could look after you" she offered as lightly as she knew how. She wasn't going to beg. She had some pride.

"Bollocks! How? You work full-time, and you can't cook."

"I'll learn to cook."

"How long would that take? At this stage in my life, that's kind of crucial."

Sanjay left soon afterwards, kissing her all too briefly on the lips before disappearing into the distance towards the escalators. She watched him go, and stared across the huge expanse of cafeteria that contained not a single boy, spotty or otherwise.

Chapter Ten

Sanjay

Poor choice of venue, thought Sanjay. If you met an ex-lover, even supposing that was a good idea to begin with, then surely somewhere more upmarket, like the oyster bar at St Pancras, was better than a café in a department store. But then spending time with Laure anywhere would probably have irritated him. Before this afternoon, he'd had no idea quite how he'd react when they had a proper chance to speak. Then they met, and he knew.

Now that Sanjay was lying on his sofa, with the speakers pumping out Pink Floyd, he realized how much he needed a rest. Normally a guy his age wouldn't have found this pace of life frenetic, but it was a different story when your lymph ducts were teeming with intruders and you didn't know where they would pop up next.

As Roger Waters eased into *Comfortably Numb*, Sanjay felt anything but. Laure lacked spontaneity, that was one problem. When she did begin to show any, she started on about getting back together.

Perhaps he'd have wanted that too, had things been different.

She hadn't known what to say, that was for sure. Probably because there wasn't a precedent in case law or something. Everything she did was by the book, while he was exactly the opposite. Strange he'd never noticed before. Anyway, now they were like dancers who just couldn't get in step again.

Sanjay stroked Dainty. Purring, she inched as close to his chest as she could. Her hot breath smelled slightly of fish. He realized that he hadn't shown a single picture of her to Laure, the one woman that already knew his cat.

He'd kissed Laure as a kind of goodbye. He liked the taste of her lip gloss but he hated goodbyes. Of all kinds.

Yesterday he'd been to see Ben as well. Obviously he hadn't kissed him.

He and Ben used to iron their underpants before a night out, while they talked about joining the Army.

"Mate" Ben would say as he pounded the ironing board. "I can't wait to get to Afghan."

"Me neither" Sanjay would agree, although he wasn't as convinced as Ben. "Are those your pulling pants?"

How things had changed. While Sanjay opted to work for charities, Ben had stayed on course. Now he was wearing bandages instead of lucky pants.

Sanjay wondered what Ben's operations had been like. The good thing about his own ops was the pre-med. That injection was chock-full of morphine, which made you as legless as a freshers' night, and some stuff to dry up secretions, so your mouth was like an Ethiopian drought. But with the morphine on board, who gave a flying fuck?

Then the anaesthetist would get him to make a fist. "Now count to 10 for me." Sanjay never got beyond four before drifting away.

Whatever delicious thoughts he had on going to sleep, there was always hell to pay when he woke up. Last time someone was moaning like a wounded animal in the recovery room. And Sanjay was in serious pain. Just because you were asleep when they plunged a knife in your neck didn't stop it from hurting like fuck afterwards.

He thought of Ben. He must have been in agony for, what, hours? He wondered if anyone had given him enough morphine, whatever 'enough' meant when you lost an arm and a hunk of leg. And whether there was someone sitting nearby, like this nurse here. There was probably just another wounded soldier, doing his best with a tourniquet and hoping the MERT would show before they both snuffed it.

In the recovery room, Sanjay had the irresistible urge to sit up, but couldn't. The pain and a nurse kept forcing him back down. Plus he had a sore throat and felt sick. The smell of antiseptic didn't help, nor did the bilious scent of dressings. Nurses insisted there was no smell, but they were wrong.

The moaning still hadn't stopped. Some poor deranged soul really didn't want to be here. The thirst was almost unbearable, but all the nurse got him was a plastic thimble of water. Most of it went down the front of his hospital gown.

Miraculously, the moaning stopped when he drank the water, which was when Sanjay realized that he was the deranged soul making all the noise.

Strange that such a small procedure would lead to such trouble. Maybe it was the drugs. It was a bad idea to mix your drugs, but hospitals dosed you with reckless abandon, with gases out of metal cylinders, and loads more stuff into his veins. One of the anaesthetists had explained it. She was one of the new docs, a woman with long red hair and a piercing that went right through a huge freckle on the side of her nose. She was flirting with him, he was sure. So he had flirted back, as best as one could when lying down and wearing a hospital gown instead of Paul Smith loafers, Armani jeans, and lucky pants. That was when he had learned about the IV anaesthetic drugs, like fentanyl and ketamine. No wonder that by the time he got to the recovery room he felt he'd gone four rounds with David Haye and had an overdose of Ivory Wave or whatever high you could get for a tenner these days.

Yesterday Ben had been in a chair. He grinned and pulled himself straight when he saw Sanjay.

"Hey, Ben, mate" Sanjay said, hugging him. It was good to see the smile was back, but somehow it wasn't right. Ben's smile reached his eyes, but there seemed to be other places it didn't go. Maybe areas of brain had also been blasted by that bollocking IED.

"Hey, mate" said Ben, giving him a lopsided hug back.

They both declared they were good.

Ben dabbed the corner of his mouth. "How's your crazy sister?"

"Still crazy. Some things don't change." Obviously, some did. Sanjay wished he hadn't said that.

Ben said his family were fine. He'd also heard from his ex-fiancée Marian. "Did you get to Prague in the end?"

"Nah" said Sanjay. "Probably won't bother now."

"Me neither" said Ben.

Neither of them said there wasn't much point in Ben's stag weekend now. Instead they claimed Prague was over-rated, with the conviction of those who'd never set foot there.

"You know what else is over-rated?" asked Sanjay.

Ben didn't have to think. "Queen. Franz Ferdinand. Paul Weller. Biffy Clyro" he replied, rapid as machine-gun fire.

"Hell yeah. And what about Coldplay?"

Ben made a retching noise. "And Snow Patrol and Keane. And those miserable fucktards Mumford & Sons."

"Dude, you're creasing me up" said Sanjay, not that there was anything remotely funny about any of those tragic bands.

They ended up playing on the communal backgammon set, improvising with a couple of coins as two white pieces had gone missing. Ben did his best to shake the dice with his left hand.

"The legs are looking good" Sanjay remarked.

"Yeah, they're coming on. Still some fucking trouble in one groin, though. Mate, I need to get back to the gym properly, not just do physio and shit like that" Ben said defiantly.

Although Sanjay loved Ben, he understood why his fiancée had ditched him. The fucking Taliban put faeces in the IEDs, which meant their victims got horrendous infections. The one in Ben's groin had taken several ops to control.

Ben may have been one of the older injured soldiers, but he looked as vulnerable as a child. He laughed with glee as he took three of Sanjay's pieces in one killer move. "After my rehab, they're going to give me a desk job" he said.

Sanjay nodded and moved one of his uncovered pieces to safety. "That's great news, mate."

"That's crap!" Ben exploded. "I want to go back to Afghan."

Sanjay wanted to ask why. But then it wasn't clear why Ben had gone in the first place.

Now he didn't know what to say to his oldest friend, so he let him win at backgammon. A while later he shook him by the left hand, said "See you later, mate," and left.

The automatic door annoyingly opened the wrong way, nearly hitting Sanjay in the face.

When he got back to the carpark, he inflicted the kicking of a lifetime on one of his tyres before driving home.

Back on the sofa with Dainty, he reflected. The whole point of life, thought Sanjay, was that you didn't know how things were going to turn out. Now he was beginning to see how things were turning out, and he didn't like it one bit.

Sanjay wasn't even looking forward to the date with Harriet, aka number 5. Yes, things had gone pretty well at the Jacaranda, or so he'd thought at the time. Now he was less sure. Would this be just another date during which he would think non-stop about Ben?

It was a coffee-date. At least it would be quick. He could feel in his bones this was going to be a massive waste of time.

Like he had time to waste.

Apostrophe was quiet when he arrived. Sanjay noticed as Harriet approached that she had a very slight belly. She was still slim, but she had a normal womanly shape instead of looking like an anorexic coat-hanger. And she'd done something pretty to her hair, maybe highlights, but way more subtle than Sita's.

The best thing was a wonderful smell, like a garden after a downpour or else a new leather sofa, the kind from somewhere classy like Roche Bobois. He knew this because they kissed on the cheek. Weird how acute his sense of smell had become since the chemo.

She laughed a lot, but that didn't stop her asking questions. "So what's this about the Lear jet and everything?"

"It was a porkie, like the George Cross and the villa in Antigua." He paused. "My villa's really in St Kitts."

She laughed some more. "So do you often make things up?"

"Guess so. Don't you?"

She admitted she did too, then went straight back to questions.

What difference could it possibly make, he thought. Who the fuck cared if he had a PC or a laptop, or whether he logged on at home or at work? "My turn now. What did you think of the speed-dating?"

She thought it was just like a cocktail party. "Only everyone there is single, or at least pretending."

"That's exactly it," Sanjay nodded. "Like a party, but my mum's not there, chasing people round the room with a tray and force-feeding them samosas, and my dad's not there boring people about his work, or fretting about crumbs on the carpet. Which you're bound to get if you ram samosas down people's gullets."

"Are those the only parties you go to?"

"No. But they're the only ones I remember in their entirety, because I stay completely sober."

"So would you say you have a lot of friends?"

Sanjay fiddled with a sugar packet and considered. "Not so many single ones now. All the guys from uni have mostly settled down." And Ben, who now reckoned he'd be single forever.

"So when you say 'guys', does that include women?"

"Do you work for a market research company?"

She leaned back in the chair and observed him. "What makes you think that?"

"Because you ask a lot of questions."

"Sorry. I'm just interested. And the thing is that we don't yet know if we have anything in common except for speed-dating."

She'd forgotten something. "And cats" he added.

"And cats."

That was the cue to show her pictures of Dainty on his BlackBerry. Not all of them, just 20 or so of the best ones. He'd shown them to Karen too, of course, but he'd had a different objective then. How else could you get someone to stop yakking about her kids and Man City and the rest of it?

Their heads touched briefly, as did their fingers on his phone. He got that leather sofa scent again.

"She's adorable" said Harriet. "Oh look, there she is waiting for her tummy to be tickled."

Harriet explained she'd had to re-house her cat when a boyfriend objected to him, especially when Pushkin jumped onto the counter and drank from random glasses. "Pushkin was the cat, not the boyfriend" she pointed out.

Sanjay figured. "Did you find him a good home? The cat, that is. I don't care bollocks about the boyfriend."

"Yes, he got a new home but it still really upsets me. Will you excuse me? Just going to the loo. Be right back."

While she was gone, he doodled on a napkin and thought about the things he still wanted to do. It was a bugger not knowing how long he might have. The doctors only gave a precise time in films and books, not in real life, when it actually mattered. Anyway, his current to-do list included:

Seaside holiday. And not bothering with sunscreen, he added to himself.

Go to Prague

Perfect date with near-perfect woman. No, scrap that. A good date with a bad woman was much more fun.

Fly a helicopter

See Shelley Ritchie again. Because there was something special about your first girlfriend.

Do something for Ben.

Like what? He had no idea. He would also have liked to add *Leave something worthwhile behind.* But how the bollocks could anyone plan that when they didn't know how long they had?

Maybe he should stop wasting time making lists. The way life was going, he was in danger of spending the rest of his days just cataloguing what he wanted to do.

When Harriet came back, he asked "Do you fancy another cappuccino?"

"No thanks, I'm good."

"OK. How about a weekend away?"

Chapter Eleven

Karen

Karen didn't know what to make of Geoff. "What field do you research?" she asked over their cluster of bowls. "Anything I might have heard of?"

He shook his head and said his work was mundane in the extreme. The only hint was the admission, made when they ordered their lagers, that he used to drink a hell of a lot as a student. As if students didn't all binge themselves senseless.

When asked, she said she had "One marriage – failed. Four kids, as you know."

He told her he too had one marriage – failed. "And one son – highly successful."

"What does your son do so successfully?"

"He plays with Duplo. He's five years old."

She laughed. Last Christmas she'd lost a tooth on a coin that Charlotte had hidden in the pudding. The gap was visible when she laughed, but that wasn't going to stop her enjoying herself.

"I'm sorry" he said. "I promised myself I wouldn't talk about my son. Kids shouldn't be taken on a date, especially not a first date."

"Don't worry. I find it really hard not to mention my children." Across the street an irritating neon sign flashed *HINESE HERBAL EDICINE CENTER*. "That could give people seizures" she remarked.

"Yes it could. Well, probably. Do you know about seizures?"

"My eldest son had one at the age of 18 months." Bang went that resolution.

He nodded thoughtfully. "That's a common age for febrile convulsions. Or so I'm told."

"It scared the life out of me." She told him about driving Damon to hospital, hitting a bollard outside A&E, then hurrying into the waiting-room with her son in her arms. A video was showing to keep patients entertained. It was *Dead on Arrival*.

"Great choice" agreed Geoff.

"He got better, but he had to have a lumbar puncture – a test where they take fluid from around the spine with a needle. They also wanted a urine sample, so we left his nappy off for hours. In the end, he peed on the floor behind the radiator when I wasn't ready with the bottle. Sorry. Well, that sign out there is really annoying" she finished. She should have remembered that no date wanted to hear about your toddler's wee.

"What do you think of alternative medicine?" he asked.

"It's just quackery, isn't it?" She had probably spoken out of turn again. No wonder Rose accused her of opening her mouth just to change feet. "What do you think?"

"I agree."

"You do?"

"Absolutely. So many people enthuse about alternative treatments and all that herbal junk. I bet they still ring 999 if they have chest pain. If they don't, they're even more stupid."

"True" she said, wrestling with bamboo shoots which kept eluding her. Rose would have had a fit to see Karen use chopsticks, because each bite took a detour on its way to her mouth.

"There are a lot of problems with Chinese food," observed Geoff, "starting with the cutlery."

"Or lack of it" she replied, even though the scattering of dark stains on the cloth said it for her.

He reflected. "Actually, starting with the menu."

"True. You never quite know what you'll get. I mean, what on earth is 'fish-flavoured aubergine'?" asked Karen. "Apart from a dish they want you not to order."

"There's a different menu for the Chinese anyway" he said.

"Yes. It's in Chinese." Shit. The kids were right. She really did say the most obvious things.

"There are probably different things on it too" Geoff pointed out.

"But I suspect everything's still got soy sauce and MSG."

His face turned into the picture of concern. "I hope you don't suffer from Chinese Restaurant Syndrome."

"What's that?"

Geoff explained that symptoms could include headache, chest pain, flushing, sweating and numbness. "Many Chinese don't believe in it, but it's possibly an allergy to MSG."

"No, I'm OK. Probably built up immunity to it by now."

"Of course the other problem with Chinese food is that you're hungry again an hour later" he said.

"That happens to me with any food."

He considered this. "Do you think that indicates some unmet need?"

"Yes. The need to have someone else prepare meals for me."

He laughed and ordered more drinks. It was the sound of a man at ease with himself. All the same, Karen thought he was a bit remote. Not buttoned-up so much as disengaged. And he kept getting text messages. He read them every time, but he didn't answer any of them.

"Sorry about that" he said, putting his phone back into his pocket.

She didn't like to probe, so she changed the subject. "Where did you go to university?"

He hesitated palpably before replying "Cambridge."

"You were trying not to mention that" she said.

"You're right."

"Not to appear a smart-arse, perhaps?"

"No, it's because I'm pissed. I only pretend I went to Cambridge when I'm pissed."

He was so hard to read. "Will you excuse me? I need to ring the babysitter, and I don't have a signal."

"I've got a signal. I'm with O2."

She preferred to use her own mobile. "Are you worried? Think if I leave the table I might escape via the toilet window?"

"Not at all" he said. "The toilets here don't have windows."

She laughed and scraped back her chair.

Standing on the pavement outside, Karen learned from Rose that the kids were being good. What was more, there were no sound-effects suggested anyone was being slaughtered. When Karen came back to the table, Geoff was reading another text.

"Sorry about all that. There's an old friend who thinks it's still OK to ask me for advice all the time." He didn't say what kind of advice, let alone what kind of friend. "The thing is" he continued, "I daren't turn my mobile off. Because of Davey."

She understood perfectly. It was good that he liked kids.

While she hadn't had much to drink, she was already light-headed, or, as Rose would have put it, tipsy. Was tipsy still a word in the 21st century? Anyway, not cool on a first date. It was strange too, because she'd only had a couple of glasses. Had he plopped some Rohypnol into her Bud?

She hoped not. If they did have sex, she wanted to remember it afterwards.

The next day, Geoff rang to ask if she would like to go to the Tate Modern. She said she would, even before looking up the artist on Wikipedia.

As well as seeing the Rothkos, they stared at the crack in the floor in the turbine hall. It surely symbolized something, but what? They speculated.

"The question is," said Karen, "who put it there?"

"Here's another question: how long has it been there? Are there any other cracks like this one? Could it be part of some arcane religion?"

"And is it getting bigger? How many coins, biros and hairpins do you think fell down it before they filled it?" She examined it like a child. Others, mostly men, were doing just the same. She asked Geoff if he thought that meant men were more infantile. Or were they more likely to investigate things, which might be why most scientists were male?

"Maybe it's in the genes" said Geoff.

This rang a distant bell. "You think all of that's down to one little Y chromosome?" she asked.

"No, it could be X-linked, like haemophilia. Which is why a few women have it, but mostly men are affected."

Karen had another theory. "How about if everyone has the investigating gene? But, in the case of half the population, they end up having to keep house, cook dinner and look after the kids. So they don't get a chance to express it."

"Are you by any chance suggesting that men are indulged and kept in a state of prolonged infantilism where they are exempt from chores?" said Geoff in mock horror.

"You might very well think so" said Karen with a smile. "I couldn't possibly comment."

Two young children came careering at them, making noises like gunfire. Geoff watched them, and she couldn't work out if he was happy or sad. Then he got another one of his infernal texts.

Geoff

He made Davey pancakes. Davey had already breakfasted before his mother dropped him off, but Geoff did not know many recipes. Ergo, it was all-day breakfasts until Davey got collected at 6pm.

Davey still had maple syrup on his chin when he put his fork down and gave Geoff the kind of serious look only a five-year old could carry off. "Daddy, can I have a bunny rabbit?"

"Davey, their fur makes you cough and wheeze. That would be bad, wouldn't it?"

Geoff was prepared for counter-arguments, but Davey only said "OK. Can I have more pancakes?"

They polished off the last two pancakes then discussed what to do. This consisted of Geoff asking Davey what he would like. In a normal family, five-year olds probably didn't get to decide. Geoff wasn't sure what a normal family was like.

On the way to the park, they stopped by the bank. Saturday opening was a bonus for Geoff. While Davey took a wodge of paying-in slips and amused himself by covering them with elaborate scrawls, chattering away as he did, Geoff stood in line.

Last night hadn't had a promising start. For one thing, he and Laure had arranged to meet in the most crowded bar in central London, where he hadn't a hope of recognizing anyone he knew, let alone someone he had seen only once. Twice he had asked someone if she was the person he was supposed to be meeting. The first time the woman had smiled back, shaking her head wistfully. The second woman appeared narked, though not as narked as her boyfriend was when he returned with the drinks.

In the end, Laure found Geoff. When she smiled, his evening began to improve. She was far more attractive than either of the strangers he'd accosted. She smiled at him again. Oh yes, she was a sure thing.

By now the bank queue had moved forward two places. Geoff waved at Davey who still seemed content with the paying-in slips and a fistful of leaflets on mortgages.

Karen was nice to be with, but it was Laure and last night now occupying his thoughts. The longer he'd looked at her, the more he realised he'd need to take a tablet. After their third drink, he had managed to slip down a Viagra. Food would slow down the effect, especially if it was fatty, so he took two tablets, just in case.

They had found a taxi. Geoff glanced at Laure in the half-light. Her face was hard to read, but her warm fingers were interlinked with his. Unprompted, the driver ranted about immigration, or possibly lenient judges. Geoff lost the thread halfway through, but the gist was that the cabbie thought the country was going to hell in a handcart, and everything the government were doing was tantamount to throwing away all they had ever fought for during two world wars.

Geoff squeezed Laure's hand experimentally. She squeezed back. He closed in for a kiss as the cab went over a speed bump. And another speed bump. Then they kissed again at length as the cabbie went on about not trusting any politician as far as he could spit.

Now Geoff was at the head of the queue waiting to see which bank clerk was free. He looked round to check on Davey. There was a trail of leaflets on the table, but no Davey. Where was he?

He scanned the bank. A couple were standing in the corner talking heatedly, but no Davey anywhere. Did nobody care what had become of him?

Sickness rose in his throat. How could he have queued there daydreaming while his beloved son ran off, or, even worse, got whisked away by a psychopath?

By the door, a young bank employee stood in her dark suit like some maitre d', dispensing smiles and leaflets. She must have seen Davey. By the time Geoff reached her, he had palpitations, his breathing was harsh, and his fingers had developed pins and needles. Although he recognized the symptoms of hyperventilation, there was bugger all he could do about them.

"Have you seen my son?" he said, struggling to keep his voice level. "Five years old, blue T-shirt. He's called Davey."

The suit woman beamed. "Is that him there?" She pointed to the desk in the corner.

Bending down, Geoff caught sight of a blue sleeve. He ran across the bank to find the rest of Davey crouching under the desk.

Davey said cheerily "The pen jumped off the table. Then it went over here but I found it. Ow, Daddy. You're hugging too tight. I can't breathe."

Feeling drained and slightly pathetic, Geoff went back to the queue where someone nice let him in. Next time he would hang onto Davey's hand constantly.

After the bank they headed to the park. The post office on the corner had just closed. Now five young black women were lined up outside it, calling out "Jesus loves you!" to every passer-by, including the faithful streaming out of the synagogue around the corner. Usually Geoff hurried past the friends of Jesus, but this time he looked at their beaming faces. Catching his eye, the girl at the end of the row ecstatically cried out "Jesus loves you!" and the other four took up the refrain. Geoff smiled back. Davey waved at them.

In the park, Davey said he wanted the time to go faster.

"Why, Davey?" Geoff was dismayed at the thought that Davey might want to go home.

"Because I want the conkers to fall off. I want pick them up."

"We'll come back in a few weeks then." It was good to look forward to something.

While Davey went on the climbing-frame, Geoff saw a woman waiting for her child. Maybe she was a lone parent too. There were lots of mothers here. While keeping his eyes firmly on Davey, he reflected that he rather liked mothers. They were nurturing. Laure, sadly, was anything but. Geoff got up to give Davey a push on the swings.

A long while later, Davey grew tired of the park and they walked home. The sun was lower but still warm. It wouldn't set for another few hours, yet the day was inexorably dwindling. Geoff hated those last few hours with Davey. Objectively they might be no different to the other hours, but he felt time closing in relentlessly. They walked past the post office where the quintet was still there, calling out just as energetically as before. "Jesus loves you!"

While they waited for the lights, Davey asked "Daddy, does Jesus love me too?"

"Jesus loves all of us." Geoff wasn't wholly convinced but it would have to do.

Davey had a little think. After they had crossed the street, with Geoff holding Davey's hand tight, Davey said "Daddy?"

"What, Davey?"

"Does Jesus love me more than you do?"

"Well, I can't really speak for Jesus, but I believe I love you more. You see, there's nobody I love more than you. You know that, don't you?"

But Davey had spotted a squirrel up a tree and lost interest.

They had a snack when they got in, then Davey got out his Lego and Geoff tried to help him make a boat. Davey laughed helplessly. "Daddy! Not like that. Here, I'll show you."

Surely Geoff wasn't meant to feel like this. Medical school toughened you to cope with birth, death and the whole random pageant of life, including the psychological torture inflicted by some of the more sadistic consultants. So how come now, well over a decade after graduating, he had grown so soppy?

If someone had told him when he was younger, when he was busy shagging nurses and fellow medical students (and one of the registrars who was totally up for it), that this would happen, he'd never have believed it.

While training there was the whole gamut of human suffering and joy, but it was diluted by being second hand. It wasn't the same as experiencing it for yourself.

He'd delivered 20 babies. Still the penny hadn't dropped. Then Davey was born, with Sonya howling and finally pushing out in three goes this tiny scrap of wet and bloody human. His tiny scrap of human, their own baby boy. When asked if he wanted to cut the cord, his hands trembled pathetically. He had cut umbilical cords on many other occasions. This time, he barely missed amputating his own finger.

Later came the August bank holiday in Devon, which was probably a lovely place when it wasn't raining. It was one night when they had no paracetamol syrup for feverish Davey, and no Vicks Vapo-Rub for their own coughs, that Geoff knew what he feared most of all in the whole world. Although Davey was eight months old and therefore out of the riskiest age range for sudden infant death syndrome, nothing would deter Geoff from staying up all night to watch over him and make sure he didn't miss a breath.

Tonight six o'clock came round as fast as ever. The hug Davey gave him before climbing into his mother's car filled him to the brim, then left him emptier than before. He sat for a moment distilling the day, keeping it for posterity, savouring it again.

Geoff turned his mobile back on. Another text from Frieda. He sighed. Her daughter had nothing more than a mild virus, but Frieda was the anxious type. She has other issues that also went way back. Every time Geoff saw her name on his phone, he was briefly transported back to the nurses' home. To Frieda insisting he should keep his white coat and stethoscope on. To his Oxford pocket guide to medicine thumping rhythmically against the hand-basin.

Every time Geoff read her texts, he wished he'd done accountancy like his brothers. Their exes never haunted them for urgent advice 15 years after a fling. This time it was *Temp 38.9 n lymph glands up, shd I worry? X*. He gave a bland reply.

When Geoff finally went up to his bedroom that night, Frieda was forgotten. He breathed in deeply as he got into bed. Laure's perfume still lingered on the sheets.

Chapter Twelve

Laure

A fellow student once asked Laure if she would like to go back and listen to music. When she got to his room, she discovered that he had no CD player, and that his nickname was Fingers Jackson.

However Laure had come a long way since her freshman year. On leaving the Bar H with Geoff, there was no pretence that the taxi ride to his home was to listen to music or sip instant coffee.

Fortified with Chenin Blanc from his fridge, Laure and Geoff soon found their way upstairs. He lit a couple of candles on the windowsill and kissed her, hard. Moments later, the duvet was on the floor.

She couldn't fault his knowledge of the female body. The curtains were open, the full moon shone, and for a long and wonderful moment, she lay face down, while he was on top of her, clutching a hank of her hair and licking her ear. She spread her legs wide to get the full impact.

The bedsprings protested as Geoff repeatedly hit home, right at the spot that made her gasp. Laure yowled like a tigress as he did something extraordinarily primeval and deeply satisfying, which led her to a noisy and inevitable climax. Geoff roared in turn. It was only afterwards, as they lay in a sweaty post-coital heap, that Laure noticed the piercing cries of urban foxes in some back garden.

Filled to the rafters, the Bar H had not been conducive to proper conversation. There was a sizeable office crowd who were loud, assertive and all over the counter. It had taken a while to get drinks. She and Geoff could have moved on to another bar, but when she tried to suggest it above the din he nodded vigorously and went to get a menu.

So they ended up sitting at one of the tables, with six mini-burgers and a huge comprehension gulf between them. Laure spooned on mayonnaise and pondered how she would weave in her job as a hairdresser with years spent in the Netherlands.

Eventually the office people moved on somewhere else, buoyed away on a tide of alcohol. When they were able to hear each other, Laure asked Geoff "What is it you do? I'm not sure you said."

He replied "Research. It's deadly dull, I'm afraid. The last woman I described my job to fell into a deep coma. They say she's still on life support."

At some point, maybe because it was Friday night, Geoff revealed he was a lapsed Jew. His ex-wife wasn't Jewish – he had married out – and so their son was not Jewish either.

They talked about pastimes. "Do you play bridge?" asked Geoff

Laure shuddered and shook her head. "Not at all. You?"

"I tried. My wife thought we should, to be sociable, but ultimately I couldn't bring myself to give a toss about the little cardboard rectangles I was clutching, let alone those in other people's hands." He paused and told her she had lovely eyes.

"Thank you. Where my mother's family come from, eyes like these are very ordinary." That was true. Almost everyone had expressive brown eyes, though there was a sizeable blue-eyed contingent from Syria. In the Middle East, eyes were big in every way. All the TV soaps focussed on the characters' eye movements. The thinner the plot and the hammier the acting, the more the eyes gyrated. Every song was about a woman's eyes, while conversations inevitably included at least one mention of the worst but most ubiquitous eye of all, the Evil Eye. Arabs believed it was responsible for everything that went wrong in the world.

"Where does your family come from?" asked Geoff.

"My father is from Bristol, my mother from Beirut. I was brought up here, and have only been to Lebanon twice. I'm a thoroughly lapsed Lebanese."

"I've never met one of those before."

Laure reached for another mini-burger. "Have you met many Lebanese then?"

"A few. And they're always charming."

"Then they must have been trying to sell you something."

"Possibly. They're big on family, which is admirable compared with the average Brit."

"They're very big on family. A Lebanese would sell his own grandmother." Laure felt mean exaggerating, but exaggeration was very Lebanese too.

Geoff was amused. "Can't say I've ever seen a Lebanese granny on eBay. Would you like dessert?"

After studying the menu, they decided against. "The cheesecake always sounds nice, but it's usually barely defrosted" he said. "And it's never as good as in New York."

Laure twiddled a lock of hair. "Or St John's Wood?"

"Or St John's Wood" agreed Geoff. "Would you care for a night-cap?"

Geoff got up, disposed of the condom, and brought Laure a glass of water.

"Thank you" she said with a trace of awkwardness.

They settled down nose to nose on a large pillow, with one strong arm around her.

"You're a lovely woman" Geoff said sleepily.

Laure sighed. "Unfortunately I'm not always a confident woman."

"Oh?" He opened his eyes.

"I don't mean tonight. I mean generally."

"But you're a delight. I'm no shrink, but you've got something wrong. Well, can't see you having trouble with guys, anyway." He leaned up on an elbow and drained his wine glass.

"No trouble attracting them, true. But it's harder to keep up a relationship with the right one."

There was a pause while he fingered the stem of his glass. "Want to tell me?"

She didn't, but it came out anyway. Her Lebanese mother was addicted to bridge, and disinclined to spend much time on Laure or her sister. Meanwhile her businessman father spent most evenings at his club. Laure gave a meaningful look. "Well, he *said* it was his club."

"Not all husbands are philanderers" Geoff pointed out. "I should know."

"He wasn't so much a philanderer as an abuser." She paused. "I preferred it when he was at his club."

"Oh!"

Laure examined her nails. "It wasn't actually rape. He didn't go that far."

Geoff said carefully "Doesn't have to be."

"It was me, not my sister, as far as I know. I confronted him at dinner one night."

"Brave of you."

"Maybe, but it didn't do any good." Laure explained that, after a couple of weeks of high drama, her parents acted as if nothing had happened.

"I'm very sorry to hear that."

She pulled the sheets up, covering her breasts. "Anyway. Probably not the best script for life."

"To say the least" he said. "Shall I get us a drop more wine?"

"I'm good, thanks." The failure of her mother to intervene, Laure added, was as bad as anything her father had done.

Geoff lay back on the pillow and shut his eyes. "According to Bowlby, the bond between child and mother forms the template for every single relationship that child will ever have." He paused. "But templates aren't actually written in indelible ink."

"Guess not" said Laure, putting her arm on his warm shoulder. It was really time to forget it all and sleep, though it was hard to sleep when you were mentally flagellating yourself. Was she going to carry on beating herself up for something she'd done years ago? And why the hell had she said so much to a man who was only a one-night stand? He might have become more, had she not said quite so much.

The next day dawned brightly. She escaped from the house before either of them started quoting Larkin.

Laure had agreed to meet Dan at the British Museum. There was no shortage of objects to admire, which might be useful in case they found nothing in common.

She paused in the atrium. A family with three children clattered through, their feet and voices echoing. Children could be unsettling.

A moment later Dan arrived, once again in a white shirt and jeans. "Hi gorgeous" he said, lifting up her hand.

She giggled as his lips touched the back of her hand. Was this the way an international lawyer was meant to behave?

"Well, I don't know if you want to see anything here" he said. "But I have to say I'm a bit thirsty. Though that can wait if you want to mooch around here first. There are a couple of new exhibits, I think."

Laure looked in the direction of his gesticulating arm and saw a poster about some pottery collection or other. "Where shall we have that drink?"

There was a pub nearby. They installed themselves between a couple of women and a table where a man sat on his own with a paper. Laure's seat offered a perfect view of most of the pub, of the street outside, and of Dan's profile. Perhaps it wasn't elegant, but it was virile and very attractive. In this light she noticed that his bald head had been shaved, and wondered how often he had to pass a razor over it to keep it that way. It was legitimate for a hairdresser to ask.

"About twice a week. I do it myself, so I'm afraid you and your colleagues don't make much out of me."

Dan didn't ask more about her work, nor did he talk about his. Perhaps he had a really boring job. Best not mention it, in case he wanted to know all about hairdressing.

"Why did you tick me?" he asked.

"Well, first I ticked everyone who made me laugh. But it turned out you were the only one. So

I broadened my criteria and ticked every man who didn't look like a convict."

He seemed disappointed. "Aw, you mean I don't look like a convict? How could you tell?"

"Intuition. Don't forget that we hairdressers know a thing or two."

He leaned across the table in mock confidentiality. "We convicts know a thing or two as well."

"Very droll. I said you made me laugh."

They got more drinks. She saw that when he put his beer glass down, he didn't straighten all his fingers.

"What happened to your hand?" she asked.

"Just a burn. I did it trying to cook."

"Looks like a serious burn."

"Yeah. It hurt like hell at the time. But let me tell you the food came off a lot worse."

She had to smile. "What dish were you making?"

"Boiled potatoes. Maybe I should explain I'm not much of a cook."

"Me neither." She didn't know how to explain this, so she played at being Scarlett O'Hara. "Back home at Tara" she said, "we all had folks to do that for us."

He smiled. "Have you been to the United States much?"

"Why of course, Mr Dan. Not to the south, though, unless you count Florida" she finished in a normal voice.

"Seems an oxymoron, doesn't it?" said Dan. "That one of the most southern states doesn't usually count as being in the deep south, when others do. Like, say, Alabama or Georgia. That's why it's an oxymoron."

Laure thought it an odd use of the word *oxymoron*.

When they parted, Dan said "We should do this again."

"Yes, we should."

"No, really." He looked straight into her eyes and said slowly. "You mustn't agree unless you mean it too."

"I do mean it."

Rather charmingly, he said "It will take me a massive amount of will-power, but I won't phone you for at least 12 hours. So you still have time to duck out of another date. We're both grownups, after all."

"I know. Grownups."

After a kiss on each cheek from him, she headed home on the tube, feeling not in the slightest like a grownup.

Dan

Dan covered his pate with a baseball cap and got on the bus.

People-watching. There was satisfaction in that. And still a little novelty too, after being stuck where the only people you could watch were those you'd seen thousands of times already. You didn't want to watch them too closely either. It gave them the wrong idea. Not good. When people got the wrong idea, they also got an irresistible urge to do you over.

He'd learned a few life lessons. That one, for starters. But Dan didn't want to think about clink any more. It was not, as tabloids had it, a five-star hotel with wall-to-wall carpet and satellite TV in every cell. Or some exclusive club where you bonded with your fellow inmates, played endless games of draughts with Ronnie Barker, and dossed around waiting for Johnny Cash to nip round.

Now he found incredible richness and colour everywhere he went. Especially in the pub earlier with Laure.

Two tables away from them and silent for absolutely ages was an Indian couple. Maybe in their 50s. He'd clocked them because Asians of that age rarely drank in pubs. Or at least they didn't six years ago. Then the couple got lively. Dan heard the man exclaim "He is so fucking bloody well thin."

"Yes, well" said the woman, wobbling her head. "I am always telling him eat, eat, you're not eating enough, *beta*."

"You stupid! It's not the bloody food. It's the bloody fucking cancer" said the man.

After that they went quiet again. Dan saw them holding hands under the table.

He wished he hadn't had to lie to Laure about his burn, but it was only a fib, wasn't it? Maybe if he repeated it enough, it would help obliterate the awful smell of that day in the kitchens, and the even more awful memory of Maxy holding him down on the hot plate until his fingers could stand no more.

Holding him down. He shuddered.

Dan's burn was treated, if you could call it that, by the prison doc. Tubby little bloke. Pasty face. Acne he hadn't managed to cure. Not inspiring. Anyway, an infection had set in on top of Dan's burn. Even then he hadn't squealed. That would have made things really bad.

So he kept schtum while the infection got worse. It wasn't MRSA or a flesh-eating bug. Still it spread through something in his palm. Part of the hand that had a fancy Latin-type name. Began with *apo*. Dan couldn't remember. He'd tried to look it up at Kilburn library last week. Hadn't found it. But found a lot of other words instead. Long words that would help him talk the talk. And for his purposes that was even better.

Yeah. Laure was hot. As hot as the curry that he and his mates shared when planning the job. They were burning at both ends for hours afterwards. The plan itself was perfect, but, when push came to shove and they eventually broke into The Jewel Box with crowbars and the rest of it, there were only four of them. Dan was at his mum's instead.

Two reasons for that. One: he hadn't really wanted to do the job. Two: he hadn't seen his mum for nearly two weeks. Hadn't realized quite how ill she was.

How he missed Mum now. More than she could know. But that was another story. She'd died before anybody took her statement. Meant she couldn't corroborate his alibi. Neither could anyone else. That was shit luck.

Anyway his coat and things had been in the van. So, his word against the others. Life lesson: when you scarper, take everything with you.

It was amazing what you learned when you didn't even realize you were learning.

His bus took in some pretty skanky areas now. You only found Burger King in a half-decent high street. This place was a dump, because it only had a Tennessee Fried Chicken. It also had a barber shop with posters of stupid-looking men with even stupider haircuts, all lop-sided, like half the hair slicked down and the rest slicked up. Why would anyone want to ask for a 'do like one of those? Then there was the medical centre, which wasn't much more than a lock-up surgery. The sign said they did NHS and private. Dan couldn't imagine many people in this neck of the woods going private. Unless the doctors did drug deals.

That trip to the pub with Laure had gone quickly. Well, 10 minutes went by in the blink of an eye when you were with a pretty girl. Einstein had said that, no less. Proved he wasn't just a nutty old boffin with electrified hair and a tongue sticking out. Dan knew a bit about relativity. A teacher had been shipped in to keep the lags occupied. Those guys were chosen because they could stomach the stench of sweat and ignorance, but some of them knew how to teach. Still, it wasn't clear why Dan's sense of time had become so discombobulated since he had been inside.

Sweet word, *discombobulated*.

These days Dan got up late. Mostly because he could. Often not waking until the postman came round. This further discombobulated him, since the postman occasionally did his round at 2.30pm, shoving mail jauntily through the wrong doors and scattering elastic bands on the pavement in his wake.

Getting off the bus, Dan walked the rest of the way. Past the mini-cab firm with its relentless yellow light. In the doorway of the shoe-shop there was a young woman slumped in a sleeping bag. Immobile, possibly dead. If anyone gave a fuck either way.

Unlikely.

The fishmonger was shut. Still smelled of fish, though. Dan noticed a place that used to be an electrical shop. Now sold Iranian food as well as *Polskie Produkty*. How about that for international?

When he got home, he'd look up tomorrow's word of the day. And count the hours till he could ring Laure without appearing to be a complete fucking loony tune.

Chapter Thirteen

Karen

It was gone 9pm and Charlotte was in the dining-room doing her violin practice.

Karen listened to the complete and utter silence. Did Charlotte think anyone was stupid enough to miss the fact that a violin was not being played, other than for those few seconds when the air was filled with the scratchy sounds of it being tuned? While Karen was not at all musical, her children were, and she found the violin, more than most instruments, intensely expressive. It could make you dance, it could make you cry. It could also tell you from two rooms away whether the person playing it was in a happy mood or having one of those pre-teen sulks, the kind Charlotte had exhibited for as long as Karen could remember.

"Charlotte? What about that new Irish jig that you like?" Karen called out. It was hard to make out what the verbal answer was, but there were a few bad-tempered flourishes followed by the sound of a metal music-stand falling over.

Karen put her Sudoku down and considered getting up again, but she had only just sat down. She had settled Damon in the kitchen with his maths homework, along with his Man U scarf and a bowl of popcorn he had microwaved. Karen wondered whether he had made any further marks on the worksheet, other than the three desultory numbers he had filled in half an hour ago and which would probably turn out to be wrong.

At her feet in the living-room, Ashley and Edward were amusing themselves with Lego. There were so many ways of playing with this hugely versatile and educational toy. In this particular version, Edward sat in one of the drawers taken out of the chest while Ashley filled the space around Edward with Lego pieces as if trying to bury him in sand. For some reason, both of them found this shriekingly funny.

Her Sudoku was progressing nonetheless. Solving it was a well-worn ritual. Some Sudoku were easy, this one less so, but, one way or another, you always wanted to drop what you were doing to finish the puzzle. Once it was completed you looked at it again, realized it was a waste of time, and wondered why you'd bothered. Sudoku had a lot in common with one-night stands. Karen sighed. Still, she wouldn't have minded one of those instead of a Super Fiendish.

Charlotte stomped into the room, dragging her violin by the neck like an abused animal. "The acoustics suck in there" she moaned.

To help him concentrate on his maths, Damon had turned on the TV in the kitchen, the little one with the snowstorm picture and only four channels. From here she could hear the forced laughter of some inane dating game. Probably a contestant making risqué jokes that were meant to sound spontaneous but were 100% scripted.

Damon had got up and now skulked in the doorway. "Mum, what's a hooker?"

"It's a kind of rugby player" she said. "But it's not necessarily the best word for a rugby player" she added quickly, wishing she could think of something better. "I don't know how you can do homework with the telly on." She went into the kitchen to switch it off before it posed any more challenges.

Unfortunately her audience was getting bigger. Ashley had appeared. Then Charlotte wandered in, scratching her back with the violin bow. "I know!" she said brightly. "A hooker is someone who goes fishing a lot. Fishy, fishy, fishy, hooker, hooker." Charlotte began to go round the room making a fish-like mouth.

"OK, that's quite enough" said Karen. If they were going to shout 'hooker' around the school, the teacher would be calling Karen in for yet another talk.

"Hooker! Hooker!" chorused Edward, who had lost interest in being drowned in Lego. When he saw his mother's face, he repeated it again, just for fun.

"Now come on, we've all got things to do." Distraction, not instruction, was the best way of getting kids to stop doing something. She picked Edward up and let him pull her necklace. "Why don't you try to finish your maths, Damon, and let me know if you're stuck. Charlotte, how's your practice going?"

Charlotte pulled a face. "I hate violin. I want to play drums."

"Drums? Why?"

"Belinda plays drums. She's the new girl and she lives in a really big house with a really cool drum kit. And she has a studio to play it in" Charlotte added, sounding hurt.

"Can't have everything Belinda has, though. We've probably got things she hasn't."

"Like what? Belinda has a *pony*."

It was going to be tough to compete with the super-cool rich kid. Violins were cheaper than a drum kit, especially when you'd already bought one. Besides, Karen wasn't sure her nerves could take Charlotte on drums.

"What about the oboe or the clarinet?" suggested Karen.

Charlotte made another one of her faces.

They were deep in discussion of the pros and cons of different instruments when Rose popped round on the pretext of borrowing a cookbook. It was really to find out if Karen had heard from Geoff.

"Not recently" said Karen.

"That's a shame. He sounded nice" said Rose, even though Karen had barely told her anything. To Rose, any single man qualified as 'nice' if he had a pulse and a wallet. To be fair, Rose had a point.

"Which cookbook are you after?"

"Any of them. My family are sick of my recipes. What's that you're wearing, by the way?"

"Remember the old curtains from Charlotte's room? Well, that's the skirt. The top is a just a random black T-shirt I sewed on." Karen was halfway to the kitchen when the dulcet tones of her mobile rang out. "Oh, hi. No, I wasn't busy. Just the usual. You know."

Edward screamed and tugged at his crotch.

"Is someone being murdered?" asked Geoff.

"No, no, everything's fine. What about you?"

"I'm all right. What's that noise?"

"One of my boys has Lego in his underpants." She pulled Edward's pants down expertly with one hand, whereupon four or five bricks and a plastic pirate fell out.

"I'm glad that's all it is" said Geoff.

That wasn't all. "Oh God, Edward, I've told you before about peeing in here" she moaned as Edward executed a perfect arc onto the futon in the living-room.

Down the phone Geoff laughed. "Don't worry. He'll grow out of it. Once he realizes everyone else uses a toilet instead of the carpet."

"I guess." But didn't that apply only to other people's children? "Ashley! What are you doing with my bag? Put that down."

Ashley had delved into Karen's new handbag from Age Concern and was now dismantling a Tampax. Meanwhile Edward tried to regain centre stage by shouting "Hooker, hooker!" again.

"Rose" she said urgently, "could you please take care of Edward, and also rescue my purse and its contents?" Rose appeared crestfallen. She'd have preferred to stay in the doorway and snoop.

"Things sound a bit manic where you are. Do *you* need rescuing?" asked Geoff.

"I'm fine, really. It's just that Sunday nights can be a bit crazy." So could Mondays, Tuesdays, or any day. People who had only one child couldn't possibly understand. "Can I ring you back in an hour or so?" she said quickly, before Edward yelled 'hooker' again.

The idea of a rescue was beginning to appeal. Anyway, she would call him back, apologize and get the conversation back on track. Yes, that was what she was going to do, as soon as she got Rose out of the door with the cookbooks, mopped the futon and collected the contents of her handbag. Maybe she should just get a bit more of Damon's maths done as well, and give the younger ones their bath?

The door went again as soon as Rose had gone and before Karen had found the foam cleaner for the futon. Not a neighbour this time, but Karen's ex-husband hoping for a bed for the night. The children rushed to greet him.

Karen saw the suitcase in his hand. Not a good sign.

His current girlfriend had turned out to be a raving lunatic, a real head-case, he told Karen while the kids screamed "Daddy, Daddy!" Anyway, he explained, she had thrown him out.

"Which floozy is that then?"

"She's not a floozy" he protested. "Karen, why isn't Edward wearing any pants?"

"He took them off to get the Lego out of his bits. Look, if it's the woman I met, she's most definitely a floozy."

"What's a floozy?" asked Ashley.

Karen couldn't very well throw out the father of her children. Luckily the living-room was too uncomfortable for a protracted stay.

There was a time when a protracted stay was exactly what Karen had in mind. For a long while she'd have liked nothing better than to have Thomas back. After all, he'd been there when each of the babies was born. He'd played with the kids as they grew up. He'd painted the ceilings. Wasn't that commitment?

So, in the weeks after his departure – the permanent one, not the two that had come before – she'd hoped he'd change his mind. They were about to plunge the kids into uncertainty and a complicated rota of parental visits. Wasn't it a crying shame to break a family up over a simple case of neo-adolescent angst?

Logic told her that it hadn't been anything to do with her that Thomas had gone off to find himself. And yet, if she'd helped him find himself, maybe he wouldn't have felt the need to leave home.

Their love-making had become sedate. Of course it had. When you were compelled to fit hushed sessions into those brief moments after the children went to sleep and before you passed out yourself, it was hardly going to be kind of sex that rocked the tent apart and pulled out the pegs. Those damp exhilarating camping trips were firmly in the past, before children.

Factor in habit and fear of a fifth pregnancy, and it was a recipe for boredom. Maybe it was also about taking each other for granted in other ways. Thomas didn't have to play nice for her to cook him dinner or keep the house clean (not that Karen's version of clean was the kind described in the dictionary).

How did other couples survive the advent of *ennui*? Her neighbour Rose had the answer. "Money" she'd said. "Or power. Or both. Can I have your meat-loaf recipe? Couldn't find it online."

The spice unexpectedly returned the afternoon that Thomas came back for his boxed sets. Karen had been sorting through these, on her hands and knees in the living-room in front of a mountain of DVDs. Just how much had they actually spent on them over the years anyway? Her mission now was to ensure that Thomas didn't make off with the children's favourite stories about wizards, talking trains, chipmunks, superheroes, lonely dragons and secret gardens.

"I haven't got long" she warned Thomas when he knocked at the door. "School run, remember."

"Well, if you hadn't insisted on taking the key off me, then you wouldn't need to be here when I popped round. Unless you think I'm going to make off with the Sponge-Bob Square-Pants video, or plant a bug under your bed because I'm morbidly jealous?"

There was a nasty glint in his eye which she wasn't used to seeing. She remembered becoming very angry with him. Her heart was pounding as heavily as the day she'd come first in the Mums' Race on sports day. Thomas too seemed surprised that she didn't hit him with the DVD she had in her hand.

What could she possibly have got out of that furtive afternoon shag, she had no idea. She knew only that she had found it completely natural.

As well as urgent and rushed. He'd left his trousers on as she climbed atop him. She was tighter than she had been for a while. He moaned. She whimpered. Someone came to the door. They ignored it. Nothing mattered but that moment.

Probably lots of other separated couples did this too. Still, she shouldn't have done it that afternoon, she'd thought to herself shortly afterwards, as she drove to school, her thighs still wet. Those eight minutes weren't worth the burden she felt now.

Well, that was never going to happen again, Karen told herself. And certainly not tonight. Why was Thomas here anyway? She reluctantly waved him and his suitcase into the living-room, pushing some of the Lego aside with one foot.

Even if she didn't bathe the two little ones, there were still the school uniforms to iron, the PE kit to get ready, and all the other things besides. Karen was going to have to shut herself away in the bathroom and phone Geoff from there, just as if she were 15.

She located a tatty pillow and a sleeping bag that smelled as if it hadn't been aired since Cub Scout camp the previous year, and chucked them at Thomas. "Here. You can sleep on the futon." She left him standing there clutching the bedding and looking pathetic.

"Karen, please, I want us to try again" he pleaded as she started up the stairs. "And what the hell are you wearing? Please tell me those aren't curtains."

Chapter Fourteen

Harriet

"I'm sure we haven't done it like this before" said Simon breathlessly, his voice emanating from somewhere behind her buttocks.

She glanced away from his feet and over her right arm at Simon's sweaty face and torso. He looked just as ridiculous as she was sure she did.

"We haven't. I'm researching a feature. And don't tell me you didn't enjoy it" she added when Simon emitted a series of satisfied moans. After that his head subsided into the bed-linen, the tasteful whatever-point Egyptian cotton that he insisted on buying, and he fell silent. He even forgot to add his usual caveat that she must desist from mentioning him by name in her copy.

She wouldn't have bothered with the Reverse Rodeo had it not been for her feature, provisionally entitled *Your Best Sex Ever: 10 fabulous sex positions to try right now*. How was she to confess to the commissioning editor that she was better placed to write an article called *Mattress Monotony*?

Right now Simon was devoid of thought. He had rolled onto his side, head embedded in the pillow. Hanks of hair, normally coaxed into a comb-over by day, had fallen over one eye. Sighing, he raised an arm above his head. His matted armpit hair was acrid, the smell of sweat and semen strong. Yet in the early days, Harriet had found it appealing, since the more he'd enjoyed sex, the worse he looked and smelled afterwards. So what had happened?

Bored in the bedroom? It's all too easy to fall into a rut. But no matter how long you've been together, a few new tricks can relight that fire. We're betting you haven't tried our top ten positions to put the sizzle back into your sex-life. So, take your partners....

As she lay next to him, she wondered when it had gone wrong. Their first shags had been nothing short of electrifying, while the more recent efforts had just been, well, an effort.

When had been their best sex? A while back, before the comb-over and the intellectual snobbery started getting to her. Must have been on one of their earlier foreign trips. Cuba was a hot contender. Harriet recalled sitting waiting for him in one of the cafés in Habana Vieja, not on the main tourist trail around Obispo or the cathedral, but nearer the waterfront. Simon had gone to see a man about some instrument that was an integral part of *Son*. It sounded like a giant cow-bell, looked like an old segment of drainpipe, and made Simon incredibly excited.

A woman was never alone long in Habana. All she had to do was show up and breathe, and soon men would materialize from nowhere with a guitar, flowers or both, serenading her with *Guantanamera* and assuring her she looked exactly like a gardenia. But Harriet had waited in the café anyway. After 48 hours during which they hadn't kept their hands off each other, she could hardly walk, let alone go salsa dancing as one young Cuban after another was now pestering her to do.

In those days, recalled Harriet, she and Simon kissed all the time too: before, after, during. She had permanent stubble rash. Yes, there too. Maybe all the kissing helped them swap vital information on pheromones and tissue antigens, as suggested in the *New Scientist*. Whatever the reason, it never happened now.

To recreate the thrill of their early passion, she'd tried creative visualization, a feature idea she'd recently pitched to a Sunday supplement. But either she wasn't doing it right or else their case was beyond hopeless. It hadn't grabbed the editor either.

The speed-dating feature was not going too well. She had gone through the tapes and notebooks but it still lacked direction. Harriet sighed. Everything she got published was so much meaningless pap on meaningless paper. Well, one day she was going to write a book, she told herself as she got out of bed. She wiped away a trickle of semen running down the inside of her knee before it reached her calf.

There were 150,000 new books published every year in the UK. Why shouldn't her novel be one of them?

Of course while writing it she could name the file something dull, like *Taxreturn.doc*, or *tapwaterdangersfeature.doc*. It would need to be hidden from Simon unless she wanted to hear a load of scathing remarks that would instantly soak up any creative juices.

Harriet tossed the tissue in the bin. Looking around at Simon and their bedroom, with its piles of music mags and its elegant ornaments, she wondered if she needed somewhere else to write. Coffee shops were one option. Starbucks served beverages so hot that you could write 500 words before your drink was even cool enough to take a sip. You didn't have to clean up after yourself when you dropped crumbs. And nobody bothered you. While the decor wasn't great, on the plus side there wouldn't be any of Simon's artefacts from foreign climes, like that cowbell thing from Cuba and the *tabla* drum from Egypt. Best of all, there would be no Simon because he abhorred Starbucks and, as he put it, everything it stood for.

She brushed her teeth, reflecting that she didn't think Starbucks stood for anything. Simon had sniffed and berated her for this, telling her she knew nothing of semiotics. Once, that remark would have intrigued her. A bit later, it would have wounded her. Now she realised she didn't give a shit.

As soon as Simon left for work the next morning, Harriet negotiated crucial extensions to two of her deadlines, then spent time tidying up her notes of the evening at the Jacaranda. She wished Pushkin was still here, pestering her for food, rolling onto his back on the carpet when he was in need of urgent tummy-tickling, or, if that didn't get him the attention he craved, trotting up to her laptop and lying on the keyboard.

Harriet's afternoon was spent invoicing, a task many freelances hated but she actually rather enjoyed. What wasn't to like about totting up sums of money that other people owed you for a change, rather than the other way round?

By the time Simon came home, she had managed to keep busy all day, without allowing herself a moment in which to think about the one thing that threatened to take over her brain completely if she opened it just a tiny crack.

"I'm home" he said, then started to walk around the flat picking up things that belonged to Harriet, looking at them with barely veiled disgust then putting them down again. One would have thought her pink scarf had been an assault on the senses.

"What would you have said if I'd left dirty thongs strewn about, instead of a few innocuous items of outerwear?" she ventured as she folded the scarf away.

"Ah, but that's not the point, is it?"

She knew what the point was. It was to make her feel stupid and slovenly. As if he hadn't done enough so far, Simon sniffed several times and said "An orderly mind and an orderly abode go together."

Over dinner, she told him she had an upcoming weekend away, one of the freebie trips that periodically came up. It was a bit of a drag, she went on with a plausible sigh, but it would probably be an excellent networking opportunity. These things usually were. He asked when and where her little junket was, but appeared not to listen to the answer.

As he stacked the plates, he said "Where are you going?"

"Barcelona. I just said." While she cut him a slice of carrot cake for dessert, she said there would be hard work that weekend, but lots of entertainment.

He made a non-committal noise and finished his cake. Then he immersed himself in some music mag that appeared to have a riveting feature on plainsong. There was some icing on his upper lip, Harriet noticed.

They didn't have sex that night. Simon's rhinitis seemed a lot worse because he snorted more than usual after putting out the light.

Sanjay

Everyone knew the bollocking big shiny pebble at the front had cost some £70,000, but opinion on it was sharply divided. Sanjay's mother thought it a shocking waste of money, which could have been spent on improving services to patients, like buying those brilliant new drugs that people were dying to have.

"But sometimes it's nice to have a bit of art to look at" said Sanjay as they climbed the stairs from the tube station.

"Oh my God, Sanjay! You call that big lump of stone art? Really, *beta*, I worry about you."

"Well, maybe the patients who come to this hospital should be allowed to decide."

"But I am one of them, and I've decided!" she concluded.

As they crossed the street and headed for the glass doors at the front of the hospital, they could see that one patient was making full use of the £70K rock. He was sitting cross-legged on it, drawing deeply on a cigarette.

"You see?" she said triumphantly. "Seventy thousand pounds on seat for smokers! What is health service coming to, ha?"

Sanjay thought it best not to get her worked up any more before her appointment or the pressure inside her eyes might rise even further. He had offered to bring her here, and more to the point to escort her home afterwards, when her eyes would be full of drops that blurred the vision for hours and hours. The morning was going to be harder than he'd bargained for if they were going to argue about everything.

Inside the eye clinic was a huge number of patients and a sizeable collection of staff. One nurse leaned against a trolley of notes and scowled intermittently at the waiting-room. From time to time, to what purpose Sanjay could not fathom, she also consulted a crumpled list from her pocket. At the computer behind the counter sat a receptionist with facial piercings and serious attitude, alongside a fat nurse who seemed wholly inert. She wasn't dead, Sanjay decided, because her eyes moved.

This clinic was nothing like the oncology department he used to attend. For one thing, most of the eye patients were going to live. So, instead of radiating banter and bonhomie, they exuded moans and complaints. They grumbled about the cost of parking, the shortage of taxis, the vile weather for the time of year, the rapid turnover of junior doctors, and anything else that came to mind. When a name was called out, they groaned that it was someone else instead of them. Sometimes they misheard the name because the receptionist's voice was unclear. Occasionally they misheard on purpose, and got halfway into the consulting-room before someone hauled them back.

Sanjay cringed when his mother got up to button-hole the receptionist. "Are you sure I am going to see the good doctor?"

"Of course, love. There are no bad doctors here."

Before long, a nurse called on his mum to check her eyesight and put drops into her eyes. She could read all the letters above the red line. The nurse congratulated her as if she'd won an Olympic medal.

Some of the people were inpatients, brought along in wheelchairs in various states of undress. One of them, an old Welsh woman, hollered for a cup of tea. An elderly man moaned that he had never been here before and didn't want to be here either. The nurse accompanying him tied his dressing-gown belt, patted his hand, and assured him that he had been here two weeks ago.

"Such a shame, isn't it, *beta?*" said Sanjay's mother. "He must have very bad eyes. Or maybe it's Alzheimer's" she added *sotto voce*, though not quite *sotto* enough.

As the minutes passed, the Welsh lady in the wheelchair got more vocal. "I want my cup of tea. Hillingdon Hospital is so much better. At Hillingdon they bring cups of tea."

Bollocking bollocks, thought Sanjay. He was wasting his time. Suppose this was to be the last day of his life. How would that feel? He would have spent the most precious day of all waiting in the eye clinic.

He wondered what he would rate as the most valuable day of his life. Possibly it was way back at school, with Shelley Ritchie, or at uni in his second term. Perhaps there was an objective way to assess value. Like you could measure eyesight, with charts and all those smart electronic gadgets that checked his mum's visual fields and took photos of anterior angles and stuff.

Mum had now been called into the inner sanctum, via trips to various small rooms where she had all these tests. It felt like an eternity, but it was probably no more than two hours, Sanjay thought ruefully. There she was with the specialist, a short rotund doctor who could barely fit in the tiny consulting-room, let alone squeeze his Michelins into the space behind the big slit-lamp machine that was used for eye examinations. Sanjay's mother pointed out that the machine was dirty, especially the place where she had just rested her chin to allow her eyes to be assessed.

Every time she spoke, of course, her whole head moved. "Sh, mum. The doctor can't see into your eyes if you keep talking."

"Why not, *beta*? People talk with the mouth, not with the eyes. My son, always so original."

To his credit, the fat doctor smiled obligingly and waited till she had stopped talking. Finally, when he had examined her, he pronounced her eyes not bad at all, and certainly no worse than they had been six months ago. There was no need for any surgery yet, and he would be happy to see her again in another six months.

"You see, *beta*? That was a good doctor" she said on their way out. "They should spend money on more doctors, and maybe nice cups of tea, not big shiny stones." She gave the offending sculpture a filthy look as they passed, as if daring it to still be there when she returned six months hence. She said nothing to Sanjay about accompanying her on her next trip to hospital. Six months was a long time away.

Mum said the bus home would be easier with her blurry eyes than the tube. The bus stop was near the mortuary, a place that fascinated Sanjay. His mum, however, gazed steadfastly in the direction of the bus stop instead of the sign that said *Chapel of Rest*.

A large Muslim family were standing outside the mortuary. All but one of them huddled together, sobbing silently. One younger man, slightly apart from the group, talked softly into his mobile phone. Sanjay reflected how quiet Muslim Indians were compared with Hindus. They were composed, restrained and decorous.

When the time came, Sanjay knew, his own family would react in a totally different way. In the Shah family, any misfortune, major or minor, was greeted with screeching and wailing, whereas in his friend Shofiq's, as in all the other Muslim families he knew, bad news was received with calm resignation and a dignified acceptance. No matter whether the roof was leaking, the car had been stolen, or someone had been diagnosed with cancer, it was all the will of Allah. It was probably their very quietness, thought Sanjay, that made Muslims so widely distrusted. That and 9/11, obviously.

Finally the bus arrived. On public transport it was always clear from Mum's behaviour that she was more used to being ferried around in a large old Merc, as befitted someone whose husband was successful in import-export. "*Beta*" she said when she had struggled onto the bus and had shamed someone into giving up their seat because she was old and, in her own opinion, nearly blind. "I hope you can have dinner tonight with us."

"Probably not, Mum. But I'll see you after the weekend."

As he delivered her to the front door of 32 Cornwall Gardens, she thanked him and said "Have a good time, *beta*, and don't forget to pack a good thick jumper." She liked to see him wrapped up warm. Maybe all the extra layers made him look like the chunky Sanjay of old, BC. Before Cancer.

"OK, Mum. But it is July."

Chapter Fifteen

Harriet

Not so long ago, everyone had the same black luggage, but there must have been a lot of cut-price sales since then. It was the only possible explanation, thought Harriet, for the hideous proliferation of pink, purple and turquoise suitcases.

Passengers didn't just have cases. They also toted jumbles of odd-shaped bags, musical instruments, random bits of sports equipment, as well as carrier bags and amorphous bundles and cardboard boxes tied up with tape and straps.

Harriet still had some two hours to the flight. By the indicator screens with flight arrivals and departures, people stood open-mouthed, mesmerized by the information before them. Did they imagine it was going to furnish them with winning lottery numbers?

Half the check-in counters were shut. The other half had people fussing over their passports and begging pathetically for an upgrade. No change there. But the fast bag drop, Harriet noted, was a slow bag drop, presumably because so many people had already checked in online. A stern woman in uniform directed passengers to check-in counters that they could surely see perfectly well for themselves. It didn't seem much of a job to Harriet.

She only had a carry-on, surely enough for her trip to Barcelona. Sexy underwear? Check. What more could she possibly need? Of course, she had pills for headache, indigestion and gastro-enteritis.

Travel broadens the mind and loosens the guts. Before you jet off to your dream destination, spare a thought for your well-being. Here are 12 health essentials for arguably your most important 'capsule wardrobe'.

She sighed. It would be another feature written in breathless prose that read easily but took her hours to perfect. She wandered past a shop selling travel accessories. No doubt she could manage the weekend without a travel pillow, a reading light that clipped onto your novel, or one of the many travel adaptors.

But would she need a pair of ear-plugs? Simon, to his credit, did not have snoring on his list of flaws. Harriet had no idea what the accommodation would be like. She thought how perfectly trusting and stupid she was being. Exactly what every single magazine feature warned against.

In a rare show of interest, Simon had asked where she was going to stay. He knew places in Barcelona, having been there on musical missions. 'I'm not sure where I'm staying' she'd replied. 'So I've no idea if it's anywhere near the Ramblas. Everything's pre-arranged. It's a press trip, remember.'

Simon was pricking at her conscience.

Stupid, really. So far she'd done nothing except exercise her imagination. Over the last few years with Simon, she had romped with Rob Lowe, coupled with Colin Farrell, starred in love scenes alongside Johnny Depp, got jiggy with Jake Gyllenhaal, bounced on the bedsprings with Springsteen and had fiery sexx with Jamie Foxx.

It was a good thing fantasy lovers could never kiss and tell because, during a particularly dull evening in bed, the security officer from *RightHere!* had played a starring role.

Today, on the other hand, was scarily real. She had condoms, of course. Rather than buy them in the terminal, she had stopped off at a Tesco on the way to the airport. She could read the expression on the check-out guy's face as he passed the sunscreen, the paracetamol and the pack of condoms over the bar-code reader. It said 'You're heading for a great time, babe.'

She had invested in an economy pack. How many condoms did people actually need?

Harriet had no idea. The other snag was that she wasn't sure how to put one on without checking the instructions. This could be embarrassing. Perhaps she should retreat to the safety of the loo now and, instead of the customary fiddling with the Dictaphone, commit the condom leaflet to memory.

All in all, her Tesco stop had not taken long, and she was ahead of time.

The queue for security snaked all the way past some souvenir-type shop. People were beginning to disrobe before they got to the front. Already belts, coats and scarves were coming off. Some were undoing their shoes.

For a feature, Harriet had once smuggled through a Swiss Army knife and three syringes with needles in her carry-on. Nobody had stopped her, probably because they were so busy examining everyone's shoes.

Ah, there he was, bang on time, coming round from the far check-in. She smiled to herself as soon as she saw him. She liked who was punctual, but mostly because she liked a guy who looked like him.

Oh yeah, she told herself. This was going to be a great trip, babe.

Chapter Sixteen

Sanjay

Sanjay couldn't fathom why hordes of tourists filled the food hall. What were they going to do with the stuff they bought? Take it back and scoff it all in one go in their hotel rooms? Those whole sides of salmon weren't going to fit in any mini-bars he'd ever seen.

On the other hand, the decor was *über*-tasteful. Fruit and vegetables were so perfect and so beautifully arranged that the displays were almost surreal.

As were the prices. He gave two of the kiwi fruit a tentative stroke. No two were exactly alike. Just like testicles, then.

According to the pre-op spiel the surgeon had given Sanjay, there was nothing new about the concept of testicular prostheses. They had started making falsies out of metal in the early 1940s. Sanjay was glad things had improved. He didn't fancy carting a cannon-ball around in his scrotum 24/7.

In the 1950s, as the specialist told Sanjay, manufacturers had moved on to big glass marbles, which sounded just as bad. Then came synthetic stuff like

Perspex, Dacron and so on, because some bright spark had realized that, as well as being light, the ideal goolie should be chemically inert and not provoke allergy, inflammation or tumours.

But they has disappointed, as had Silastic and silicone rubber. The specialist was one of those young guys that looked really old. Maybe he'd spent too much time researching other people's genitals. Anyway, he said, apparently what the market really needed was a nut with a natural feel, a prosthesis that was the right shape as well as trauma-resistant. Sanjay had nodded.

Which was why, Mr Carmichael went on, they were made of silicone these days. Except in the USA, of course (he injected a snigger of disdain at his transatlantic brethren). Across the pond, they decided to pull their silicone prostheses and use saline instead. Experience with boobs had not been good, apparently.

Looking closely at silicone breast implants (which sounded like a very fine line of work to Sanjay – why hadn't he gone in for this?), studies had shown that two-thirds suffered a degree of so-called 'device disruption'. But mostly, said Mr Carmichael, this was just a little disintegration of the outer silicone casing and minimal leakage of the contents. Only the Americans worried about auto-immune disease. The consultant made their concerns sound like an advanced neurosis.

Sanjay was getting a little nervous now too. He wondered what his new testicle would be like and how it would perform.

Perform. That was the word Mr Carmichael used. Sanjay had never thought of testicles having to do anything much during the show. After all, his cock was the principal actor here.

There were some three or four manufacturers, Sanjay learned. However, as far as the patients were concerned, the differences were negligible. Casting director Mr Carmichael would have trouble choosing between them.

Then he brought out examples of varying sizes. Sanjay had picked one up and weighed it experimentally in his palm. Those were bollocks? They were shiny and not nearly heavy enough. But no. Those were just the dummies, made to ensure the prosthesis would match the patient's own testes.

It was funny how nobody said 'testes' outside of hospital. They always said 'testicles'.

Sanjay wasn't bothered about terminology, but did care about possible problems. Occasionally the size or position wasn't quite right. So how, thought Sanjay, would his *perform?* Mr Carmichael had insisted he shouldn't worry about rupture. This little silicone beauty should be durable for years.

'What about on planes?' Sanjay had asked.

Good God, yes. Mid-air rupture was an urban myth, much loved by the tabloids. He'd be perfectly OK on a flight or any other method of transport.

Good to know, thought Sanjay.

He put back the fruit and left the kiwi aisle, carrying with him a twinge of anxiety along with a dragging sensation. After the produce section, the space opened out. Fortnum's tiled floor was elegant, Sanjay thought, and there was no sawdust smell, even around the meat counter.

He peered into a glass case with an array of cheeses, some of them larger than his head, and asked himself if this was the last time he'd ever go to Fortnum's Food Hall.

Bollocks. That was ridiculous. This was the *first* time he'd ever been to Fortnum's Food Hall. He pushed morbid thoughts aside and pointed at some nice-looking fish. The woman behind the counter didn't query why he only wanted 100g. She wrapped it as carefully as if it were a cashmere tie, secured it and handed it over with a smile.

He considered deviating to get earrings for Shelley Ritchie. Pierced? He wasn't sure. All the girls at school had worn massive earrings, but he had no idea how they were held on. When you were a 16-year old boy, there were lots of zones more erogenous than earlobes.

Sanjay went home and put on The Doors. He poached the fish in a pan with a dash of lime. Dainty disliked it plain. Using the kitchen timer, he cooked it for exactly nine minutes, until the flesh was tender but not yet disintegrated.

While this was going on, Dainty made a huge fuss of his legs, walking on his feet and rubbing herself vigorously on his trousers. She was the only woman who did that these days. And Dainty probably wasn't even going to miss him. Or was she?

To the sound of *Light My Fire*, Sanjay checked the hob and the light sockets, and moved all the plants out of the way. Dainty had a taste for greenery. Her five-a-day. Finally he pushed the battery into place and pressed the start button on the cat feeder. It would have to do until Sita popped round tomorrow. Oh bollocks! Suppose she forgot?

He killed Jim Morrison but left the lights on and exited the flat. After lugging his case down the road to the tube station, he negotiated the stairs. There was no easy way to manoeuvre wheeled cases, even this small one, without straining your shoulder and jabbing yourself in the armpit with the handle when you went down stairs. You'd think if you had only a few months to live (and those doctors were hellishly vague as to how many), you'd feel carefree, but the snag is that if you'd got only a limited time left then you were bound to feel crap from whatever it was that was trying to kill you.

Unless you were on death row, of course. Then you might feel physically fine, but you wouldn't have the opportunity to enjoy your last moments properly. You couldn't win, Sanjay decided. Impending death was such a bitch.

As he passed Hammersmith station, he wondered if he would ever be seeing it again, then told himself not to be so stupid. He was seeing it again in three days. By the time he got to South Ealing, he wondered how the weekend would pan out. He hoped his arm would get better. Right now it ached to the bone. He'd packed in such a rush. Had he brought enough pain-killers? Possibly not.

At Osterley several young people left the carriage, armed with shoulder bags and jawing about working for Sky News. Soon the tube reached the first of the Hounslow stations, where the airport proper began, as did the twilight world of all the workers, mainly Sikh, who serviced the many-headed monster that was Heathrow airport. Sanjay was already worn out, without doing anything like the mopping, polishing, scrubbing, toilet-cleaning and bin-emptying that made up these people's daily lives.

By the time he reached the terminal, he felt drained. He bumped into someone changing money, and narrowly missed sending him and his Euros flying.

She was here! He'd hardly believed she'd turn up, but there she was, a guidebook tucked into her shoulder bag. Instantly he felt more awake. He gave the crotch of his Levis a little tug and told Kiwi to behave.

It was a bloody relief she was travelling light, unlike women who lugged outfits for every hour of the holiday, along with the obligatory changes of shoes, sandals and what have you, not to mention hairdryers, hot brushes and straighteners. She had only one case, a compact functional wheeled thing.

Right there and then in front of security, they had their first kiss on the lips. Her laugh was tinged with embarrassment, as well it might be, since she probably didn't do this often. Not that he knew for sure. He had no idea what she was like. He didn't do this often either, but since the cancer it had become usual to live an unusual life.

He would explain all that to her, but it would have to wait till somewhere quiet.

At security, he hovered over his bag. He glanced up just before his case rolled out of the x-ray machine and saw that she was equally protective of her own luggage.

They passed through to airside, where the duty-free dominated, and you could also find all the other shops that were in any street. "Do you need any duty-free?" he asked.

"I'm good, thanks."

She didn't look good at all. She looked wicked as hell. Fine by him.

She suggested a coffee. This could have been the moment to tell her, but their flight had just lit up on the notice-board, so instead he said "Shall we go to the gate now?"

He wanted to hold her hand, which was next to impossible on travelators with people overtaking all the time. The gates were so far, much further than they used to be, he was sure. Perhaps he could have asked for one of those golf carts. But he wouldn't have cut much of a dash by hitching a ride with the pensioners, cripples and plague victims.

When they eventually got to the gate, there was a bus. Bollocks! Weren't these piers or things meant to go all the way to the fucking plane?

Some ground-staff bloke funnelled them on. As Sanjay got on the bus, he leaned across to him in mock confidentiality and said "Maybe I got it wrong, but when I booked my ticket I was expecting something a little more streamlined. Possibly with wings, I don't know." The bloke didn't get it, but she was amused, which was more important.

Only when they were on the plane, cruising at 37,000 feet, did she ask Sanjay "How many rooms did you book?"

He told her.

She said nothing. She didn't have to. The answer was the green light in her eyes.

Chapter Seventeen

Dan

In Dan's opinion, the Flatiron Building should have been torn down ages ago. Never mind its beaux-arts charm. Or the fact that it was a massive feat of engineering for 1902. It was looking tired. If he'd had the cash, Dan would have put something entirely different there. Not necessarily another skyscraper. It didn't even have to be a building. Hell, it could be a poster of a wild animal, or even a flower. Stylized, obviously. He didn't want anyone thinking he was gay.

Anyone? Who the fuck was he kidding? Nobody came to visit. Probably never would. Dan waited until the bathroom was free. One advantage of living here was that he could hear the bathroom door on the landing below. Another was that few of the other residents seemed to use it. Especially not that repulsive couple with rap blaring out. Whether they chose to pee in the basin and crap in the garden with its forest of nettles, he didn't know. Since he'd been behind bars, he himself had the Lady Macbeth thing. Shakespeare. He was reading the sonnets at the moment.

While he waited for the bathroom, he went through the job adverts in the local paper as well as the Guardian. So far he'd found that employers were wary of someone who couldn't satisfactorily account for a six year chunk of his life. He hadn't been able to construct an alibi for one single night, that October night when the Jewel Box was raided and he was genuinely somewhere else. He'd have to work a fuck of a lot harder to explain away a couple of thousand days.

The craving came on again. He'd done OK without nicotine so far today, but now there was the familiar tightening in his muscles. Dan reached under the bed for the Lidl carrier bag and extracted a giant bowl. Without spilling any of the precious contents, he set it on the table, leaned over and took several deep breaths. Those 20 or so fag ends, together with a collection of matches and enough ash for a crematorium, provided just the hit he needed.

As he inhaled repeatedly, he got a few lungfuls of old ashtray that would last him a good few hours. Cheaper than the real thing. Cheaper than nicotine gum and all that. And it worked. Another lesson from the book of life: never underestimate aversion therapy.

Dan left the telly on while he used the bathroom. It was on a lot. Telly was the refuge of the single male. As well as the not-so-single male, of course. And it taught him a lot about current affairs and stuff. Too bad there weren't more programmes on Slovenia.

After his shower, he put on his signature outfit of clean shirt, jeans and leather belt. It was nothing short of a miracle, he thought, that he had a second chance with Laure.

She was quality! The clothes she wore, the way she carried herself, everything. He'd never met a woman like her. He'd certainly never been out with a woman like her. Well, the impossible could happen. He knew that.

But she was a hairdresser, she'd told him. So whence her classy style and expensive looks, not to mention her lovely voice?

Whence. Nice word.

Mellifluous. Even better word. Perfect for her voice. His dictionary said it meant 'like honey'. Which, as it happened, was also the colour of her hair.

Maybe she was a top hairdresser. Like Vidal Sassoon or Nicky Clarke. Chain of shops. Her own product range. Celeb endorsements. He should check out the shelves at Boots and Superdrug, see if there were products with her picture on. On the other hand, maybe she was just a top liar. Anyway, after that evening in the pub he had phoned her. Listened to her mellifluous voice. Remembered her mellifluous hair. And tried not to scare the crap out of her by being too keen.

Which was how they now came to be in Regent's Park, watching a huge silver-grey dog nudge one of the women on the park bench, practically bulldozing her onto the ground.

As far as Dan was concerned, dogs came in three sizes. Dog-sized, which was to say anything from a spaniel up to the size of a Labrador or police dog. Chihuahua sized, designed for designer handbags. And racehorse sized, like this one. It even had rippling muscles to match.

"That's some dog" remarked Laure as the owner arrived to yank the dog away.

"You're not wrong" said Dan.

They watched the lake for a bit. Even with his eyes shut, Dan would have known it was summer. A man was cramming his whole family into a boat, accompanied by squeals from the kids and arguments about who would sit where. On a bench sat two seriously wrinkly geezers arguing loudly in some language or other. They would probably still be yelling at each other when they popped their clogs. Or, as he must now think of it, shuffled off this mortal coil. Shakespeare again, that was. Class.

Another dog went by. "Do you like dogs?" Laure asked.

"Most of them, except the kind that yanks your arm out of its socket. I had a friend with a dog like that. A Rhodesian Ridgeback, I think." Dan had walked that dog once, or rather the dog had dragged him around the block, much to the amusement of a bunch of schoolgirls at the bus-stop. There was another kind of dog that Dan wasn't too keen on, but no need to tell Laure anything about those, so he just said "Actually I prefer rescue dogs."

"Me too. There's something special about mongrels."

"Have you got a dog?" he asked.

"Not had one since I was a kid. Until lately I was travelling a lot."

Surprising. But then a hot-shot hair stylist probably had clients around the world. Perhaps did the Beckhams' hair. Or Shakira's. That would fit.

"What about you?" she asked.

"No. I wasn't allowed a dog the last few years."

They walked a little further along the path. On either side, people sat on the grass trying to sun themselves, or reading or talking. Another exercise junkie with headphones jogged by.

"That's a shame" said Laure. "Family against it?"

"Pretty much." That would have to do for now.

Laure yawned. "Sorry. Not been sleeping well."

"That's too bad. Why?"

She paused before saying "I just beat myself up about things sometimes."

He never needed to beat himself up, he jested. "For years, I had plenty of volunteers to do that for me."

"Sounds nasty" remarked Laure.

"I guess it was."

She gave him a sideways glance. "How did you get it to stop?"

"I moved."

"I'm surprised it took you that long. You don't look like a victim."

"Well, I had to stay put a while. Commitments and all that. Perhaps I should have tried doing a runner, but there wasn't really the chance." Damn right there wasn't. It hadn't exactly been *The Shawshank Redemption*. He should change the subject. "Did you rate the speed-dating evening then?"

"Well, I'd been once before" said Laure. "It's a nice venue, and it was pretty well organized. There's always a quota of no-hopers, of course."

"And would I be one of those no-hopers?"

"What do you think?" she replied, with a broader smile than he thought possible. He noticed her eyes had crinkled up too. Was it really the sun?

He replied by working his eyebrows. Now that he was bald, forehead movements conveyed huge amounts of expression, as his mirror had told him. But he had no idea what effect they had on Laure because the big grey thing had given his owner the slip again and bounded up to spoil the moment.

Despite the dog's massive chest and jaws, Dan wasn't worried. Neither, to her credit, was Laure. The hound's big yellow eyes looked even bigger now that he was up close and personal. He started sniffing Dan's bottom. It didn't get much more close and personal than that.

Dan tried to shoo the dog off, to no avail. "Were you travelling for work?" he asked Laure.

"Yes, I was. Have you travelled a lot?"

"Oh, no. Not been anywhere much." It was tough to think straight, let alone come across as suave and sophisticated, when some outsized canine was trying to get his conk right up your crack.

"It's a bitch" Laure pointed out. "If you ignore her, she'll probably go away."

Eventually the owner came lolloping up, with a gait just like his dog's. "Sorry, she's such a naughty girl. But Weimaraner are hunting dogs, do you see?"

She won't find anything up there, mate, thought Dan.

With the Weimaraner out of the way, they wandered past some huge plants that were like giant cabbages, and lots of other things he didn't know the names of. Some uppity swans had installed themselves on the grass like they owned the place. There was a clutch of moorhens or something too, Dan wasn't sure. Their feet were incredibly pink. While he didn't always know what things were called, it gave him enormous pleasure to be out of doors. Especially in places that weren't exercise yards, with birds that weren't dead pigeons.

They found a bench, unoccupied except for lavish amounts of bird poop down one end. That meant only limited space. Fine by him. When they sat, her right knee touched his left thigh. Even finer. OK, she was wearing jeans too. Meaning that there were at least two layers of denim between their naked bodies. But it was a start.

A small kid passed on his bike, all wobbles. He fell over a couple of feet away from them, and bawled till his mother arrived. Dan watched her as she fussed over the grazed knee, hugged the boy and promised him an ice-cream.

"How's the mum in the *niqab* going to eat her Magnum?" asked Laure.

"Maybe she won't have one."

"True. She probably doesn't eat unless she's in a room with other women." Laure sighed. "I wish there weren't so many Arabs here."

"Well, we could have chosen a park a little further from London Central Mosque" he said reasonably. He wasn't about to spoil the mood by suggesting she was a teeny bit racist.

Laure considered this. "If you could be anywhere at all, where would you be?"

He looked around. A young bloke, maybe a student, was playing the saxophone to himself and to the rest of park, as if it were the most natural thing in the world. It was all good, thought Dan. "Here. Right here" he said.

She was smiling back, big-time.

As he closed in, he just about registered another couple of tykes running past their bench, howling for attention. Laure was still smiling.

He gave his plate a little nudge with his tongue, just to check. Then he kissed her. Oh, she wouldn't have been smiling, let alone kissing him, if she knew his secret.

Dorottya

In her large and pleasingly-proportioned drawing-room, Dorottya's lips pursed as her mobile emitted the sound of a child playing the recorder. For years she had wanted to change the ring tone to something more bearable, but that would have been difficult since she'd always told Roger how delightful his children were and how angelically they played.

Yes, if angels habitually covered the wrong holes, spat all over the recorder and still expected praise for their efforts. A newborn Hungarian baby had more musicality in its little finger than any English child.

The mobile displayed an unrecognizable number. "Hello?" Dorottya said huskily.

"Dorottya?"

"Who is that?"

"It's Michael. We met a couple of weeks back."

"Where?" she snapped.

"At the Jacaranda club. I wonder if you'd like to –"

She could hear Roger in the hall, treading on the squeaky floor-board he hadn't fixed yet. "No, I absolutely do not want any of your double-glazing."

"If this isn't a good time to talk, can you call me tomorrow?" he said.

"Neither do I want any patio doors" she said by way of reply.

"When can we speak?"

"Maybe when I need new windows. Thank you" she finished, as Roger approached.

"Sweetie, which company was that?"

"I have no idea, *dahlink*."

"You must know. I want to lodge a complaint." He sounded more officious than usual. "They shouldn't be ringing your mobile. One wonders where they got the number."

"*Dahlink,* I really don't know. I suppose he did mention the company but it was all so quick because he was rushing to tell me about a special offer on windows, and how they were in our area right now."

This seemed to placate Roger. "Ah well. The usual sales patter."

"Yes, and of course there wasn't any caller ID" she said, sliding the mobile snugly into the pocket of her Versace jeans so that Roger wouldn't be tempted to check the call history.

"Sweetie, would you just help Olivia with her bassoon practice? She needs a little encouragement to get into the orchestra."

A hefty bribe was the only way to ensure that, since her bassoon was even worse than the recorder. Dorottya put one hand to her brow. "Can't you do it, *dahlink*? I have such a bad head trouble."

"Poor you" said Roger.

Dorottya squirmed as he began to massage her shoulders. "Careful, *dahlink*." She still had a bruise from last time. Men weren't very gentle.

Chapter Eighteen

Harriet

"If you've got cancer, you totally deserve room service" said Harriet, stretching for the phone from the comfort of the bed. Phrasebook in hand, she ordered *dos desayunos. Jamon y uevas* would be a good start. Sanjay should have the works, she decided. In every possible way.

It had begun with her saying something banal about deadlines, the bane of every freelancer's life. Bland though his first response was, she'd become hotly defensive, the words 'What do you mean?' rising up in her throat, as when Simon had a go at her for not having a proper job.

Then he explained. He had testicular cancer, followed by a recurrence. It had become inoperable and untreatable.

Now that was a deadline, thought Harriet.

In a towelling robe, Sanjay sat on the edge of the huge expanse of bed. The Spanish called it *una cama de matrimonio,* but they had already christened it their play-pen. Half-light from the shuttered window cast shadows on his face as he told her about the first operation to remove the testicle, then biopsies of lymph nodes here, there and soon, it seemed, almost everywhere. Radiotherapy followed, after which came chemotherapy, baldness and other unwelcome effects, all interspersed with numerous consultations and his family's intermittent hope and hysteria. Conventional weapons seemed to work for a while, but, when the Taliban tumour ambushed and invaded his lymph system, pessimism set in. The war had been doomed from the start.

Sanjay pointed out small silvery scars from the surgery he'd had. Harriet had noticed one already. She'd also registered that his body was almost hairless (perhaps the chemo), and that one testicle was much firmer than the other.

"I don't know how long I've got. But I'm almost certain to last the weekend, unless you treat me very badly." The look in his dark-rimmed eyes suggested he might enjoy that. "Put it this way: if I were a washing machine, then a three-year extended warranty would be a shocking waste of dosh."

The way the shade fell on his face, she couldn't tell if he was smiling or not. She herself found it unbearable, to the point where she either wanted to cry or drag him back to bed. Unable to decide, she did both, quietly and tenderly.

Sanjay lay on his back. She shut her eyes because watching him just piled on the agony. Now that he had told her, it was more meaningful, more precious, so much more than just a shag. She had to be careful. He had been injured enough already. Could pressure in the wrong places damage his fake testicle or, even worse, send tumour cells racing through his body? She wasn't sure, so she kept her weight light as she moved in a circular motion. Her orgasm, when it came, took her by surprise. She had not thought it possible when weeping so persistently.

Room service delivered a shiny silver tea service, fruit juice, croissants, butter and the rest. Croissant crumbs laced her breasts, and butter fell on his chest.

"Do you think jam can damage latex?" she asked.

"No idea."

"Want to Google it?"

"Nah. Better things to do." Sanjay gave a meaningful look. "I might like to see Barcelona too."

"You may get tired."

He looked exhausted already. "Almost certainly, but I won't get another chance."

"I think Barcelona was a better choice than Prague" she said, trying to keep it light.

"I only wanted to go there because of Ben." Staring at the carpet, he told her about his best mate who'd been planning his stag weekend in Prague. "He's not going there either now. He lost an arm. His leg injuries are healing, but I think his genitals are pretty much shot to pieces. Not that he actually said, but he got an infection after the blast. The antibiotics didn't do the trick so he had to have loads of surgery. To clear dead tissue, they told him."

It was impossible to say the right thing. Harriet made do with "Poor Ben."

"To be expected, I guess, if you go on patrol near Lashkar Gar. Anyway, when he came back, his fiancée scarpered. That did him in but he doesn't like to let on how much it hurts. All he wants to do is go back to Afghanistan, which seems even nuttier than before." He sighed at length.

She kissed him then took herself off for a much-needed shower, locking the door behind her. Right now she wanted some privacy to shave her armpits and pluck her eyebrows so they wouldn't go wild and meet in the middle. That was what she told herself.

Standing in the tub, she cried, her tears as warm as the water that fell on her face. Shampoo got into her mouth as she wept for Sanjay and his illness, for Pushkin, the beautiful and beloved cat she might still have had she only met Sanjay instead of Simon. Lastly she cried for herself and the tough decisions she faced. But those things, she told herself, were either yesterday or tomorrow. Today was today.

When she emerged with a towel around her head, Sanjay was studying the guidebook. "We should definitely visit the *Sagrada Familia*. You know, I always thought it was the same as the cathedral, but it's not. The *Sagrada Familia* is the unfinished Gaudi church, which actually is still being built, whereas the cathedral is Gothic, real Gothic as opposed to neo-Gothic. In the courtyard there are always 13 geese to represent a martyr called - what's wrong?"

"Got shampoo in my eyes. That's all."

She turned away and sat at the dressing-table mirror. Deception was difficult when you had no Dictaphone, no notebook, nothing to hide behind. Slowly, she unwound the towel from her hair. In the mirror she could see Sanjay studying her face. To compose herself, she brushed her hair bit by bit, giving it far more brush-strokes than needed.

"Do you want to go to the Nou Camp?" asked Sanjay. "It's the biggest stadium in Europe."

"Nah. I'm not really into baseball."

"It's football, silly. Oh. You're pulling my leg."

She grinned. "I'll pull something else if you're not careful."

Later, much later, they went to Montjuic. Sanjay was fascinated by the fact that the park was no longer used for Grand Prix races because it was deemed unsafe, yet it was a popular circuit for learner drivers. He said it was like allowing amateur cooks have a go at recipes that were too tricky for top chefs.

On the funicular she finally found time for her confession. "I've got something to tell you too. When I went to the Jacaranda that night, I was researching for an article on dating. But don't worry, I won't put you in it. This weekend's not research, and neither are you. I wanted you to know."

He listened then laughed. "It makes no difference, you know. The long run, well, it's not that long."

"I wasn't looking for someone that night. But I found him anyway." As she threw her arms around him, people smiled indulgently.

They stopped at a restaurant, choosing one that didn't have fish swimming in a tank in the window or baby pigs lying on platters. Spaniards were good at producing whole animals and calling them dinner.

"Are you vegetarian?" It was shocking how little she knew about him.

Sanjay finished his mouthful. "No. I eat everything."

"You don't look as if you eat everything."

"Well, I eat most things." He raised one index finger. "With the exception of cauliflower."

"What's wrong with cauliflower?"

"I hate it! It's the white trash cousin of broccoli."

"You mean it's loud and tasteless, or what?"

"I don't know. It's just wrong. Cauliflower doesn't taste like food. It tastes like candle wax. A candle scented with cabbage water, in fact."

"I don't think I've ever eaten candle wax" she reflected. "Scented with cabbage water or not."

Over lunch, something seemed to occur to him. "If you weren't looking for anyone, was that because you were already seeing someone then?"

"I was." She was choosing her words carefully. "Yes, I was seeing someone."

"Simon who?" he asked. "You said you were seeing Simon."

Panic smacked her in the face. Was he a mind-reader now? "I said *someone*, not *Simon*!"

"Oh sorry, I heard *Simon*. My mistake."

"No worries. Anyway, it didn't have a future."

He put away a mouthful of rice and appraised her critically. "Do things need to have a future?"

Some questions were too tough to answer.

As planned, they visited the *Sagrada Familia*. Sanjay was thrilled to find it exactly as described in the guidebook, unfinished yet magnificent. 'See?' he said. Harriet knew what he meant. Things could be amazing even when they were incomplete and imperfect.

As he enthused about the geese, his eyes grew animated again, and he looked fit and healthy.

But of course he wasn't, and no number of church visits could effect that transformation. Although Harriet wasn't religious as such, she thought about this as she lit a candle. The coins clanked in the slot. Peace on earth and a cure for Sanjay's cancer. It seemed a lot to ask of a couple of Euros.

They ambled down the road. He was looking drained now, with circles under his eyes and beads of sweat on his brow. He blamed the heat. It had been a long day already but still he kept going, driven by some force. They had stopped at a bar. By then he needed a breather. Besides, as Sanjay put it, what was the point of going to Barcelona if you didn't take in a bar?

Harriet wondered if a gay bar was on his bucket list. The place had an old-fashioned oak door, ironwork sprouting everywhere. They were greeted by lounge music and a waiter in leather chaps. His cute bare buttocks wiggled as he showed them to a booth.

A whiff of marijuana drifted their way. It was a fun place, full of laughter. Over their cocktails (obviously more appropriate than beers) her mood lifted. Had she ever seen so many beautiful young men? The lesbians were equally stunning. The place was a palace of pulchritude.

She'd sipped a seriously intoxicating orange drink and looked into Sanjay's eyes. Was she going to dump Simon for a terminally ill guy she had just met? An inner voice, one sounding not at all like Harriet's inner editor, whispered that yes, she could do exactly that. Before Heathrow she'd acknowledged this wasn't all in the cause of journalism. Surely it was only another small step from there.

The only way to cope this weekend was to hang a sign on part of her brain, like the one on their door that said *No molestar*. It worked, in a way. As long as she didn't think too hard.

They stopped in some market on the way back to the hotel. Sanjay didn't want to accumulate any more things for himself, he said, but he chose two necklaces. One was for his sister and the other for someone called Shelley.

"I was at school with her" he explained.

Harriet felt herself stiffen when Sanjay added that she'd been a girlfriend. Stop it, she told herself. It was stupid to feel threatened.

He picked out a pair of long dangly earrings and held them up to Harriet's ears. "Like them?"

"They're stunning."

"Then they're yours" he said as he paid for them.

"What about earrings for Shelley?"

Sanjay shook his head. "Not even sure if she has pierced ears."

So he hadn't studied her earlobes. Good. Harriet put on her new earrings immediately, removing the cubic zirconium studs she normally wore. The new ones were light considering their size. She tossed her head. They made her feel different.

As they walked back to the hotel arm in arm, Harriet began to wonder if *My Baby for a Birkin* wouldn't have been simpler after all.

Chapter Nineteen

Laure

Regent's Park had been lovely, thought Laure as she got off the train. All of it was lovely. With a man serenading them with his saxophone it was like Central Park, except there weren't any guys playing baseball.

When she got to her tube station, she noticed there was another text from that Michael, pleading to see her again. It was just as well it was only the cheap pay-as-you-go. Even so, he was beginning to get to her. There was something so wrong with that man.

She got as far as the lighting shop when her iPhone rang. "Laure *chérie*" screeched Tante Victorine as if she hadn't spoken to her niece for a year, not a week.

She could hear Tante Lina try to wrestle the phone from her sister. "*Mais je veux aussi lui parler, chérie.*" They came from Beirut so they could have been heard in Peru. As they were Christians, they usually shouted in French, using Arabic only for occasional idioms.

When Tante Lina got the phone, she said exactly the same thing, that it was high time they took her out for lunch.

Laure said she'd love to. She walked on, holding the phone 20 cm from her ear while Victorine and Lina debated where the three of them should eat. The two sisters lived together and disagreed about everything, yet never bore a grudge. Finally the date, time and venue were decided, and both aunts declared they couldn't wait to see her, and what a delightful young woman she was to agree to spend time with two boring old widows like themselves. "By the way, *chérie*, how old are you now?" asked Tante Victorine.

"I'm 38, *tante*."

"What a coincidence, *chérie*. That's exactly the age my Sophie would have been." Victorine sighed.

Laure sighed empathically. The baby had lived for an hour. And Victorine was still eating for two though she had never been pregnant again.

When the conversation ended, Laure had reached the corner of her street. A couple stood arm in arm waiting for the lights to change.

Laure had never intended to have married boyfriends, but they'd often been the most attractive men of all. Chemistry transcended rules, written or unwritten. Mark and the motorway services were a case in point. Their destination had been the nearest Travelodge but they'd never got that far. Casting caution and Armani jackets to the wind, they'd made do with his Mini. She'd come first, then him. The grubby feeling came last, when Mark was wandering around the carpark in search of a suitable bin for the scrunched-up tissues in his hand.

There was always a grubby feeling afterwards. But there was something much worse, something that topped the list and made her feel far dirtier than that.

She crossed and turned left.

Dan, now. There was something insanely attractive about him. Funny too, but she didn't want to go too fast. She still knew too little about him. Of course she wasn't naive enough to think you had to know everything about someone. On the other hand, you had to know enough to keep yourself safe instead of ending up chopped into little pieces and chucked to the seagulls.

This time she definitely wasn't going to talk kids. He himself never gave away anything serious. All his banter probably served to hide stuff, just as surely as an *abaya* covered all those Gulf women up. There might be rolls and rolls of surplus fat lurking under there. Or there could be the latest Gucci outfit.

Then there was Sanjay. Well, that was going nowhere. Besides, thinking of Sanjay reminded her of something she needed to forget.

Geoff. Lots of good things about Geoff, she knew from that one night, but she had told him far too much.

Dan still hadn't asked about her work, she thought as she punched the lift button. His own job was no doubt dull. Or was it for the same reason she hadn't asked about his work – that he too lied about his occupation?

The lift arrived, and in it one of the Japanese women with her toddler. They flattened themselves courteously to make more space for Laure, even though it was unnecessary. The child looked up at Laure, and Laure smiled back. Once again she wondered if she would ever have a child, and, if she did, whether it would be as docile as this one. Probably no, to both.

She unlocked the door to her flat. There was something else about Dan. She put the key down and tried to remember.

Hadn't Dan said he'd been living abroad? She frowned at the sofa that still looked stupidly short even though she'd moved it. He'd said it at the Jacaranda, she was pretty sure of it. Her memory was good. It had to be, in her line of work.

Yet this afternoon Dan in the park had distinctly said he hadn't travelled much at all. A man that lies. OK, he wouldn't be the first. Or maybe there was a simple explanation. She'd have to ask him.

Chapter Twenty

Geoff

"You're in a good mood today, Geoff" said the person next to him.

The person was wearing mustard-coloured cords, a blue shirt with a button-down collar, and a jacket of the type dubbed 'sports'. The whole ensemble looked familiar, but sadly GPs didn't wear name badges. Obviously they had met before, since mustard trousers knew him. "Yes, I suppose I am" Geoff replied to play it safe.

Mustard Trousers sprinkled salt liberally all over his salad and then on the steak and kidney pie that was on the same plate, as if he'd never heard of high blood pressure. Geoff noticed that thin gravy had run all over the lettuce. But then the postgrad centre was the home of continuing medical education, not healthy eating or *cordon bleu*.

"Was I in a foul mood the last time?" said Geoff, fishing for clues.

"I should say! You'd lost the keys to your car and didn't know how you'd get to your afternoon clinic."

"Oh yes, I remember. I was pretty angry with myself."

Geoff thought that was last year sometime. Unfortunately he could not recall how Mustard Trousers had got involved, and no more hints were forthcoming. Geoff concentrated on his lunch which, by the miracle that was drug company sponsorship, was completely free. Free to the GPs anyway.

He was famished after a mammoth morning surgery and two home visits, one being to the Thing family, where someone had slobbered liberally on his feet. Could have been the baby, the dog, or Mr Thing senior. Who knew? Anyway, body fluids were the reason why GPs didn't wear suede shoes.

"It's New Horizons in Stroke Management today" Mustard Trousers informed him as he chased the pie around his plate.

"Bugger!" said Geoff. "I'm here for the update on basic life support."

"Ah, no, that's been postponed. Didn't you get the email?"

Geoff couldn't leave immediately after his lunch, especially since the drug rep was eyeing every doctor in the room. So, when they were summoned, he too went into the lecture theatre where the seats were comfortably padded and the lights were specially dimmed to enable the audience to see the slides, or to catch up on some sleep. For Geoff a little doze won. It was an almost imperceptible glide into anaesthesia induced by too many Powerpoint slides, which were not remotely improved by dinky animation sequences.

He woke with a start when the young Sikh doctor on his left brushed against him while picking up a fallen biro. "Sorry" whispered the younger GP, and resumed copious note-taking. He had scribbled three pages already.

Good for him, thought Geoff. At this rate, Young Doctor would end up knowing more about strokes than he knew about his own family.

It was admirable having a new framework for dealing with strokes, trying to fast-track them during a narrow window of opportunity. But they'd still land up festering on some ward where the physiotherapy was non-existent and the nurses were more interested in eating the patients' grapes.

When the lights came back on, Geoff woke with a dry mouth and heavy legs, and shambled out of the room.

He left the postgrad centre feeling like a very old man. He was barely 38. At least, he told himself as he patted his pocket, this time he had the keys to the Toyota.

By the time he'd reached his practice, there was another text. Laure, he thought, as he'd phoned her twice the following morning. Geoff did have some bedside manners. But once again it was only Frieda. Now she wanted him to know that she too had a cough with a fever, and was bringing up phlegm, *w flcks of grn like avcado.*

He banished memories of the nurses' home and white coats, and texted back advising her to see her own doctor.

Geoff thought he'd lure Karen away from her kids to see *The Sentinel Crossing*. The reviews were good and it might be nice to see the film with her, even if the title was forever linked in his mind with anal fissures (as in *sentinel pile*). Going to the cinema had the drawback of sitting in silence, with no clue as to what your companion was thinking. But 126 minutes later you could chat about the film over a drink, which provided something to talk about. On that particular evening he had finished surgery as early as he knew how without actually removing the patient's chair to cut consulting times.

But Davey was ill. Even if his ex-wife had known how to look after anyone but herself, Geoff wouldn't have wanted to be at the movies with his mobile turned off.

On the phone, Sonya was sure it was appendicitis. Or possibly meningitis. Maybe even both. It took a while to establish that Davey had abdominal pain, along with fever and vomiting.

Geoff went round to find Sonya in a flap. Davey lay on the sofa cuddling an old soft toy called Little Bun that looked like it harboured every single species of micro-organism ever known. Davey looked very sorry for himself, but he didn't have a tender tummy. When Geoff examined it, he laughed and complained that it tickled.

Geoff peered down Davey's throat. "He's got tonsillitis."

Sonya gave him a look that said he might not actually be the most useless doctor in the world, but it was close. "Can't we get a specialist?" she asked. "I'm with BUPA."

"It's not necessary" said Geoff. "It's just tonsillitis." Then he patiently explained how lymph nodes inside a child's belly often enlarged and caused pain, even if the focus of infection was somewhere else.

"Well, I've never heard of mesenteric adenitis" Sonya said flatly.

"I'll get him some paracetamol and penicillin." It was legal to prescribe for your own family, even if it was ethically dubious. But for something simple it made no sense to call someone else, especially after hours.

She furrowed her brow as much as Botox would allow. "I don't know, Geoff. I'm worried about him."

So worried that she eventually decided to go out. "Well, if you're sure it's only tonsillitis. I mean, it is late-night shopping night."

Davey was left on the sofa surrounded by toys for which he had less than his usual enthusiasm. Geoff rang Karen to make his excuses, got Davey the medicine from the boot of his car, then, instead of watching *The Sentinel Crossing*, settled down on the sofa next to his son. Truth be told, an evening with Davey was a bonus.

Davey perked up when the paracetamol began to work. He asked for some tropical juice drink, and got most of it on the arm of Sonya's sofa. Geoff rubbed it with a wet tissue. The stain worsened but he found it hard to care, even though Sonya would no doubt discover a way of making Geoff foot the bill for having the cover cleaned or replaced.

"Every day the world ends for someone" said Davey, snuggling up to the nest of pillows on the sofa.

Davey never ceased to surprise him. "Yes, I suppose it does."

"Daddy, is it true doctors never die?"

"Well, they do die in the end, Davey, because they are human beings too." This was dangerous territory.

He could see Davey getting upset. "But Daddy, they live a really, really long time, don't they? Because they're doctors, right?"

"Yes. Because doctors look after themselves and stay healthy" Geoff said glibly, even though this was the biggest whopper of all time after Father Christmas and the tooth fairy.

Davey seemed satisfied with the response. "I'm sleepy" he said, clutching Little Bun.

Geoff arranged the pillows for Davey, then sat back with the paper. But he did not turn many pages. He was too busy distilling the moment in one of his precious bottles. When he came to pour it out, he might perhaps alter the label – erase the fact it was his ex's house – but it would still be liquid gold.

How soon this would become precious, he had no idea.

Geoff later gave Karen a précis, omitting the bit about diagnosing his own son. Karen understood about cancelling. Not to worry, she said. She'd been there.

Ten days later, *Sentinel Crossing* was no longer showing but *Parle-moi de ces choses* was on. This time Davey wasn't ill, and miraculously neither was any of Karen's mob.

Geoff thought she looked lovely. Karen duly replied "It's only an old thing from the back of the wardrobe." Women always said that even when the dress was fresh out of the shop with the label still on, though Geoff wasn't sure what kind of shop sold such a startling mix of tartan and polka dots.

Inside the Odeon, they studied the posters and hoped the film would be good. French films fell into two main categories, wacky and certifiable, and he didn't mean with an 18. He liked the wacky kind, he said. So did Karen.

As they got their tickets, an elderly lady with a hat like a turquoise loo-roll cover patted Karen's arm and confided "If you're seeing *Parle-moi de ces choses*, you're in for an absolute treat."

As in every cinema foyer, the place reeked of popcorn and the lighting was designed to make you look washed out. Considering everyone these days had Sky movies and DVD players, it was surprisingly busy. Maybe the film really was worth seeing.

He and Karen examined the posters for upcoming features. "Oh, this one's got Denziel Washington in it" she said.

"And lots of other big names too by the look of it" added Geoff.

Karen mused. "The director is the one who did *The Gathering*, isn't it? I loved that film, though not the bit with the priest. Did you see it, Geoff? Geoff?"

Geoff was hot-footing it to the other side of the foyer where two Odeon staff were bent over someone lying on the floor by the assorted sweets.

Right away he could tell she was old. Her skirt was hitched up around her knees, and a turquoise loo-roll thing had fallen off her head, revealing a mass of grey curls. Ah. The woman who'd said they were in for a treat. Her mouth hung open and it didn't seem to be moving. Nothing was.

Geoff waded through the popcorn strewn on the floor around her and shouted "Hello? Can you hear me?"

No response.

Although unconscious, she appeared to give a breath. Geoff knelt beside her. With a finger, he checked the woman's mouth for food and loose dentures and extracted a half-chewed piece of popcorn. He wiped his hand on his jeans.

"Anyone know who she is?" he asked as he listened, watched and felt for breathing. People shrugged. More people arrived. Someone had seen her before but nobody knew anything.

She had a pulse and she was breathing. Good.

By now there was no shortage of onlookers. Geoff selected one of them. "Ring 999 and tell them it's an adult female, unconscious." His knee had become damp through his jeans. He hoped to God it was Coke.

Karen was bending over the woman as well. "Geoff, shall I see if there's a medic here?" she asked, and Geoff was just saying it wasn't necessary when he noticed that the finger he had on the woman's artery was no longer moving. Even more obviously, she wasn't breathing.

It was pointless yelling 'CRASH!' as you did in hospital. It was also pointless wishing the last lecture had been the update on life support skills. He would just have to do his best.

She needed chest compressions, but what was the ratio supposed to be these days? His last cardiac arrest had been 10 years ago, unless you counted plastic dummies. Was it meant to be 30 compressions to two breaths, or maybe 15 to one? And was he going to clamp his mouth across hers or go with chest compressions only?

He decided that the niceties of the latest resuscitation guidelines made no difference since this poor old woman was already on the brink of oblivion.

Kneeling at her left side, he placed his hands on her breastbone one over the other, and pressed down rhythmically with most of his weight.

One, two, three, four, five, six, seven, eight, nine, ten. Cardiac massage was much harder work than he remembered. He stopped at 30 and assessed her.

Something had worked, because her lips began to move as if tasting a dish she was cooking. And, miraculously, her heartbeat was back though it was very slow.

The ambulance arrived swiftly and Geoff gave one the paramedics the gist.

"She was lucky you were here" said the deputy manager when the ambulance left.

"Just happened to be in the right place at the right time" said Geoff.

The deputy manager offered him two free tickets for next week. "And if someone collapses each time you come here," he added optimistically, "you won't ever have to pay again."

When Geoff had washed his hands with lots of soap, twice, he came out to find Karen waiting. "I had no idea you were a medic" she said.

"Who said I was a medic? I'm just a perv who likes to feel up old women."

"Silly! You saved her life."

"Well, it's no biggie." Still, it felt bloody good, he had to admit.

"Have you been called to duty in cinemas before?"

"Nope. Couple of emergencies on planes, but they weren't cardiac arrests. I'm a GP now and my CPR skills are somewhat rusty. But hopefully she'll be OK." If truth be told, he was feeling ashamed for not having loosened her blouse and her belt. It was the first thing the paramedics did on arrival. Not only had Geoff improvised with his resus, he had forgotten basic stuff even a first aider should have known.

Incredibly, they had only missed the opening credits of *Parle-moi de ces choses*. And it turned out to be a lovely film.

Karen smiled at him in the dark. Whenever Geoff glanced to his right during the film, he noticed that she was still smiling. Maybe she was one of those people who did synchronized smiling.

As soon as they left the cinema, Geoff found he had a text from Sonya.

Need 2 tlk soonest. V imp.

Well, it couldn't be about Davey, because she would have phoned to have a rant. Geoff tried not to think about what it might be. He didn't want it to spoil the after-film hour or so he spent with Karen over their Bloody Marys.

"Looks like we made a good choice" said Karen when their drinks arrived, each with a huge celery stick, leaves and all, poking out of the blood-red juice.

"Yep, plenty of fruit and veg there" Geoff agreed. "It provides at least two of your five-a-day."

"Would it be stretching it to count that slice of lemon as well?" said Karen, licking the salt-coated rim of her glass.

"Not at all" said Geoff. "A Bloody Mary is a perfectly balanced meal." They sipped in amiable silence for a moment. Geoff remembered he hadn't taken a blue tablet. These days things had to be planned like a military campaign. Well, perhaps tonight he would see how it went. He could take one later if needed. After all, the stuff was supposed to work pretty quickly.

"You've got tomato juice on your chin" Karen pointed out.

"Oh? Have I?"

She dabbed at his chin with one finger. "Gone now."

He smiled. "Thanks."

"So tell me. What's the best thing about being a GP?" asked Karen.

He stirred his drink with the celery stick. It was tempting to say 'Locking the surgery door behind me' or 'Making my son better', but he actually replied "Times like earlier this evening, I guess, though they're few and far between. But really any situation where I've been able to make a difference. Sadly, there aren't as many of those as people imagine."

"Delivering babies must be quite gratifying, if you can block out the screaming."

"Ah, I haven't delivered a baby for ages. Far too traumatic for a mere man. I leave all the messy stuff to nurses and midwives."

They both agreed they had loved the film. "French actors don't take themselves too seriously. Maybe that's why it was such fun" Karen offered by way of analysis.

"True, on camera. But they compensate by taking themselves intolerably seriously in every interview I've ever read."

"You're right. Wasn't there that French starlet of about 17, can't remember her name, who talked about herself in the third person as if she was France's answer to Isaac Newton?"

Geoff couldn't remember her name either. What the hell could Sonya's important news be? Perhaps she was getting married to that irksome shit she had been bonking. Irksome shit or not, he would be doing Geoff a huge favour because if they shacked up or got married then he wouldn't owe Sonya maintenance for herself.

"I can't recall what she was in either" Karen persevered. "But perhaps you know who I mean?"

"It's on the tip of my tongue" said Geoff, which wasn't quite true. Maybe Sonya had to go into hospital for something. If he had to look after Davey, that was fine by him. He'd love to have his son more often.

"Actors lead such privileged lives" Karen was saying. "But they're obviously desperately insecure."

"Well, if the ones I've had as patients are anything to go by, they're difficult as well as insecure. What did you do before you had kids? I hope you're not going to say you were on the stage."

"Not at all. I was in human remains."

He laughed. "Like me, then."

"I mean human resources."

"Ah. I see."

"It's silly, I know, but I always say 'remains'. The more time I spend with my family, the more juvenile I get. Just as well I stopped at four kids, eh?"

"Well, I don't mind at all. Would you like to see another film soon? After all we do have two free tickets."

He thought her eyes lit up. "Sure. What's on?"

"Next week I think there's *Toy Story 5*, *Nemo Returns*, and a rather good remake of *Bambi*."

Her laugh, her shiny hair, the polka dots, the tartan. They were all very attractive. The closer they sat, and the more Bloody Marys they drank, the more intoxicating she became. He thought about taking a Viagra quite soon.

By the time they left the bar, he was far more relaxed, and had convinced himself that Sonya's news could only be good. It was too late to ring her back now. No matter. It could easily wait till the morning.

Chapter Twenty-One

Sanjay

"I don't want to leave this hotel." Harriet was putting shoes into plastic bags with utmost slowness.

"I don't want to leave this *room*" said Sanjay.

"If only I'd brought more clothes" she complained.

"Why? You're much nicer without them."

She mocked exasperation. "Not to wear, silly. To pack."

"Yeah. Right. Because packing is such fun."

"I meant that it would take longer to pack, and then we wouldn't have to leave the room so soon."

He rolled his eyes. "I'm not convinced that's how check-out times and airline departures work. But why are you taking back annual reports on fisheries and a catalogue of soya bean products?" he added, peering into her case.

"It's just some bumf I picked up from a random conference downstairs."

"Yeah, I can see. But why would you want to take it home?"

"I'll explain some other time." She glanced at her watch. "By the way, we check out in 20. So if you want a final fuck on Spanish soil, it's got to be now."

Yes, indeed. A life-enhancing weekend. He felt more alive and energetic than he had for a long time. Well, he had at some points. At other times he'd felt completely drained. There was the distinct possibility that if they stayed another two nights he'd be going back in a pine box. But what a way to go.

He put his jeans back on, dumped the suitcase back on the bed, and resumed his packing at double speed, smiling as he shoved in T-shirts and jeans. The new CD went in the centre of the clothes.

The music shop had been a bit of a detour but it had to be done. The shop assistant claimed to speak some English, though it wasn't quite enough to understand what Sanjay was saying.

"*Un artisto que e muerto*" explained Sanjay, having rehearsed beforehand. "*O una artista. Non fa nada.*"

The assistant found him a CD of Verdi's Requiem. Very tasteful, but Sanjay wasn't in the mood for burials.

When the man finally got his drift, he explained to *señor* that dead musicians, they do not make the big money. In the end, Sanjay and Harriet scoured the shelves themselves.

"Look, Sanjay!" She had found Andrés Segovia. "He's a classic, and he's very dead."

"Are you sure?"

"Positive. Dead about 20 years. Possibly longer."

Andrés Segovia would make a worthy addition to his collection.

Sanjay felt good on landing at Heathrow. He had to say goodbye to Harriet, but that was OK. This trip he'd brought home something more significant than a tatty straw hat or a crop of mosquito bites. They kissed at length before she went her own way, each of them promising that they would talk soon, very soon.

Sanjay took the long tube journey home, texting Ben when he had a signal. Nothing profound, just to keep in touch. *How ru m8? Just got bk from Barca. Tell u more when icu S.*

Normally he'd have texted during the trip as well. This time, Sanjay realized guiltily, he hadn't sent a single text, not even to Ben. Well, bragging to Ben didn't feel right.

When Sanjay got back to his flat, Sita was curled up on the sofa in front of the TV, mesmerized by some mind-numbing drivel. It looked like an ancient episode of *Law & Order* or one of the thousands of spin-offs thereof.

"Hey, bro! You had a good time, innit?"

"The best. Where's Dainty?" She hadn't greeted him in her usual way, with trills of pleasure as she wound around his legs.

"She's there. Look."

She was sitting in the shape of a meat loaf on a dining-chair, glaring with big green eyes. As well she might, given his unexplained absence. He gave

Dainty a rub behind the ears, and she bent her head for more, purring loudly. That was more like it.

Then Sanjay did his customary visual sweep of the flat, in case Dainty had been sick somewhere. "Hey, thanks for cleaning the cat tray" he said when he came out of the bathroom.

"I didn't" said Sita. "She didn't go."

"What do you mean, didn't go?"

"Well, she, like, peed over the side, cos she holds her bum in the air. I washed the floor, obviously." She gave a look of exaggerated patience. "But she didn't do nothing in it."

"You mean she didn't do a dump in three days?"

"Yeah, that's what I mean. Unless she did it under the sofa. I'm sorry, bro, but you never said to check under the sofa."

Sanjay bent down to look, but there were no deposits of any vintage under his sofa. He took his case into the bedroom and hauled it onto the bed.

This was weird. The stripes on the duvet were meant to be horizontal. But now they were vertical. He checked and found the poppers were on the side, not the bottom edge. Had he actually put the duvet wrongly? "Hey, Sita, you make my bed or something?"

Sita dragged herself away from Lenny Briscoe and the other stalwarts of the 27th Precinct. "What do you mean exactly?"

"Well, did you come in here and straighten up the bedcovers?"

She stared at her fluffy orange socks, looking as guilty as hell.

"Bollocks, Sita, don't tell me you actually slept in here!"

It was when she said she hadn't, like, you know, slept, not as such, that he knew.

"You never asked if you could use my place as a shag-pad! Bloody hell, there's someone else's spunk in this bed and you didn't even change the sheets!"

"There's no spunk on the sheets. We used condoms."

"For God' sake, spare me the details. Who the fuck was it, anyway?"

She said it was nobody he knew, and that it didn't matter anyway. "Besides, didn't you just say to spare you the details?"

Bollocks! This meant it was either a one-night stand or else the guy was already hitched. "He's married, right?"

"I don't go with married men." Her face was like an old boot. Even as a child, Sita could really work a look.

"Then you could have gone back to his place. But you didn't. That's why I think he's married. Or else he's about 14."

"Think whatever you like." The sulk had reached Oscar-winning status.

It didn't really matter. Life was too short, like he always said.

That night when he went to bed it was just like being in the anaesthetic room, only obviously more comfortable. He felt himself slipping away, a delicious sensation enhanced by the knowledge that he would not be waking up to that hospital smell, or to the sound of someone retching in the recovery room.

He surfaced in the night to the realization that Harriet's arms were not around him. Neither were her legs entwined in his. He could however hear the distinct sounds of someone being sick.

Dainty was in the hall, her sleek little body racked by retching. Her paws slid on the wooden floor from the force of her heaving. It was distressing to watch, even though he should have been used to it by now. She'd have won medals for chucking up. Only this time she hadn't eaten anything. Sanjay cleared it up and waited for the vomiting to subside before carting Dainty back to bed with him.

When Sanjay came home from work the next day, he was done in even though he'd left the office early. The charity was very understanding. They'd even let him know there might be someone to take over, eventually, should he ever need - as they put it – more time off. They were a good bunch, thought Sanjay, including the boss. Although maybe they just didn't want him to snuff it while actually at his desk.

He sighed as he removed his shoes. It was frustrating to feel so tired when he still wanted to do so much.

He put on the Traveling Wilburys. He liked them, and as a bonus they counted twice, for both George Harrison and Roy Orbison.

The Wilburys didn't do much for him this evening. He was worried about Dainty. She hadn't eaten a lot, apart from the top of the ornamental grass by the telly. Not that it looked so ornamental now. Once she ate a Holy Palm. That was when he had an Irish girlfriend. Lovely face, a bit plump. Anyway, the palm Ciara brought back from Mass had disappeared, much to her consternation, but it reappeared two days later, sticking out of Dainty's rear end.

Sanjay considered the situation. Apart from one tiny pellet, Dainty's tray was still pristine. Obviously she was seriously bunged up.

Time for lactulose. His GP had prescribed it a while back. It happened to be exactly the same syrup, only cheaper, that the vet had sold him for Dainty a couple of years ago when she needed a laxative. Unfortunately Dainty hated it, even though she liked other sweet sticky things like baklava, which didn't taste much different in Sanjay's opinion.

He got out the little syringe for giving medicines by mouth. What was the dose of lactulose for a cat? He wasn't sure. Oh, bollocks. Now he remembered. The dose was whatever he could get down Dainty's throat before she ripped his arm to shreds.

After he had wrapped Dainty in an old towel and syringed some of the gunk into her mouth, things seemed normal. Dainty escaped as soon as she could, leapt onto the cooker with a bound, and turned the hob on. Funny how nobody warned you about that when you bought an electric hob with touch controls.

Exhausted by it all, he lay on the sofa. Dainty came and sat on him. The fur around her mouth and chin were sticky from the medicine, but she had forgiven him because she was purring. She might not be the friendliest cat in the world, but she loved Sanjay. It went without saying that he loved her back.

After a while, Sanjay found the energy to ring Harriet.

"Hello?" Her voice was guarded.

"Hey, it's me, Sanjay. Can you talk?"

"Can I get back to you when I've checked my diary?"

Strange, thought Sanjay. "OK, sure."

Three hours later she still hadn't rung back. Couldn't be blowing him off, could she? Or maybe someone else was there. He preferred not to think about that one.

It was all too complicated. He made a few more calls, including a long one to his mum who updated him about her leg, the long and short of which was that there was no change. After that, he gave Dainty a light supper of Whiskas followed by another dose of lactulose for good measure, and subsided into a profound and featureless sleep.

When he got up, he gave Dainty a kiss on the head because she had not thrown up anywhere that he could see. Then he opened a text from Harriet.

Got 2 tlk asap xxxx

Sanjay ran water into the Dualit kettle that was made to last a lifetime but didn't need to. What the fuck did Harriet mean? Women and their mixed messages!

Chapter Twenty-Two

Karen

So far she had fallen over twice. Not bad considering the grass was wet and she was in trainers, while her kids wore proper boots with studs.

"Come on, Mummy. You can do it." Five-year old Ashley tried to haul her up.

If she had a partner, they'd be able to play football in the back garden a lot more easily. As it was, they had to make do with a sort of two-and-a-half-a-side footie which included Damon and Ashley on one team, with Charlotte, Edward and herself on the other.

It was time for her to be subbed off and spend some time on the bench. The children were still full of go, Charlotte in a pink T-shirt just like Belinda's. The boys' football shirts were hand-me-downs. Replica kit was expensive.

Breathless, she clutched at the stitch in her side. If she had Thomas back, not only could someone else go in goal, but the kids might have this season's shirts.

Thomas had wanted to move back in. For nearly a week he had occupied the futon, ignoring the books, puzzles, soft toys and bits of Stickle Brick that landed on it. That man could doss anywhere, as long as it was the wrong place and the wrong time. A plantation of dirty coffee mugs, used tissues and general debris grew around the futon, as if reclaiming the space.

"I'll tidy it later" he lied. "Sit down with me for a bit."

"Thanks, but I'll pass." Did he think littering was some kind of foreplay?

His presence exasperated her though it would at least be good for the children, she'd thought. Wouldn't it be fun for them to be together for a while, other than at McDonald's, where all the kids and Sunday dads went?

Except that 'fun' wasn't quite the right the word since Thomas didn't show much interest in playing with them. The only thing that really mattered to him was the six inches of trouble nestling between his legs.

The children had tried. "You can stay in my room, Daddy" Edward had said.

Thomas hadn't even ventured into Edward's room. He did however turn up in Karen's, complaining that the futon was damp. She assured him it was as dry as a bone, and turfed him out. Then he asked her to sort out the MOT on his car. Outraged, she then called him something she didn't want to explain to the kids. But she took care not to get too angry, in case rage crossed over to whatever emotion had taken hold that afternoon with the DVDs.

Thomas tried another tack. He ambushed her in the kitchen while she was scrambling eggs, the one dish she really did prepare to perfection. "Do you remember that time in the back of the Volvo?" he said.

For eight years, the Volvo had carried groceries, furniture, tins of paint and rolls of wallpaper, stuff to and from charity shops, various dogs, grubby sports gear, grandparents, a bonkers old uncle and of course gaggles of kids. One night, however, the old estate car was involved in a more delightful transport.

It took a fraction of a second for it all to come back to her. The hotel in Cornwall. The bottle of red wine that she and Thomas had consumed on the beach, to keep warm while the kids amused themselves in the sand, unaware that with wind-chill the temperature was hovering around zero. Then at the end of day the feeling – rare in those days – that they just had to have each other now.

But there were the children, snoozing in their beds about two feet away in the family room. Fear of waking them led to 10 stolen minutes in the back of the Volvo. It was quite possible that a passing villager had seen them, or that the hotel's CCTV had captured images of them writhing among the travelling rug and the wind-break, Karen's legs akimbo. But that didn't stop them.

It was a powerful memory. Karen sighed. "Do you mind? The toast is done."

Thomas persisted. "What about when we christened our new kitchen worktop in Crespigny Road?"

She shooed him out on the pretext that brunch was burning. Back then, they'd had each other all around the room, and it was a big room. It was distracting to remember the moment when they realized that the butcher's block had wheels, and she didn't want any impromptu dramatizations.

"Why can't we try again?" he pleaded while he watched her load the dishwasher afterwards. His face displayed the kind of detached curiosity that people can only manage when they have no intention of dealing with the dishes themselves.

"Why should we? Because she threw you out?"

He had no answer to that. She'd hit home.

Karen rubbed her lower ribs and made an easy save. Charlotte had taken a lazy shot from the far side of the garden, at the same time going on about a drum kit, please please please, Mummy.

What about Geoff, thought Karen. He was nice. They had a lot in common, but alas not that much spark. As yet, anyway. According to Rose, you had to give it time. It sounded like getting a barbecue going.

Karen looked around her now. The children weren't fighting, and the slanting afternoon sun made the garden shimmer in perfect light, even though in reality it was neglected, with ragged edges, a surfeit of dandelions and multiple bare patches from football boots.

She often looked back on the earlier years as a golden time. The days when the children were tiny, and she was not. Either she was expecting another baby, or had just had one, so she was always round and fat. There was eternally baby sick on one shoulder, and a variety of deposits around the house. At that stage of parenthood, every lump on the floor was a turd till proved otherwise.

That wasn't so long ago, maybe three years. Before Charlotte and Damon realized that Santa Claus didn't exist, and that grown-ups had sex. Also before her husband had declared he was a lost soul and decided to go and find himself.

Still, afternoons like today were just as golden. Especially now that she'd finally persuaded Thomas to get off the futon and try again with his floozy.

"OK, you lot are going to have to do without me" she announced as she went into the kitchen.

Ashley promptly followed her in. "Damon just called me a plonker" he whined.

Damon yelled "I did not."

"You did too. Mummy, what's a plonker?"

"I want a biscuit" said Edward, trailing in behind them.

"Right" said Karen. "Now who's going to help lay the table for supper?"

This had the happy effect of making her sons rush out to continue playing.

Geoff

In medicine, every lump was a cancer until proved otherwise. At least, that's what you had to assume when a patient came in with a new swelling. The young man in front of Geoff was 23 and had a lump on his shoulder-blade. The fact that it had doubled in size within a month was a bad sign. He had also lost about 10kg. There were so many red flags here it could have been a map of China. Geoff spent some time explaining that an urgent scan was in order, and not the course of antibiotics the patient had in mind.

Sonya rang in the middle of this. "Don't you want to hear my news?"

"Of course but I'll have to ring you back. I'm doing my surgery." To be exact, Geoff was halfway through. And, it went without saying, he was running late, because that was inevitable if you did the job properly.

Mrs Thing came in next. Her symptoms were like a black hole, swallowing up every doctor she consulted. Today she had ankle pain which she feared might be serious. As she reminded Geoff, "I did have poliomyelitis as a child, you know."

"And you made a wonderful recovery. Many children with polio didn't do well at all."

She was shocked. "Oh no, doctor, I'm afraid you're very much mistaken. I never had polio. It was polio-*myelitis*."

There was no point trying to explain to Mrs Thing that they were one and the same. She was adamant that poliomyelitis was much worse, just as she was convinced that tuberculosis was more lethal than its little brother TB, and that influenza was far more contagious than the flu.

True to form, the last patient was an oddball. This one complained that when he ate he could taste the food in his ears. Geoff told the man that this symptom wasn't anything too terrible and was bound to pass. He would have preferred to tell him not to be pathetic and that some people had MS, for fuck's sake.

When he finished he was desperate for a sandwich, but he had to ring Sonya back.

She picked up immediately. "The thing is, Geoff, we leave in a fortnight. I thought you should know."

"OK. Where are you going?" he asked, not that he actually gave a monkey's where his ex-wife went on holiday.

They were going to Perth, she said. At first, he couldn't see the attraction of Scotland. It was cold, damp and dark. He was a bit surprised that Sonya would like it. She usually preferred more exotic destinations. Maybe if he'd had that sandwich, his brain would have been working better. As it was, it didn't sink in until after she said he might like to have Davey for an extra weekend.

"Of course. I'd love to."

"It's just a holiday at this point, a little recce if you like, but after that you probably won't be seeing him for a long time. And I know you think I'm heartless, Geoff, but I'm really not."

"Excuse me?"

"All in all, we're going to be away 18 months to two years."

He felt like letting out a scream that emptied his lungs completely, forever, because there was no point in ever breathing again. But he didn't scream or stop breathing. He just said "Why?"

"Because Drew has got a job in Australia, that's why. I knew you weren't listening. You never do."

She launched into a long explanation of why Drew's job was so good, it was an offer he couldn't refuse, and so on. Australia was a superb place to live, with a fantastic lifestyle, as she put it, although Geoff knew for certain she had never been there. Anyway the long and the short of it was that Drew was an engineer, and he couldn't just work anywhere as a doctor could. Geoff grew tired of Drew's CV.

Eventually he found a gap in Sonya's monologue and asked if Davey had been told yet, and whether he'd said anything, because he, Geoff, would much rather he stayed in the UK, and of course he'd be happy if Davey came to live with him instead of going away. "He is my son."

There was a bang on the door. Probably the practice manager. "Wait. I'm on the phone" he called out.

Sonya hadn't said anything to Davey yet. "I'll be telling him today. I wanted you to know first."

"Well, can I be there when you tell him? I can be done here by 6.30."

"I don't think so, Geoff. It's Drew's job, so I think it's our call. And I'm the one who has custody, remember."

Oh, how could he forget?

"He still needs two parents" she continued. Geoff thought this was a nod to his input, which showed how wrong one could be. "He'll be with Drew and me, and living with two adults will be a much more normal set-up than the current one."

Heartless, and incredibly obtuse as well. He wanted to negotiate a way out of the dilemma, but it was clear she'd finished her say. Anyway he now had things to do. Like find a shit-hot lawyer.

The practice manager must have been lurking outside the door, because she knocked again as soon as he'd put the mobile down. "Geoff, Mrs Montgomery's daughter-in-law wants you to visit. And the nursing home at Hillside called. They say Mr Andrews had another fall and needs checking over."

Mrs Montgomery was 96 and her family thought of themselves as very caring, the downside being that they were a complete pain in the arse. Geoff ended up seeing Mrs Montgomery at least once a week if not twice, even though he could no longer do anything useful for her. Once he'd mumbled something about *anno domini* and gently mentioned that it was not always possible or even desirable to prolong life indefinitely. The daughter had looked at him as if he'd suggested a lethal injection.

"Mrs Montgomery junior did say there was no hurry. You don't have to visit until after evening surgery. And I'm going home now" added the practice manager.

"Fine, but before you go, I'd like you to ring Mrs Montgomery junior and tell her to get stuffed." As soon as the words were out, Geoff felt as guilty as hell. "I'm sorry, Barbara. I shouldn't have said that. It was totally unfair of me and completely out of order. Just get me the fucking number and I'll do it myself."

Chapter Twenty-Three

Harriet

"You haven't stopped yawning all evening" remarked Simon after dinner.

Well," said Harriet, "everything in Spain is so late. They don't even have lunch till half two, then dinner ends up being at 11. I'm rather jet-lagged."

He stretched out on the sofa, put one arm over the back and gazed at her through narrowed eyes. "I hadn't realized you'd gone to Barcelona solely for paella and tapas."

"Of course not. There were other activities as well." But she certainly wasn't going to describe them. "It was a working weekend, you know."

He picked up a glossy brochure and sniffed twice. "I can't imagine what anyone finds riveting about soya bean products."

"Ah, but it wasn't the products themselves. There was a simulated press conference, with each of us playing a reporter from one of the papers – and from different radio and TV stations – and we fired questions at a spokesman from the soya bean industry. The weekend was mainly for freelancers, so that workshop was a very helpful. I feel far more confident now." Though not necessarily about press conferences.

"Which one were you?"

"What do you mean?"

"Which publication were you from?"

"Oh, I was *Good Housekeeping*."

There was an audible snort from Simon before he said "Women's magazines are so trivial."

"They are not! They're often very well written, and the topics are important" she said, her voice rising to a squeal despite herself. She hoped Simon had forgotten her feature *What your loo roll says about you*.

"Really? Then why do they rabbit on about fashion or cooking being the most vital thing in the world, and why is every article written in such a breezy condescending way?"

She shrugged. "That's a matter of opinion."

"I know you agree with me. You just don't want to admit it. Anyway, how did the press conference work?"

It must have been a rhetorical question. Sure enough, he lost all interest when she began her prepared description of the damage-limitation session, where people accused the fishery and canning company of using dolphin-unfriendly nets, or of farming salmon too intensively. Instead he examined the contents of his mug critically and said "Did you use a pot?"

"Of course! I said so, didn't I?"

Sanjay's call came at a bad time, but then on this particular evening there were no good times. Simon seemed to be watching her tonight. And his hearing was excellent too.

"Can I get back to you when I've checked my diary?" she said, as lightly as she knew how. As soon as she ended the call, she noticed that Simon was holding out her shocking pink Filofax.

"It was on the sofa next to you."

"Thanks. But I didn't really need it. I was just trying to fob off someone boring from the trip to Barcelona." She felt a twinge of disloyalty.

When she brushed her teeth that night, Simon started kissing her neck. She squirmed and got toothpaste on the wall tiles as a result, which normally would have irritated him beyond belief.

Simon couldn't wait to get out of his clothes. He whipped off his boxers as soon as he could, hooking them onto the bedpost. His skin was like undercooked chicken, pale and a bit flabby, except for his genitals. Clearly he had clearly missed her. She turned the light off.

"Why can't we have it back on?" asked Simon.

She muttered something about itchy tired eyes and dehydration from the flight. The darkness helped that. If he stopped talking it would be a whole lot easier to pretend he was someone else. She was wet, of course, but that was just a reflex.

"You missed me" he remarked.

She made a non-committal sound and continued to fantasize. But kissing him seemed too intimate. Prostitutes never kissed their clients either. Somehow the thought cheered her up. This was duty sex.

Simon must have noticed she'd been dodging his mouth because, after he'd finished grunting, he got up to go to the bathroom. She lay on the pillows and watched him through the doorway as he viewed his teeth from all possible angles in the mirror before giving them a thorough flossing.

He returned from the bathroom with renewed vigour, and began to lick her nipples, flicking each one briskly with his tongue.

During round two she still didn't kiss him. Afterwards, he nestled in her arms and mumbled "I'll make an appointment with the hygienist." She nearly chuckled when he got up to sloosh some Listerine round his mouth again. Rarely had she seen him this eager to please. He wasn't so bad after all.

"I've got a question" she called out when he'd stopped gargling. "What's your opinion of Andrés Segovia?"

Simon spat extravagantly into the basin before replying "Hugely over-rated."

Harriet's text the next day was far from inspired. It would have helped, she thought, if she knew what to say. He had to be told about Simon. Or did he? How long did he have left, anyway?

Sanjay rang five minutes later and asked how she was.

"Can we meet?" she countered.

"I was hoping you'd say that. Especially considering what a good time we had last time we were together." The anticipation in his voice didn't help any.

She took a deep breath. "To be honest, we do need to talk."

"I've already been honest" said Sanjay. "But I think you have something to tell me."

"I guess I do."

She had spent most of the night thinking about it. During their weekend away, she had forced herself to live entirely in the present. That might have been a great way to defer anxiety and delay decisions, but now the present had turned into the past. The current present was reality, and the reality was that she had no place of her own and little chance of affording one anytime soon.

Worse, she was in debt. Harriet wasn't stupid enough to have huge credit card bills, but she still owed Simon a pile of money. While she'd bought the new laptop herself, he'd bank-rolled two journalism courses, as well as five spa trips that had unfortunately not led to the publication of her feature on *The Wonders of Water*. Some titles had gone belly-up, while others had been slimmed down or relaunched, making it harder than ever for a freelancer.

Harriet got up to go to the loo, inching quietly around Simon's side of the bed. Commissions still came in, but many publications offered the same rates as 10 years ago. And then the writing often turned out to be a massive effort, however enthusiastic Harriet may have been at the start. No zip, no zing. She pushed the button-flush, as usual trying not to displace the toiletries Simon kept on top of the cistern.

There had been a connection with Sanjay. Harriet knew it. He was wonderful and unusual.

He was also running out of time. Being with him long-term was impossible. Therefore, as tough as it was, the only thing to do was to forget about him and stay with Simon. She crept back to bed, shut her eyes and tried to sleep.

They met next day at the Jacaranda. "Convenient for my office" Sanjay had said.

That was fine with her. No point wasting time he didn't have.

Sanjay was conversational. It was almost like being back in Barcelona, sight-seeing. His head swivelled around to take in all his surroundings, as if he hadn't been there before. "You always notice more the second time around" he said.

True, thought Harriet. They had kissed on arrival, giving her a whiff of Sanjay's aftershave. She didn't know its name, but she recognized the potent mix of musk, sandalwood and pure passion which transported her straight back to room 427.

"You're wearing the earrings from Barcelona."

That was true too. As they sat down, their hands touched briefly on edge of the table. That fleeting contact sent 220 volts shooting through her fingers, but it was just the fear of being seen by a colleague of Simon's, or, worse, Simon himself. Why the hell had she agreed on the Jacaranda? It was perilously close to all his contacts at the BBC, not to mention that Royal Music place in Marylebone Road.

Sanjay had finished his study of the ceiling, the window frames and the coving. Now he looked at her expectantly.

She traced a knot on the oak table with her finger before she could speak. "I need to tell you something. I hope it's not too much of a shock."

"You'll have to be quick. Did I mention I've got a terminal disease?" He grinned, showing two canyons of dimples. God, that made it hard.

"Sanjay, I really enjoyed our weekend" she said, her mouth so dry it was practically clicking. "It was terrific, and not just because Barcelona is awesome. But I'm sorry, I haven't been totally honest. I'm seeing someone. We were going through a bad patch, so I guess I fell for you. But I'm still seeing him. Actually I'm living with him, and – well, that's it really." She had got the whole lot out, but she didn't feel any less awful.

His dimples had gone. "I kind of suspected."

"You did?"

"Well, you told me you were – past tense – seeing someone, but I wondered if it was still on. I definitely got the impression you wanted to mislead someone about where you were that weekend. One way or another, I sort of knew."

"I'm sorry. I didn't mean to hurt you." Cliché as it was, it was true.

He chose that moment to examine his cuticles with forensic attention. "It was a great weekend, and it was on my to-do list. You know, Harriet, life's too short" he said, finally looking up. "At uni my friends and I used to say this all the time, but in reality we hadn't a fucking clue. We were talking out of our arses. Now I know exactly what it means, so I care a little less about some things, more about others."

"So. A list." She'd guessed he'd have one. She just didn't know she'd be on it. "What else is on there?"

"Well, catching up with old friends like Shelley Ritchie is on it, but one of the things on my list is to stop adding to the bloody list."

He had been gracious. "Thank you." What else was there to say? She made a vague hand movement on the table towards his, whereupon the electrical thing threatened to erupt again. She really had to escape before any of Simon's colleagues showed up. The Marylebone studios were much too close for comfort. To lessen her unease, she asked after the cat.

His cat wasn't that well. She'd become constipated, he explained as the bill arrived, which they split. "And she's gone off her food."

It didn't sound serious. "That happened to Pushkin all the time, but then he'd go out and eat grass, or else savage a bird or a field mouse, which helped. Anyway, I hope your cat's better soon." She'd forgotten his cat's name, but no matter.

"Sure. Thanks" replied Sanjay without conviction.

She studied him one last time. His latte-coloured face. His ink-well eyes. Hair that looked like a burnt field. But she didn't get long because he soon scraped back his chair and was gone, leaving words unsaid on her lips. In the air there was still a hint of his aftershave, a scent that would forever signify great sex. She wondered if anything that amazing could ever happen to her again.

Feeling gripped her chest as she walked out in the street, mingling with rich tourists, yummy mummies and terribly important people who worked at the BBC. Maybe there was a reason why she and Sanjay had met.

She crossed the street. Or maybe not. It was all random, after all, even if the weekend in Barcelona had felt otherwise.

Too upset to go straight back to the flat, Harriet wandered for a bit. On the pavement outside one of the cafés, a slim waiter was practically dancing between the tables while balancing a metal tray laden with coffees and patisseries. She crossed the street by the Emma Bridgewater shop. The crockery was gorgeous but it didn't make her feel any better.

On impulse, Harriet went into a florist. Looking around at the roses, lilies and gladioli, she instinctively knew that none of these showy blooms would fit the bill. A potted plant was more the thing.

The assistant pointed her in the direction of hydrangeas in a selection of colours. When she looked doubtful, he showed her some potted daisies, rosemary, lavender and little bay trees. Better, though still not what she was looking for. The only thing she knew for sure was that Simon liked topiary, so she bought a *buxus* that had been severely clipped into a tight little sphere. It was hideously expensive for a small plant that didn't even produce flowers, but it was a safe choice, and it kept its leaves all year round, which was good. You knew where you were with topiary.

Chapter Twenty-Four

Geoff

"Daddy, what's Vegemite?"

"Well, Davey, it's a bit like Marmite, only different." Geoff slid another pancake onto the pile keeping warm in the oven. This latest effort was a little rounder, a lot less burnt. By the time Davey left for Perth, Geoff would have perfected his pancake-making. But for what?

"Mummy says I will like Vegemite and koalas and kangaroos and our new house."

It was tough to compete with koalas and kangaroos. Geoff just said "Ready! How many pancakes do you want?"

"Lots and lots! Daddy, do you think our new house in Australia will be nice?"

"Davey, why don't you wait and see? You might not be moving to Australia." Not if he had anything to do with it, he added to himself. Having custody didn't give Sonya the right to take Davey to live anywhere she liked, as Geoff had discovered after getting legal advice. He intended to pursue this through the courts.

"Daddy, will you come and visit?"

"Of course I will. I'll come as often as I can."

Davey nodded sagely. "You can stay in our house."

Geoff didn't think Mummy and Drew would like that. "Let's just see, Davey."

"And we can go swimming every day."

Obviously Sonya had filled his head with Oz propaganda. Geoff knew that the beaches in Perth were only warm and inviting when viewed from a long way away, like Siberia. The sunsets might be spectacular, but the coarse sand was littered with dead creatures, and the water was cold even at the height of summer, unlike the beaches of South Australia. Despite a few nice buildings and a large park, Perth was dull and sterile. It also felt like it was at the very end of the earth. Geoff was sure little had changed since he'd been in his gap year. It was unfair of Sonya to trick a small child into thinking it was going to be like the Algarve with cute furry animals thrown in.

"Why aren't you having any pancakes, Daddy?"

His appetite had vanished, and nothing could induce him to do more than push a piece of pancake around his plate, especially not the fact that Davey was being transported 9,000 miles away. While the solicitor was encouraging, the little holiday Sonya was planning with Davey worried Geoff. Suppose they didn't come back? Perth was horrible and soulless. It would suit Sonya and Drew perfectly.

"You should eat, Daddy. Every day, your tummy is born again."

Children's tummies could recover even faster than that, Geoff reflected, remembering the number of times Davey had thrown up and then, ten minutes later, begged for crisps or wolfed down a whole pack of hot cross buns.

Today Davey's appetite seemed boundless. He wanted to take some sweeties for their visit to the park. Davey went in goal, chewing one toffee after another. Geoff feared he might inhale one of them by accident, but Davey had this covered. "Goalies always chew something, Daddy" he pointed out. "It never goes down the wrong way."

At the park there were children of all ages. He glanced at two girls on the roundabout. As a doctor, Geoff was pretty good at estimating ages. The girls were much bigger than Davey. They were about the age he would be in a couple of years.

A Japanese father was playing football with his son. He kept dribbling the ball away and exhorting the lad to catch up and tackle him. Since the dad was very quick, all the kid could do run after him, squealing with frustration. It bordered on cruelty, thought Geoff, but then parenting was an inexact science. Who was to say this man's methods were wrong? Maybe he was just teaching his son to keep trying.

Geoff let Davey make a few saves, then, when the toffee was finished, he volleyed a ball that went straight past Davey and into the back of the net, or what would have been the net had there been one. Davey's face lit up with admiration. "Nice one, Daddy."

Geoff wondered if Drew played football. He hoped to God he was rubbish.

After the park, they walked down the main street, Davey with muddy ball and grassy knees. The five young black women lined up outside the post office as usual called out "Jesus Loves You!" Davey responded "I know", which had them in paroxysms of appreciation.

"Why do I have to wash my hands?" asked Davey when they got to Burger King.

Geoff explained there were all sorts of germs that could do you harm.

"What sort of germs?"

Although you couldn't see them, lots of parasites and bacterial spores lived in soil. And you didn't want them in your tummy because they could make you ill. Geoff explained that some parasites could even make you blind.

"I don't want to be blind" said Davey washing his hands carefully. "You can't play very good football if you're blind." At this rate he was going to be the best medically informed child in the class, thought Geoff. If he stayed in England.

"Uh-oh" said Davey as some of the burger oozed out from the bun, disgorging sauce and a slice of tomato. Geoff handed Davey one of the scratchy napkins to wipe his chin.

This too Geoff would distil and keep safe. He needed lots of little memory bottles to sustain him, so he could preserve the whole day, though without the horrible gnawing that occupied the middle of his abdomen and had nothing to do with hunger.

There was the usual empty space when Davey left that weekend. Geoff did the washing up and took out the rubbish. He wasn't up to tackling anything demanding, especially not reading the *BMJ* or replying to Mrs Montgomery junior's complaint about his intolerably rude phone call. Truth be told, the only thing he was inclined to do right now was throw himself on his bed and sob his eyes out.

Sonya and Drew would probably marry soon, and she would no doubt encourage Davey to call Drew his new daddy. He would only be Davey's stepfather, but if he pointed that out to Sonya she'd only say 'Step-dad, dad - what's the difference? You always did split hairs.'

Geoff needed to be positive so he could fight, and crying like a little girl wouldn't help. He was the strong one. The one you could text with all your worries, or ring in the night when you were scared that your chest pain was something serious, rather than induced by too many Bacardi Breezers. Just now he'd got another text from Frieda. At this point he needed someone to help him out, rather than have to go on giving.

The two mates he'd spoken to about Perth had tried to jolly him along, insisting everything would work out fine. The last thing it felt was fine.

But perhaps there was someone else he could talk to, someone neither depressing nor judgmental. Whenever he'd seen her, she was upbeat. If she didn't manage to infect him with cheer, well, it would hardly matter if she saw him cry.

Karen

The trouble with some ex-husbands was their unwillingness to remain ex. After vacating the futon and returning to his floozy, Thomas had then come back one evening, bringing a random selection of groceries and leaving puzzlement in his wake.

"Is Daddy moving back in?" asked Ashley.

"No, darling, he isn't" she said, although it wasn't clear what Thomas wanted to do.

She discussed this with Rose. By the time she'd finished the call, a tea-party was in full swing, with Edward and Ashley drinking imaginary tea and coffee out of a plastic tea-set. As Edward explained, they had real coffee with grounds in it. "It's Cup o' Chino" he said, handing her a cup of mud from the garden. Everyone else had already had some, including Edward's best friend Mr Cow, and it was delicious.

Karen added sugar from the bowl Ashley was holding out. "It's really sand from the sandpit" he confided.

"Ooh, is it? I thought it was the best Demerara sugar from the Caribbean." The three boys beamed as she made slurping sounds. "Lovely! Is there any more?"

"Sorry. Mr Cow had it all" explained Edward, waving at the sofa where the soft toy sat surrounded by three or four plastic cups. "He looks like a cow, but he's really a pig" Ashley added, while Edward contributed a few snorting noises.

Karen now saw there was fake coffee all over the sofa. "Oh crap!" she cried without thinking.

"Oh crap!" echoed Edward. But it wasn't the sofa that worried him. "Mr Cow's got a wet bottom!"

"Now look" said Karen patiently. "You can't put drinks on the furniture, because it can spill and make stains, like this."

The two boys stared. Edward clutched Mr Cow and said "But Mummy, *you* put drinks on the furniture."

"No, I don't."

"Yes, you do. A table is furniture. You said" said Ashley.

"OK, a table IS a kind of furniture. I meant, don't put drinks on the sofa, chairs, beds or any upholstered furniture."

"What's up-hostel-er?" asked Edward.

"It means furniture covered with cloth."

Ashley immediately spotted the flaw in this logic. Karen was just explaining why a tablecloth wasn't actually upholstery when her mobile rang.

"Hi, Geoff. No, not that busy. I'm just explaining what upholstery is."

"Up-Hollister" corrected Edward.

"Not that well, actually" she said into the phone. "It's now a semantic debate, and I'm losing. How are you?"

He'd had some unwelcome news so he wasn't at his best, especially now that it was Sunday and Davey had gone back to his ex-wife's.

She was sorry to hear that. "Do you want to talk about it?"

"Actually, yes. When's convenient for you?"

"Well, tomorrow and the day after are pretty busy, but I might be able to do Wednesday. Or just tell me when you can manage, and I'll see if I'm free."

"How about in an hour?"

Geoff

The GPS got Geoff to Stanmore without any trouble. Parking his Prius about 100 metres from her house, he sat for a moment taking in his surroundings. He patted his pocket. No blue tablets there but he didn't think he'd want them.

Over the years he had visited countless homes, seen hundreds like this 1930s semi. This one had some plant draping itself over the door and climbing into an open bay window upstairs. By the front door sat a discarded tricycle. The downstairs window had a Lego pirate ship on the windowsill. Homely.

He knocked because a faded sign said *Knock – bell not working*. The letter box did not look as if its spring worked either, since the flap was stuck open. Karen wore a smile and a subdued pair of sunshine yellow culottes, and was clutching a pile of laundry. "Come in" she said as she kicked a football aside to let the door open wide.

"Thank you. It doesn't look as if this is a very good time for you."

She laughed. "This is as good as it gets. I've just removed the washing from the radiator in your honour."

"You didn't need to" said Geoff, meaning it.

"We'll go in the living-room where the kids are." She introduced Ashley, Damon and Edward. "Charlotte's upstairs running up a phone bill."

Geoff smiled at the three boys. There was one of about six who looked a lot like Karen, and an older lad with freckles and a sensitive face. The youngest had a round face and deep-set eyes that reminded Geoff of raisins in an Eccles cake.

The furniture included a battered futon and some seriously wonky lamps. On the large sofa, the cushion covers had been removed and a tartan blanket draped over it instead. When Geoff sat down, he realized how scratchy it was, but it was all exactly as it should be, a family home with an actual family.

The assortment of discarded shoes was devoid of Louboutins, Ginas and Jimmy Choos. Geoff also noted with pleasure that among the clutter of magazines, newspapers and children's books there did not appear to be a single Harvey Nicks catalogue. The room itself contained nothing fancy, nothing ironic and (thank God) nothing Prada. While most of its contents probably belonged to her children – he doubted she read books on helicopters or magic tricks, but he might be wrong – the whole place reflected Karen and her exuberant imperfection.

Karen got him a glass of wine, with fizzy water because he was driving, and the same for herself.

Somehow, between a neighbour popping for a plunger, one of her boys needing help with maths, and a sullenly pretty daughter, probably around 11, coming downstairs in to talk about a sleep-over, Geoff told her about Davey's imminent departure.

Karen was shocked. "But that's dreadful. Isn't there anything you can do?"

"My solicitor says there is, but it will be a battle."

"Oh shit. Sorry." She looked at him seriously. "What kind of battle?"

"Long, bloody and expensive. Sonya has custody, and I have access. Therefore I have every right to try to stop her taking our son to the other end of the earth. But there's no guarantee I'll succeed."

She said nothing. One of her boys gave her a tree he'd made from Lego and she nodded distractedly.

"This holiday, though. Sonya says that's all the trip is, but I'm concerned she may be lying. Karen, can you smell burning?"

She sniffed thoughtfully.

To Geoff's nose, it was like burning blanket. There'd been a night as an undergrad when, in bed with a fresher he had just met at the Societies' Fair, his cigarette end had landed on the bedclothes. They had been enjoying a post-coital smoke, which was coincidentally also a pre-coital one, all of which meant that he and the woman had been slow in noticing that the bed was smouldering.

Karen identified the source as the table lamp. She extracted a soft toy from under the shade. "Who put Edward's cow on top of the light bulb?"

Edward flapped his arms and howled "Mr Cow! Mr Cow!" as if his own bottom had been singed.

Karen hugged him, and said she could shave some of the scorched bits off Mr Cow, so his bum wouldn't look so bad. Ashley began to blub. "I only wanted to dry him after he got wet." So Karen hugged him as well.

Geoff would have liked another glass of wine, this time without mineral water. Most of all, he too would have liked a hug in her reassuring arms. Hell, he wanted to stay the night, tucked up in bed close to her lovely face, feeling her healthily rounded hips and exploring her totally natural anatomy which had surely never had a Brazilian.

But that was impossible. For one thing, Edward, now more or less recovered from the damage to Mr Cow, was sitting on top of the sideboard. Perched next to a pile of papers and magazines, he glared malevolently at Geoff. It was a look that children gave Geoff when he mentioned injections.

Geoff ignored him at first, but then came the missiles. To begin with, Edward threw a couple of magazines experimentally onto the carpet. Emboldened by the first few attempts, he aimed further, and a comic landed at Geoff's feet, followed by a copy of *RSPCA Today* that was unmistakeably directed at his knee.

"Edward, stop that" warned Karen.

Edward gave a sideways glance that sized his mother up, then threw a TV guide at Geoff.

Karen got up, plucked Edward off the sideboard and dumped him by a hillock of Lego. "He likes you really" she said to Geoff.

"Sure" said Geoff. The child liked him about as much as Sonya did.

It was time to go. At the door, Karen said she would speak to him soon. She was there if he wanted to talk, she said, but otherwise she'd keep out of the way because he probably needed as much time with Davey as he could get.

As the front door closed behind him, Geoff heard one of the children ask "Is he going to be our new daddy?"

"No, he isn't, sweetheart."

Geoff walked slowly down the path, the family noises fading as he approached the Prius. He was already someone's daddy, and he was going to hang onto the job as long as he could.

Chapter Twenty-Five

Laure

Laure had timed it perfectly. Dan was already there. As always, he was neatly dressed, in great jeans and a white polo shirt that emphasised his shoulders.

Instinctively Laure held herself straighter and smiled, before she reminded herself that this time she wasn't here to make an impression. She was after the truth.

Dan rose from the table and kissed her briefly on the lips. "Mmm. You smell wonderful."

"Thanks."

"So, how have you been?" he said before she even sat down.

"OK."

"Just OK? Or better than OK?"

She gave a tiny shrug. "Just OK."

"It's wonderful to see you again. I know it's been less than a week since Regent's Park, but a guy can get seriously addicted to your presence. But you know that already. There must be dozens of men going through the pain of cold turkey."

She waited for him to stop wittering on. "Look. One thing puzzles me."

"Only one thing? I'm usually puzzled by at least three things at once." He glanced down at the menu. "Shall we get drinks?"

Under the presence of the hovering waitress, Laure asked for a small glass of white wine. She didn't plan to stay long.

"Bite to eat?" offered Dan.

"I had a big lunch."

It had been a huge lunch. "Have the fish, Laure. They have excellent fish here" Tante Lina had pressed. "*Garçon!*" she'd called out, waving her arms like a person drowning. When the waiter approached, she had asked him what she'd ordered the last time she was there.

The waiter smiled courteously and said he didn't know, *signora*. The aunts talked to him in French, because he was Italian. The rules they lived by owed nothing to logic.

Another rule was that no guest could be trusted to rely on their appetite. They had to be told to eat. If that person was under size 18, force-feeding was the only way to prevent imminent death from starvation. Victorine herself never deprived herself of food, least of all meringue Chantilly, *tarte tatin* or anything with a kilo of sugar in it.

"So tell me again, *cherie*, how old are you now?" Tante Victorine asked Laure when the first course had been cleared away.

"I'm 38 now, *tante*."

Laure dutifully feigned surprise when Victorine said that was exactly the age her dear Sophie would have been, God rest her poor innocent soul.

After putting away enough food to feed the whole of Sicily for a year, and leaving a tip to match, they parted. Laure tried to hail a cab for them, but they insisted they could manage, so off they went down the street, whirling their arms at every passing taxi.

Laure's phone had vibrated several times during lunch. She could see the number. Nothing would have induced her to take his calls.

Now, in the basement brasserie with Dan, she was relieved she had no signal. It meant that Michael couldn't bother her. She could concentrate on talking to Dan.

Dan beamed at her. "Cheers!" he said jauntily, clinking glasses.

Dan

"Cheers" she replied solemnly.

It wasn't going well. He had no idea why. People used to smoke in restaurants. What the fuck had become of that great British tradition? Even though he'd quit, he was dying for some snout right now. But he could hardly scarper up the stairs and join the nicotine junkies on the pavement. It would be like getting up to make tea in the middle of a shag.

After the tiniest sip of wine, Laure said "This might sound a bit weird, but I was wondering. What exactly have you been doing the last few years?"

He tried not to pause for even a beat. But he did, just the same. He also tried to look to the right. People looked left when they were lying. "I've been abroad. In Slovenia."

She seemed doubtful and determined. Not a good combo. Dan knew this from prison adjudications. "The other day in Regent's Park, you told me that you hadn't travelled much."

He opted not to contradict and say she had misheard. Instead he spread his hands to look convincing. Palms open, natch. "But I haven't travelled much."

"'If at all', you said." At this point she put her chin on her hands, which made her look adorable. Her next few words were anything but. "Explain it to me."

"I was working in Slovenia." He emitted a huge weary sigh. The sort you gave when a metal door clanked shut behind you, and you knew you had very few options for the next few hours. Well, he might be a free man now, but he still didn't have much choice. Lesson from the book of life: lie only if you can get away with it. Looking at his thumb, Dan began "Well, the truth can be hard to explain sometimes. Can you tell me where you were seven years ago?"

"I was here in London, working at – well, it doesn't matter where." He seemed to be getting on her nerves. "Why?"

"Can we get olives or something?"

She just about endured the delay as he flagged down a waitress, gave his best smile, ordered bread and marinated olives. Then he asked Laure "Do you remember the Jewel Box raid?"

"Yes," she said tersely. "Again, why?"

He chose his words carefully. "Then you probably recall that several men forced their way into the jeweller's. They grabbed some gems, then assaulted a woman as they escaped down the street."

"Yes, I do know. Vaguely."

"Here's the thing." Dan leaned forwards. "Daniels was innocent. It was actually Miller who masterminded it, and he was the one who whacked the woman in the street. Not Daniels."

She dipped a piece of bread in oil. "Wasn't it Daniels that the injured woman picked out in a line-up?"

"Yes. And he got sent down. But he was innocent. Look, line-ups can go wrong. Daniels wasn't even there. It was Miller who thumped the woman, broke her nose and her arm and landed her in hospital and then in a nursing home. There was someone else too, but that's not the point. What's important is that Miller implicated Daniels to spread the blame, which worked out even better than he'd intended."

"And it's important because?"

She still wasn't getting it. He looked at her meaningfully. "Because it was almost exactly six years ago."

"Is Miller the one who escaped?"

"Yes."

Her eyes widened with alarm. "Are you saying Miller escaped to Slovenia?"

His short laugh seemed to throw her. "Not at all. Miller is on the run somewhere. I suppose it could be Slovenia, but I doubt it. No, you could say it was Daniels who was in Slovenia."

"But Daniels went to jail. Didn't he?"

Deep breath. A slow nod. "Yeah. He was in Bedford jail six years. But here's the thing. Daniels likes to reinvent himself. Pretend he was in Slovenia." Now he could really imagine the calming feel of a ciggie between his lips. He went for a change of tack. "Look. I'm Martin Daniels. I changed my name to Dan. And I'm the innocent one. Innocent because I wasn't even there, but when push came to shove they demolished my alibi."

He had taken a fucking huge risk. But what choice did he have? Now his plate was misbehaving as well. Bad enough having to explain it all to her without the sodding plate working loose. Should have used a fuck of a lot more glue. He touched the denture with his tongue again as he chose his words. But she didn't leg it. She listened intently as he told her about the night at the Jewel Box, his sentence, and why Slovenia had seemed such a cracking idea for a fresh start.

"I know this may be a shock to you" he said. "In your line of work you probably don't come across people who've done time."

Laure drained her glass first. "You'd be surprised."

"Then hairdressing is more dangerous than I thought. Would you like another drink?"

She agreed. Dan was fucking amazed. He rashly ordered a bottle.

When the waitress had gone, Laure fiddled with the stem of her glass. "My turn now. Actually I'm not a hairdresser. I haven't changed my name, but I have changed my job, at least when it comes to meeting new people." She smiled enigmatically. "Would you like to guess what I do?"

A lawyer. A fucking lawyer. Well, that explained it. Dan had noticed from the off that she was pretty damn smart for a crimper. But then she wasn't a crimper, was she? A fucking lawyer!

"I can totally understand if it puts you off seeing me." He felt he had to say this. In reality he wanted to fuck her more than ever. She was the hottest thing he had ever seen. Ever. Now that he could see how brainy she was, it was giving him a hard-on. Clever women were off the scale of hotness. And there was also, he had to admit, a tiny bit of him that wanted to screw her because she was a lawyer. That fucking bunch of parasites incensed him. Now he was mighty confused. This needed sorting.

Over a huge burger and the rest of the wine, he told her a lot about being banged up. Losing touch with his long-time girlfriend. And now picking himself up and looking for a job. Nearly found one too. "One day I'll tell you about Maxy as well" he said. OK, maybe just the bit about his hand. Not everything.

It was amazing she was still talking to him. Not only talking to him, but actually beginning to tell him stuff. Her age, for a start. Now that was a surprise. He'd thought she was no more than 32 or 33.

After those confessions, he wanted to say something more. He'd had a bit to drink now. Way too clumsily, he said "I don't know where this is going with us. But I just want to say that I'll be honest with you from here on. And I hope you'll be honest with me too." He wanted to smack himself in the gob when he heard how that came out. Too late.

"How honest would that be?" she countered.

He smiled. "Like they say, the whole truth. Nothing but."

"So if you fancy the waitress, will you feel obliged to tell me?" Her smile was triumphant, like a lawyer who'd stitched you up.

"No, I guess I would draw the line at that."

"Very sensible."

By now, the restaurant was empty apart from them. The waitress had brought the bill a while back. Nobody had said 'Excuse me but we're closing now', because it wasn't exactly necessary. If you didn't realize that stacking the bentwood chairs on top of the tables and getting a broom out meant they wanted to shut up shop, then you had to be a bit of a retard. But, just to make sure, someone brought in a giant floor polisher.

He and Laure finally took the hint. As they went up the stairs and out into the street, he heard her pocket chime around half a dozen times. It was the same doorbell sound his own very basic mobile made. She had a lot of messages, but she didn't seem bothered.

Gratifyingly, she continued to show interest in him, though possibly the interest was purely professional. "Have you ever considered the possibility of a retrial?"

Of course he had. Who wouldn't want a chance to reclaim six years of their life as well as their reputation?

She'd have to look into this because, she said, it wasn't at all her area of expertise. "I'm not a criminal lawyer."

"You must be the exception. All the other lawyers I've met were criminals through and through."

Chapter Twenty-Six

Harriet

When Harriet got in from the PR event, she found Simon sitting on the 70s sofa with his headphones on, gesticulating in time to some music. He barely looked up. Normal.

"Hi" she waved as she wandered into the kitchen. Her mouth was dry from generous helpings of Chilean Shiraz. She ought to have water before bedtime. All the glasses were in the dishwasher, so she used a random mug off the counter. It looked clean enough, though it was possible that Simon might have already used it. She made a face.

Way back, she had liked using the same mug as him. She also loved finding his stray hairs on the pillow after he'd got up. Sometimes she'd collect a few strands together and roll them between her fingers, wondering if it might help her possess him. He was shedding just as much hair these days, but now she brushed it away.

Simon finally took off his cans. "Aren't you going to tell me how your PR thing went?" he asked through the hatch from the dining area.

"Didn't know you were interested. It was OK. All the usual people there."

Simon said nothing.

"Does this need watering?" Harriet asked as she prodded the soil around the box plant.

He blew his nose and sniffed. "Maybe a drop."

She gave it a little sprinkle, taking care not to get water on the Habitat glass table.

"I won't be up much longer" he added, putting the cans back onto his head.

"OK."

Harriet brushed her teeth, had more water and went to bed. Burrowing into her pillow, she reminded herself that she was satisfied with Simon. It was cosy. It was fine. You didn't have to have great passion all the time. As everyone knew, but didn't always care to admit, it was impossible to sustain the first bloom of lust forever. She still loved Simon, she was sure of it. Perhaps she should actually say so from time to time.

So, much later, when he had left his music and joined her in bed, she said "I love you, you know."

The light was just enough for her to discern a smile. "I did know, but thanks." After a pause, he said he loved her too, then he rather spoiled the moment by asking if she might make him a late night cup of Lapsang. But, she rationalized, weren't human beings all stuck in their ways?

After his tea, he showed his appreciation in the usual way. She was never going to come like this, underneath him, but at least she didn't have to make any effort. A couple of scratches down his back with her nails would probably do. All the while she encouraged herself by thinking of Daniel Craig. It was harder than usual as his blue eyes had turned brown, and his short fair hair had mysteriously become black.

A bad dream woke Harriet in the night. It was the editor of *RightHere!* barking at her about Christmas. This year, she had a really, really fun feature idea. All Harriet had to do was find three women who'd had an immaculate conception. They had to be willing to give their real names and be photographed, of course. And it would be a real bonus if their partners were carpenters.

It was difficult to go back to sleep, so Harriet got up to work on a feature. She'd had a bit of a reprieve on *The Seven Ages of Dating*, which was just as well, given that she didn't have that angle yet.

What exactly were the laws of attraction, she wondered as she let Twitter distract her. Somewhere she still had a press release from an American outfit that aimed to match couples from their DNA profiles. It had to do with scent-based characteristics. They offered to help clients find someone who was not only attractive, but could also provide eye-watering sex, enhanced fertility, healthier children, even a lower risk of being unfaithful. Now where was their info? She wasn't going to sign up for the service herself, but it might be useful for a future article.

Looking for the perfect match? Now you don't need to ask your best friend or consult the stars to discover if you're compatible. Based on a simple mouth swab, a cutting-edge DNA test will tell you all you need to know for a lifetime of bliss...

It was getting light when she went back to bed. He was still asleep, rasping with each breath because of his sinuses. She inhaled the bedclothes deeply as she got in, as if to check that she and Simon had the same scent-based DNA. Or was it supposed to be different DNA? She was too tired to remember.

Despite only a few hours sleep, she rose before Simon and went back to her laptop. It was to work on that feature, of course.

Opening the wooden blinds in the living room, she reflected as usual that they weren't to her taste. If she had her own place, she'd have curtains, maybe pink and navy. With a full pelmet. The furniture would not be at all Scandinavian. Provençal style would be nice, with mountains of scatter cushions. She'd have coasters with cats on them, and the fridge would be covered in kitsch magnets. Or maybe magnetic words, like *cat, mouse, wonderful, tabby* and *pounce,* all perfect for writers who liked cats.

Where would she live if she moved out of Simon's flat, with its sleek sofas, its *objets d'art* from foreign trips, and a whole wall of CDs which obstinately reminded her of a certain shop in Barcelona? As a freelance, she'd have trouble proving her income when applying for a mortgage. She would have to rent.

Not that there was any need. She and Simon were OK.

While the kettle boiled, she noticed the plastic mosque, minaret still in place. From a certain angle it was a bit wonky, but Simon had not spotted it. Just as well she had kept quiet. Sometimes that was the best plan.

She took him a cup of tea and a smile. As usual, the alarm clock had not gone off yet, but he woke easily and quickly. "I used a pot" she told him before he got a chance to say anything.

Karen

At the risk of a scald, Karen glugged the hot tea gratefully. In this job you didn't get many chances for a break. She rinsed out the chipped mug which informed her that she was mysterious and kept her emotions hidden. According to the curly silver script, she was also strong-willed, determined and a natural leader. Karen did not consider herself to be any of these things, but then she wasn't a Scorpio. Nobody cared who used which mug, or how the tea was made as long as it was hot and wet.

She rushed back to the classroom. Beneath the paint and crayons lay the aroma of lost plimsolls and unloved school-bags. That always catapulted her back in time.

She started mixing powder paints with water, pouring carefully into each non-spill container. The new job was great. How many people were lucky enough to work term-times only, in a place with a burst of golden-yellow sunflowers all over one wall? This wall, this classroom, the whole school, evoked a simpler and easier time.

The other wall displayed collages which shed macaroni and glitter even if you didn't touch them. The corner table had an array of all things yellow, including a pile of paper napkins, a vase, a patchwork quilt, teddy bears, a box of tissues, a jar of lemon curd and a bar of sulphur-yellow soap. Books were arranged so that you could see their front covers. They looked cherished, unlike the ones at home.

It was nothing like working in human remains. It was like being at home, except with other people's kids to help with their reading and their nose-wiping. She surveyed her charges and wondered how they would all turn out as adults. There was a risk of the quiet ones being last in the queue of life, although you never knew. It was like that with children.

As on her first day, Karen wore a red velveteen pinafore dress teemed with leggings, a practical choice when the chairs were so low. One of the boys was stroking her hem now, just as he'd stroked the class hamster earlier. Imaginatively, the animal was called Fluff. The kids took him home at weekends on a rota basis. Karen hoped Fluff would survive all that TLC.

Now the little boy was holding his legs together. "Do you need the toilet, George?"

George nodded vigorously, but judging from the front of his shorts it was too late.

It had been a fabulous day, Karen thought. Not as high-flying as her previous job, maybe, though here too one needed skills in negotiation, diplomacy, creativity, communication, leadership and teamwork.

Even better, she was going out to dinner with Geoff this evening. Rose was coming over, and Karen was going to wear a new outfit. Well, new to her. Doubtless parts of it would give a sense of déjà vu to a people who dumped unwanted sacks in charity shops.

Life was good.

Geoff

Life was shit. Karen held his hand while he rambled on about difficult patients, the letters from the General Medical Council and the impending loss of Davey, which he could never begin to accept. There would be a battle with Sonya, a battle that his lawyer explained didn't look quite as hopeful as it had initially.

Separation would be tough for Geoff, but what might become of Davey? The surgery was full of directionless youths who would have been a lot better off for a spot of real fathering as they grew up. He couldn't bear Davey becoming one of them.

That wasn't all. Geoff was enjoying work less and less. The prolapses, bunions, arthritic knees, lumpy breasts and dental abscesses – despite the notice in the waiting-room that reminded patients this was a

GP surgery, not a dental clinic. The asthmatics who regularly lost their inhalers. The girl who asked for her third termination in under a year. And of course practice politics, which really got him down. Was this all he had to show for his existence?

"Your life's hardly been wasted" Karen reassured him.

Those, Geoff reasoned, were just kind words from someone whose occupation involved teaching children which way up to hold a pencil.

On the coffee table, his vibrating mobile told him that new texts were arriving. He didn't care, though briefly he thought how incongruous it was to be lying helpless on his sofa, just like a distressed patient, and being consoled by someone he still barely knew.

They had been out to dinner, and she said she had to go soon.

"Can't you stay?" he pleaded. Karen and a blue tablet could turn the evening around.

She could stay part of the night, maybe, if the babysitter was agreeable.

While she was on the phone, he nipped upstairs and took two 50mg tablets. The dinner they'd had would slow down absorption, he reasoned, and he didn't have long. He swallowed a third tablet to make sure.

"She said I'd need to be back by 2am" said Karen as she put down her mobile.

It seemed a bit early to Geoff, but it was the best she could do, she said as he led her upstairs a few minutes later. He hoped the pills would work soon. There was no way he wanted to fail at this too.

As they undressed, he nuzzled the nape of her neck and breathed in deeply. Viagra had already made his nose stuffy, but he could smell enough to appreciate her mesmerizing scent, far more feminine than the expensive artifice of most women.

Her skin was soft, as were her breasts and her belly. Just a small tattoo on one thigh, and her bush was tidy, trimmed yet completely natural. He touched her and she responded. Equally promising was his growing erection.

As they moved to the bed, he took in a caesarean scar, stretch marks and on her calves just a hint of veins. None of the unsexy hardness some women had, the kind of woman who would shriek all the way to some overcharging clinic if she ever spotted dimpling on her thighs. But, as he explored, he found she wasn't loose and baggy either, like patients of his who'd popped out their fourth or fifth baby without any stitches or anaesthetic.

Now his eyes were stinging and his head was throbbing. On the plus side, the tablets had had an outstanding effect. He had dreaded wilting when rolling on a condom, but that wasn't going to happen tonight.

She lay on her back at first. He lingered playfully for a moment. She was warm, moist and alive, drawing him inside as if it were the most natural thing in the world.

With her legs around his neck, he could feel every inch. Then they rolled over. She rode him like a mustang, which was exactly how he felt. His face was hot with blood and the top of his head was threatening to blow off, but it was worth it. With her on top, he could see and feel how utterly turned on she was.

She wanted to change position, so she flipped over and lay face down. By now he had developed into the BT Tower. He stood by the side of the bed, his legs slightly apart. This way he could feel her clamped around him, moving, squeezing, pumping. Perspiration ran down his temples into his eyes as he bent forwards. He grabbed her pelvis to steady himself. This hard was going to last forever, he thought as the bed edged closer to the window with each push. She was crying "Don't stop, don't stop" before she gave one long final scream.

He let his eyes close as the explosion engulfed him.

Karen had to leave. Geoff watched from the doorway as she hurried down the path towards her beaten up RAV-4.

The cramp in his calves was vicious and he felt faint, which was no surprise after the mega dose he'd taken, but he felt peaceful now. The sense of achievement helped.

Although Karen's car had disappeared up the dark street several minutes ago, Geoff was still at the door. He sniffed his fingertips to savour her sweetness.

Somewhere in the distance were the shouts of yobs trashing the neighbourhood. Typical weekend sounds. Geoff heard them progressing down one of the streets. Sounded like a tin can was being kicked.

A plume of clouds wafted across the moonlit sky, and a helicopter clattered from somewhere or other, unseen. Police, probably. Those were the usual type in London, though obviously that wasn't the case in other countries.

The thought, when it came, hit him with the force of – well, he had no idea, because he wasn't used to being hit, except when Sonya used to make a point by jabbing a manicured finger at his sternum. This blow was far more powerful.

He asked himself why it hadn't occurred to him before, when he was young and idealistic. Then he remembered. He had been busy studying hard, then chasing something elusively known as quality of life.

It was hard to define, but everyone imagined that they would recognize it as soon as they grabbed it. Well, sometimes they didn't spot quality even when it landed in their laps. If someone had told him that his marriage to Sonya, and being a dad to young Davey, were just temporary phases, he'd have said 'Yeah. Sure.' But only now did he really, really know what temporary meant.

He wiped his streaming eyes. Now he also knew what he was going to do if Davey went to Australia. Geoff knew it with all his being.

Chapter Twenty-Seven

Dan

Dan checked his mobile again.

She still hadn't called back. Or answered his texts.

Christ. He wished he hadn't said anything. Now she'd probably rush right away from his life. Like one of these fucking cockroaches under his sink.

Not the most apt analogy, though it was hard not to think of cockroaches right now, given that they were threatening to take over his bedsit. He was on their case but they scuttled to safety whenever he got within striking distance.

On his hands and knees, with a paper towel in his hand, Dan surveyed the area beneath the sink. He had managed to crush one of the buggers into oblivion. Now he inspected the corpse on the paper.

Fuck! Things with Laure were in a similar state. That too would be his fault. Another lesson from the big book of life: don't kill anything if you might regret it later. He dumped the cockroach in the bin.

He wasn't a natural killer, and he wasn't a cheat. But even he was prepared to admit he was a liar. This morning he had lied at a job interview. Not only had he given the Slovenia spiel, he had also said he loved plants. It seemed the right thing to do. Seeing as it was a garden centre and all.

That was a narrow escape, because the gaffer interviewing him then asked, not unnaturally, what his favourite plants were. Dan didn't know any plants other than the kind you ate or smoked. He couldn't say 'marijuana' so he opted for 'vegetables.' When pressed to say which vegetables in particular, he said he hadn't grown many since he'd left Slovenia. There, he had grown lots of tomatoes. The gaffer hadn't seemed to mind that Dan couldn't name any strains he'd grown. When asked, Dan had replied "Big. Round. Tasty. Bit shapeless." It was the kind of description he'd once used for his sister-in-law. Bloody hell, he could still taste the cut lip it had earned him.

"Marmande?" said the garden gaffer.

Dan wasn't at all sure, but the gaffer didn't seem to mind. After all, it was to be expected that the names would be different in foreign.

There was another dodgy moment when the man had said he would call over Stefan from the paving department, because he was Slovenian and they could natter together. "Or maybe he's Slovakian" mused the gaffer. Yes, that was it.

Ah well, Dan had said with a sigh of relief, Slovakia was an altogether different place, see. Anyway, they must have been desperate, because the gaffer rang Dan an hour later and offered him the job, no references needed.

He would start on Monday. Dan didn't care where he worked. One, he needed to keep busy. Two, he needed money. Perfect. Something he did like at the garden centre was the paving, fencing, lumber and DIY materials. He'd learned a few building skills during his stretch. While it didn't compare with a proper builder's yard or a large DIY store, the range at Mr Tubbs' Garden and Outdoor Centre was far wider than anything on offer at HMP. One day, he'd like to build stuff. Maybe have a shed. He couldn't explain why he hankered after a shed, not after being banged up in a tiny space for years. It was just a guy thing.

He was glad to be starting the job, but there was still a terrible feeling about the other stuff. In an ideal world, the only thing he'd have hidden from Laure was his fucking tooth plate. But what choice had there been? If she'd known the truth about him, she wouldn't even have met him for a drink.

He'd managed it badly and he had probably lost her. OK, so the last time they met, they talked for ages. But maybe she was just letting him down gently. Women were world-famous for that.

Now that he knew about her, there was just one thing he was sure of. He wanted her more than ever. For all kinds of reasons.

He crushed another cockroach and dumped it in the bin.

Laure

Many of the Magic Circle firms were in the City, with another sprinkling in Docklands. Dicklands, thought Laure. She much preferred this small London Square where most of the businesses were media-related. It was a bright day as she walked through the square littered with old leaves and new conkers. Here there were no schoolchildren to pick them up, only adults passing through, and they were absorbed by entirely different trivia.

For lunch Laure would grab a sandwich and take it back to the office. No grossing out at a fat-cat blow-out like some of the senior partners. Odd that anyone in the legal profession dared describe themselves as a senior partner when no such thing existed in law. But then, thought Laure, lawyers were experts at stretching things.

Dan's revelation had been a shock. Now that Slovenia story of his really was stretching the truth. But he'd been brave enough to admit it.

Was it right to forget his whopper? She wasn't sure. Yet what if someone had asked her exactly what she'd been doing that December day five years ago? Obviously, she'd have left out all mention of the clinic, and instead concocted something plausible based on her activities on a different day that same week. The day before, say, when she'd gone to the office, then met Sanjay for drinks at The Hog in the Pound. The pub was barely a mile from her office, but it was literally over a lifetime away.

It had been full of people sheltering from the rain, standing too close and acting too jolly.

Laure had said nothing that evening to Sanjay about the termination. She was never going to, even without the rain and the inevitable crowd of Christmas shoppers.

Only after the event did she tell him. His face had clouded over, and his features had furrowed. To Laure he looked strangely like someone faking anger. Unfortunately, as she discovered, it wasn't feigned.

The clinic was in south London. Disorientating, but, Laure reasoned, good for anonymity. On arrival she'd found someone filing her nails, and a nurse on the phone in the corridor, apparently complaining about the deductions on her wage slip. Finally the manicure was over, and the woman attended to Laure and someone else who was waiting. The other patient was young and had a tat on her left shoulder, bare even in December. She was laden with carrier bags which all seemed too much for her stick-thin arms. The profusion of plastic carriers suggested no fixed abode, as if she simply relocated from one clinic to the next. Laure told herself to stop being so judgmental. But she wasn't just evaluating others. She was judging herself too.

Laure had sat there on a hard orange chair, still wondering why she was having the termination. Sanjay had been non-committal about the baby, and Laure reckoned it wasn't up to a tiny fetus to provide cement to keep them together. Then there was her work, as she often said. But that was just an excuse. In reality, her career provided a solid financial base to raise a child in comfort. The real reason went a lot deeper than physical comfort.

The pregnancy was an 'accident', whatever that meant. It happened all the time. Although lots of women coped on their own, Laure didn't think she could summon the confidence to fly solo. It was years since her father had done the things that no father should do. She thought it was in the past, but still it echoed. One way or another, it had shaken her world, dislocating all her notions of family.

At the clinic they had told Laure there was no need for guilt about a little procedure like this one. She tried to recall exactly what one of the doctors had said. That she was still young, and could always change her mind and conceive again in six months if the tide turned. Yes, that was it. But how could having a baby become right in six months if it wasn't right now? It was ridiculous, thought Laure, to be sitting here relying on strangers like these two medics to help her make life-changing decisions. She wasn't sure why the Abortion Act needed two doctors anyway.

Well, they'd been wrong at the clinic, Laure knew now. Guilt was exactly what was needed. A termination was for life, not just for Christmas.

As Laure paid for her chicken, bacon and avocado sandwich, her thoughts returned to Dan. There'd be a certain symmetry if she overlooked Dan's lie. She couldn't be sure he was as innocent as he claimed to be, but at least he hadn't killed anyone.

Back in the lift with her sandwich, she observed the usual etiquette. It was a quick smile and a hello if you recognized anyone in the car. If you didn't, then it was a quick smile before looking down in the direction of your feet.

The lift stopped momentarily on three and Charlie Postie got in. He was a so-called senior partner, one of the most senior of the lot. Word was that he knew all there was to know about criminal law, though he still behaved like a naughty little boy who was about to get caught with his hand in the cookie jar. *Postie* wasn't his real name and neither was *Charlie*. Nobody knew where the *Postie* bit came from, but *Charlie* was widely reckoned to be a nod to his favourite recreational substance. Laure already knew what his favourite recreational activity was, which was why she stood a safe distance away.

"Well hello! It's the lovely Laure" he said, as always. His eyes darted from her chest, where they first alit, to the mirror behind Laure. No prizes for guessing he was using it to study her derriere.

"Hi Charlie."

"How's the exciting world of corporate governance?"

"Good, thanks."

"And when are you going to grace me with your company over a drink? I've been pining for eons, you know."

Laure couldn't count the number of times she had told him to keep pining, but this time she said "OK then. This evening at seven?"

You could tell from his open mouth that he hadn't expected that. Someone else got into the lift on the next floor but Charlie was oblivious to the extra presence. "Wow, yes."

He exited the lift on the sixth floor with a hideous smile. At least he wasn't punching the air and going 'Woop–woop.'

Ten past seven and the bastard hadn't showed. Laure sometimes suspected that men tried deliberately to be awful, like forgetting birthdays and showing up late, just because they could. The point was that, no matter how abominably they behaved, they could still get a woman. And they knew it.

When he finally arrived, he managed to make the cosy table even cosier by inching his chair closer to her, explaining that it was always so difficult to hear in this pub.

Charlie also managed to spill some of white wine into Laure's lap. Wisely, she refrained from saying she loved a guy that splashed out on a woman. Charlie Postie could find a double entendre in everything.

Why was she here in pub full of incredibly young creatives, having a drink with Charlie Postie? Maybe she cared more about Dan than she wanted to admit.

Charlie downed a couple of glasses before she got much out of him. By then, his forehead was shiny and his nose, thimbled with pores, began to emit amounts of sweat that threatened to cascade down his face.

He got his face close enough for Laure to have a good guess at what he'd had in the partners' dining room, and said accusingly "You shagged Stephen Jamison yonks ago." The emphasis was on how long ago it had been. It clearly didn't seem fair to him that she hadn't got around to him yet.

In fact she had shagged not only Jamison, but quite a few others in the office besides, more than once in the office itself. They were mostly lapses of taste that Charlie Postie did not need to know anything about. "I'm taking the Fifth" she said.

Unfortunately this only whetted Charlie's appetite. He demanded to know what Stephen Jamison had been like, and he didn't mean during nine to five. Laure eventually managed to steer him onto his other specialist interest.

"But why are you asking me all this? Has the lovely Laure taken up with a bit of rough?"

She gave a dismissive laugh. It was nearer the truth than she cared to admit.

Charlie, to his credit, talked generously about his area of expertise, even if he did imply that it was easy for a legal genius like himself. He gave Laure a lot of information, spilling a little wine in the process.

He was a multi-tasker, she gave him that, because he managed to stroke the wine stain on her lap while quoting one obscure case after another. It was hard to follow everything he said, what with the media crowd around them and the need to remove his hand repeatedly. She placed it on his own knee once again and gave her most non-committal smile.

They had nearly finished the bottle of Sancerre by the time Charlie told her what she needed to know, along with a good deal that she didn't need to know, like some of his sexual preferences, which seemed an integral part of his holiday in Thailand. By then, he was ready to return to his theme of Stephen Jamison and wanted to know if Laure operated a waiting-list system. She told him not to be so smutty. Predictably, he took this as a compliment.

One thing admired in Charlie was his complete confidence. A lot of men wouldn't have dared say or do half the things he did, for fear of allegations of harassment. This clearly never bothered Charlie, which was maybe how he got away with it.

"Actually, Charlie, you may be a bit of a lech but you have your plus points. Thanks for the drink and all." Seeing her get up, Charlie bobbed up to kiss her, but she dodged his sweaty face and patted him on the head like a puppy.

She couldn't wait to see Dan.

Chapter Twenty-Eight

Harriet

There weren't enough days like this, filled to the brim with activity and free meals.

The early morning press event had kicked off with freshly squeezed orange juice, steaming coffee, toasted bagels and scrambled eggs the like of which Harriet could never manage. And watercress. Normally Harriet associated watercress with salads. Until today, she hadn't realized it was versatile enough to use in scrambled eggs, as well as magical enough to keep away scurvy, colon cancer and a host of other dread diseases.

With time to spare before she was due in Soho Square for her next meeting, Harriet ambled down Oxford Street, past the shoppers and tourists. She peered into windows, took in street stalls flogging fruit, scarves and fake football shirts. A bicycle rickshaw nearly mowed Harriet down as she gazed at pashminas. Surely nobody wanted any one of them for a fiver, let alone three for £10. And why were there so many mobile phone shops? By now every single soul in London probably had at least half a dozen hand-sets.

She dodged someone handing out flyers and crossed over to a bookshop.

There was a slew of self-help books, as well as a proliferation of new fiction, celeb biographies and cookbooks. Browsing the tables, Harriet considered how many things cost under £10 and yet could fill your head. CDs were around a tenner, but they didn't always occupy all your attention or stop your mind from straying into areas you wanted to avoid.

Books, now. Different matter altogether.

As she checked the titles on display, Harriet tried to convince herself that anyone could do it. The snag was that she was overawed by almost every book ever written. Even if it wasn't very good, it had been published, for God's sake. *Ergo*, it had succeeded where she hadn't.

She studied a luridly covered paperback with loopy lettering that was meant to make you think 'zany chicklit'. According to the blurb, the author had a baby that never slept, but she would drive around every day until her baby nodded off, then amuse herself by writing in a lay-by until her little darling woke up and howled his head off.

Harriet picked up another book. This one, she knew from a piece she'd once done on first-time novelists, had decided to write a book because she was worried that her job at a fashion company might evaporate. The firm did go belly-up, but by then the woman, aged all of 22 or something, had one paperback on the shelves and a deal for another two. By comparison, Harriet felt little short of middle-aged and retarded.

Some people had all the luck. But then maybe they didn't have an inner editor like the one that kept Harriet from finishing what she started. Her inner editor sounded a lot like Simon.

Harriet succumbed to a special offer, paying for a clutch of new paperbacks including one entitled *Tennis for Cats*. It was the cover that attracted her. Long-haired tabbies were always going to remind her of Pushkin, last seen six years ago.

By then, she'd been with Simon and his sinuses for two years. He looked ill all the time, and a tissue seemed permanently anchored to his nose. Not long before his birthday that year, Harriet asked what he wanted. After that, she resolved she'd never ask him again. It would be gift vouchers.

In theory, she appreciated Simon's problem. One of her friends told her to get him put down. At first Harriet thought it was a joke, and that the friend was referring to Simon. Wrong on both counts. "Just take him to the vet. Isn't your man more important than a cat? Especially since the sex is amazing."

Harriet would never have Pushkin put down. "It's just ailurophobia" she'd told Simon at first. But he wasn't just scared of cats. His breathing was really bad, beyond the help of inhalers, pills and sprays. She had tried products that promised to keep down fur and dander, to no avail. It would have to be the

RSPCA or the Mayhew. She tried to think of an alternative, other than leaving Simon, and couldn't.

It was raining on the day. Simon got the cat basket out from the cupboard and Pushkin promptly fled under the bed.

"He's gone into the bedroom!" cried Simon. "Now I'll be sneezing forever."

"Well, he won't be here much longer, will he?" Harriet retorted.

Pushkin eventually emerged warily, though not warily enough.

"Grab him, Harriet. I'd rather not touch him."

Harriet picked him up and cuddled him, kissing the area between his ears. It was too awful to let him go. "It's raining" she pointed out. "Pushkin hates rain."

"Put a towel over his basket if you're so concerned."

The car was parked two streets away. Simon offered to get it, but he drew the line at driving to the shelter. "I've got work to do. And frankly I'd rather not spend the next hour about a foot away from him."

Harriet, of course, wanted to be close to Pushkin, preferably forever. Instead she lugged the basket downstairs and into the car. As Simon got out of the driver's side, he warned "Don't bottle now, Harriet." He didn't add 'It's only a cat', but he may as well have done.

It was December 18. People who looked forward to Christmas lived on another planet, thought

Harriet as she negotiated the traffic out of London. She thought the RSPCA place off the A1(M) would be best, as there'd be more chance of finding him a suitable home in a rural area. Plus with a shelter that far she might be less tempted to rush back and adopt Pushkin herself.

Traffic was always bad here, even more so in the rain in December. She got stuck in a fierce bottle-neck along the A41, trapped between a bus and a Chelsea tractor. When she finally moved off, an aggressive van driver (was there any other kind?) nearly clipped the wing of Simon's Peugeot.

As soon as Simon had gone indoors, she had transferred the basket from the boot to the passenger seat. Pushkin yowled and stared at her through the grating with huge eyes.

"Come on, big boy" she said, her voice catching. "Everything's going to be fine."

Her words failed to reassure Pushkin, who did what he often did when he was stressed. Soon the car was filled with an unmistakeable aroma. Fresh dog turds occasionally smelled of coffee grounds. Cat shit, on the other hand, only ever smelled of one thing.

Harriet began to weep. The kindness of the RSPCA staff when she got there only made things worse. "My partner's allergic to cats" Harriet explained.

"Has the cat had any health problems?" the girl asked.

"He has slight irritable bowel." What kind of luck was it to have a fastidious boyfriend and a cat with loose motions?

Tears still streaming, she left Pushkin and a large donation and returned to the car with the empty basket. There was nothing to look forward to this Christmas. She was sure that Simon was getting her the cashmere and silk top she had wanted. But there would be no Pushkin to climb the tree or bat the baubles off it.

Harriet replayed the tape of that day many times since. After her trip to the RSPCA, things with Simon began to change. Whether this reflected the loss of Pushkin, or the natural shelf-life of their relationship, she had no idea.

The book Harriet had picked up did not aim to teach felines racquet sports. It was, apparently, a hilarious picaresque novel set in the world of health clubs, which made reviewers laugh till they cried, should be required reading for everyone who was over 30 or had ever breathed, and wasn't *Anna Karenina* but people couldn't put it down.

Harriet was relieved that it wasn't Tolstoy or any of the other impossibly slow-moving writers like the ones on Simon's shelves. She often read books in the hope of gaining insights on writing successful fiction. However, once the narrative drew her in, she invariably lapsed into admiration for the writer's talent, concluding that she would never be able to carry off a similar feat however hard she struggled.

Simon was right to discourage her, thought Harriet as she left the shop with her purchases. If she ever tried to write a book, she would be wasting her time.

She took a detour through a department store to get Simon some more tea. Yesterday she had eked out the Lapsang with PG Tips to make it last, but his lips had pursed into a moue that showed exactly what he thought.

Passing through the handbag department on her way to the food hall, she saw two women admiring a giant handbag. While one of them held it up, her friend stroked the black patent leather and, in a Manchester accent, pronounced it gorgeous, absolutely gorgeous. They thought £350 wasn't bad at all. Clearly neither of them realized it was a lot to pay for something that looked like a crumpled bin liner. Some people, thought Harriet, had no critical faculties.

By the time she got the Lapsang, it was later than she had planned and she grabbed a taxi for fear of being late for the press launch.

At the end of a full day, armed with shopping, press packs, memory sticks and other give-aways, she stumbled through the door of the flat. Her heart sank as she found Simon in his usual pose, in the Eames recliner with his headphones over his combover, his head swaying gently.

As his eyes were shut, it was a few moments before he noticed her. When he did spot her, he sniffed eloquently. His sinuses did not seem that much better since Pushkin had gone. Simon always said that any improvement would take time, but surely six years was pushing it.

He asked about her day, managing to imply that her time had once again been frittered away.

Nothing she told him managed to turn his lips into a smile, so she fell quiet as she put her things away then made tea. She couldn't recall when she and Simon had last had a decent conversation, but surely they must have done. Tonight the atmosphere was nothing more than a rancid silence.

No sooner had she brought the two mugs into the living room than Simon gave her a mean stare. "Did you use a pot?"

Anger rose into her throat. Instead of letting it go, she spat back "What the fuck do you think?" Leaving her mug untouched, she got up and headed for the bathroom, her heart racing.

Simon didn't come after her. She knew he wouldn't bother. Harriet locked the door and sat on the toilet lid with her head in her hands. Maybe she lived with Simon, but she felt totally alone. Trite but still true.

She took a few deep breaths and fixed her gaze on the shower-head. Concentrating on something might calm her down and help her regain some equilibrium. It didn't work.

Then she washed her face in cold water and patted it dry. Still no better.

There was a Hindu belief, she recalled hearing a while back, that when God created you He made two of you. Even though He separated you at first, you were nonetheless connected to each other by an invisible piece of string. The string might be long or it might be short. Whatever its length, one day you would each climb up your end of the string and be together just as He intended.

She wasn't sure who'd told her, but she knew what must have happened. Her string had got tangled up with someone else's, and she needed to undo the knot. Was she ever meant to be on the same string as Simon? If she was, then God was having a laugh.

Harriet felt far from composed when her mobile rang in her pocket. "I hate to bother you so late, pet. Really sorry."

RightHere!'s commissioning editor didn't sound sorry at all, but that was no doubt down to the pugnacity of her Glaswegian accent. "Thing is, I'm going tae need 700 to 800 words by noon taemorrow."

"Sure" said Harriet, without finding out what the piece was about.

"The peg is this week's *EastEnders*, you know, when Janine - "

"I'm in a bit of rush right now" said Harriet, although she wasn't. "Could you ping over the brief in an email?"

Sounding surprised, the editor agreed, and they ended the call.

Harriet replaced the mobile in her pocket. She needed something miraculous to happen, for both of them to suddenly climb up their length of string.

Didn't miracles sometimes need a nudge? Reaching into her pocket, she extracted her mobile slowly. With uncertain fingers she composed the number.

After a long while, someone answered but there was only sobbing.

"Sanjay?" she tried, her heart doing gymnastics in her chest.

There was no reply, only another series of desperate sobs. Harriet found it hard to breathe. Clearly Sanjay must have just died, and one of his relatives had taken the call.

Harriet was too late. He was gone forever.

Not trusting herself to speak, she ended the call without saying another word. She knew now how much she missed Sanjay, and that nothing she could do could possibly sort out the mess. Harriet stared at the floor tiles, trying to assess the weight of her loss.

Chapter Twenty-Nine

Karen

That morning, Karen decreed they would walk to school. It had less to do with global warming than the fact the car wouldn't start. She threw a raincoat over her default get-up of green corduroy tunic and the shiny leggings that looked black in most lights but were actually purple. According to fashion wisdom, cheap clothes should be neutral in colour, but Karen ignored that. Colours made her feel alive, while black, beige and navy were deadly.

Today she would have felt good anyway. It didn't matter that the kids had put up the usual resistance to being woken up for school, then built up to the customary fight over cereal and milk.

Now the untidy gaggle progressed down the street. Ashley skipped ahead, Damon dragged his feet, Charlotte dawdled so that she could text her friends, and Edward scraped a stick noisily along every fence. It occurred to Karen, not for the first time, that a sheep-dog might have been handy.

"Charlotte, where's your coat?" Karen asked.

Charlotte looked up from her mobile long enough to make a disgruntled face. "In my schoolbag, duh!" As if there was anywhere else coats should be on a cold morning.

Edward said "You're stupid cos you don't wear enough clothes."

"Like the ladies in the papers" said Ashley helpfully. "They don't wear any clothes."

Karen smiled again at the memory. Geoff had been feeling sorry for himself, but it was far from a sympathy shag. Besides, Karen could do sympathy perfectly well with a kiss on the knee and a Mickey Mouse plaster. Duty shags, now. Those she knew.

She went to bed with Geoff for one only reason: she'd wanted to. It had been a long time since that had happened. In fact a long time since any traffic had passed up there, unless you counted hygiene products from Procter & Gamble.

It had been surprisingly simple. She'd thrown her clothes all over his floor, in exactly the same way she had told Damon never to do again, or else.

Geoff was unexpectedly muscular for someone who claimed never to work out. His back was hairier than most, though sensibly he hadn't gone in for poncy waxing.

They didn't have long, but long enough. She was tighter than she remembered being, yet every bit as aroused as ever when he drummed into her, knocking at the boundary between pleasure and pain. When she was on her front he really hit the spot, the spot that magazines always went on about yet never managed to describe in all its glory.

Entering her front door in the early hours, Karen felt like a teenager who'd broken her curfew.

The first thing she'd discovered after Rose had gone was that Edward had wet the bed, right on cue. As she changed the sheet, Karen tried not to kneel in any sharp-edged toys or use bad language in case Charlotte made an entrance.

Charlotte did appear in the doorway. "Where were you, Mummy?"

With great satisfaction, Karen replied "Out."

By the time they turned at the end of the road before the school, the children had accepted the inevitability of the day ahead. They were almost docile. That was only temporary. Outside the gates they'd see their pack of classmates and turn feral again.

Relaxing, Karen basked in contentment again. She often got these moments of pure joy, usually unexpectedly. There were a lot more of them since that shag.

As soon as she had steered Edward inside and deposited him in the reception class, she reached for her mobile to savour the text he had last sent. *You're one in a million*, it said, without any abbreviations. That was followed by a line of xs.

Some women might have wondered why there had been 11 kisses (why not 10, or 12? Or had he just pressed the button too long?). Or they might have worried about the other 999,999 women he must have screwed to come to his conclusion. Karen wasn't going to agonize or dissect. She was happy. That was enough.

Dorottya

As a rule, Dorottya was thoroughly dissatisfied with her lot, and today was no exception. Now that the rain had stopped, she opened the patio doors and installed herself in the garden on a Lutyens-style wooden bench. Because it was under the pergola, the seat was barely damp, but even if had been Dorottya would not have cared. This was the only place where it was safe to smoke. While enjoying a Benson in the conservatory the other day, she'd had to stub it out in hurry when Roger returned early from his golf. He hadn't noticed the smell – were men completely devoid of senses? – though he did later spot the hole Dorottya had made in the plastic flower-pot. She told him it had come that way from the garden centre, a reply that seemed to convince him.

Dorottya extracted a cigarette from its shiny gold packet and lit it, inhaling deeply, as you did when it was your first smoke in over 24 hours.

So what if the Versace jeans got spoiled by rainwater? There was always a pair of Josephs to put on instead, or, if she was slumming it, her Sevens which were only four or five times the price of Gap jeans. She had not worn Gap for a very long time now.

She glanced above the room she had had as an au pair. Roger was right about the chimney stack. It needed repointing or something. He said he would do it himself because you just couldn't trust anyone.

It was good for a man to work at something, thought Dorottya. Especially for sex.

As she slowly exhaled a lungful a smoke, she pretended for a moment that she was in a café in Budapest, in the company of someone cerebral and impossibly beautiful, rather than in the garden of a dull ageing Englishman who did not have a fortune quite as large as she'd imagined.

Dorottya got up and picked off several dead rose blooms. It was one of the things that Roger had taught her. Although she had no interest in anything garden-related, she now began to dead-head enthusiastically, applying a vicious twisting motion with more force than was required.

Treat them mean, she thought, tossing the dead heads into a corner of the border. That way they lasted longer. Everyone knew that, not just rose-growers.

When her mobile rang, Dorottya immediately saw who it was. She let it ring. She was in no mood for talking double glazing or anything else with that man.

It would have suited her better to turn the phone off, but that, Roger had made clear, was unacceptable. Because of his precious children, there always had to be a way of getting hold of either Roger or Dorottya in case of emergency, such as some horrible accident that might befall one of them at school or on the way home.

As she continued to smoke, she relished a moment musing on what might lead to an urgent phone call about one or other of Roger's offspring. Not the oldest girl, though. She was sweet, pretty and not at all conceited, all of which distinguished her from her siblings. Dorottya would hate anything to happen to her.

Her phone rang again a few minutes later, as well as several times at lunchtime when she was watching one of her favourite talk shows. It was a confessional-style programme she once loved, which had helped a lot with English idioms when she first came to the UK. She used to watch it with one of the other au pairs in the area, and they'd sit mesmerized on the sofa, toes touching as they marvelled over the messy problems that the English got themselves into. But today Dorottya had trouble concentrating, especially when the mobile rang. She steadfastly refused to answer.

It went silent during the afternoon. He must have given up. Later, however, just as the children came home, throwing their bags down in the hall and asking what was for dinner, she saw that she had a text.

I know just where you live, you screwed up bitch. Call me.

Dorottya's heart skipped a beat but she told herself to keep calm. How could he know? She powered off the mobile immediately and kept herself busy by tidying the assorted shoes in the hall, just like a good au pair.

Michael

The screwed-up bitch hadn't picked up, nor had she replied to his texts, but that did not surprise Michael. She would respond in the end.

Michael got home at precisely 6.45pm, right on schedule. He carefully placed his jacket on a suit-hanger, went into the kitchen, and selected an apple and a knife.

The woman was a tease, and he hated a tease, but he would win. His original plan had been simple: meet her for a drink and make sure hers was a double. Or treble. Now that she was jerking him around, he had little option but to get firm with her. Women were gullible, especially when it came to technology. Yes, she would believe that he knew where she was and exactly what she was doing. Then she'd agree to meet him.

He might send her a text to warn her that he could spy on her as if her mobile were a webcam. It wasn't even possible, but she wouldn't know that.

Dorottya wasn't the only tease, he reminded himself as he finished his customary snack of apple and cheddar. Those bitches needed sorting.

When he powered up his Lenovo, Michael quickly found what he needed. He didn't want anything complicated, just a simple silhouette of a naked woman. With his porn collection, it took him only minutes to locate one. It didn't matter that it was copyright. Nobody would trace it back to him.

He opened a program, copied, pasted, adjusted the font size, changed the border and inserted some more text. It looked great. Just one thing missing. Now what was a derisory rate for a blow-job? He'd never paid for sex, beyond the usual level of investment that most males were prepared to make.

Twenty pounds would probably do it, and serve that stuck-up bitch right. He added the words *Busty Lusty Laure, 23, wants to give YOU a blow-job, special offer only £20! Limited time only! Phone now!* He followed this with her mobile number before printing off a test card. His initial print run would be a hundred or so, which was plenty to be getting on with.

As they rolled off his Epson, he smirked with pleasure. Next he cut the sheets using a guillotine. The cards looked very plausible.

Oh, yes, yes. This was very good. Almost as good as sex. He rubbed his hands with glee. He hadn't felt this great for a long time.

Predictably, he now had a hard-on. He unzipped his flies and shut his eyes. Laure had caused it. She was going to be really sorry.

Chapter Thirty

Geoff

The woman opened her mouth wide. It looked like herpes. Maybe she even had the full house, SHAG: Syphilis, Herpes, Anal warts, Gonorrhoea.

Medical school had taught Geoff that any woman with chipped toenail varnish had chlamydia till proved otherwise. Nowadays he used urine samples to make a diagnosis, but the saying still stuck in the mind.

The next patient had just returned from holiday. "I hope you had a good time" said Geoff automatically.

Yes, the weather had been fabulous. In the daytime, it was in the high 20s, with barely a cloud in the sky. The evenings got a bit chillier, but the temperature dropped no lower than maybe 12 or 14. Couple of days were overcast, apparently, and the visibility hadn't been that good.

The man must have been a bloody meteorologist.

Geoff had to keep busy, not to leave a moment in which to brood. Davey was back, maybe for good, maybe not. Geoff would have him this weekend. He told himself that was all that mattered for now.

The last patient took longer than planned, mainly because she didn't have her hearing-aid on. At the end of a dysfunctional consultation about her bunions, she explained that she needed to save her hearing-aid batteries for important matters.

After evening surgery Geoff had to visit a child with croup. He didn't mind. He wasn't going to be at the practice forever.

It was one of those streets where there weren't many lights. The council would probably claim it was for the sake of the environment, but it was obviously cost-cutting. He peered at the houses in the gloom. Pretentious people lived everywhere. There could be no other explanation, in Geoff's view, for the glut of house names.

Where his patient's home was, he had no idea. Going up the hill he drove past The Orchard, Osbourne House, Holly Hedge. Down the hill there were Nelson Cottage, Rose Cottage, Everton, Journey's End, Nothing Matches. What the fuck possessed people?

No sign of Manton House. And no mobile signal.

He couldn't recall the last time he'd used a call-box.

Ah, there was one. It sat on a sad little triangle of grass, right by a zebra crossing, making it difficult to park. He pulled in as legally as he could and locked his car.

The phone-box didn't smell too bad. Geoff wondered who actually rang these numbers on the postcard-sized adverts for women of the night, as his ex-wife used to call them. The name Laure was familiar, of course, but obviously this couldn't be her. *Busty Lusty Laure* couldn't possibly be Lebanese Laure. For a start, she wasn't 23 or particularly busty. He remembered her breasts. Not the sort of thing he forgot.

He turned his mind to his patient's elusive house. Miraculously, the phone actually worked, and the mother replied at once. She gave what seemed the vaguest directions, her best tip being that there was a tree out front. Like other houses didn't have trees. Geoff sighed and asked the family to leave the porch light on for him.

The child turned out to have most of the same toys as Davey, but the similarities ended there. The parents had delayed calling the doctor. How had they failed to notice the little girl's breathing had become so bad?

Geoff sent the child to hospital. He didn't think the parents would be able to cope. The family that lacked for nothing was missing something vital. Common sense maybe. It was hard to define but every GP would have understood exactly what he meant.

Some people found parenting so difficult. He sighed as he pulled away, thinking inevitably of Davey.

The last call was to a flat in the worst block of town.

"Are you the probation officer?" asked a youth. He had hostility in his eyes and the crotch of his jeans around his knees.

"Sorry, dude" replied Geoff.

It was no use trying to press the button for the lift. It never worked. Geoff took the stairs to the 9th floor two at a time, trying not to inhale the stench of urine and Dettol. His medical case made him a marked man. Why hadn't he thought of wearing a hoodie and carrying his medical equipment in a Primark carrier?

The mum turned out to be anxious, and her baby was fine. She offered Geoff a cup of tea, which he refused. You never knew what you were raising to your lips. Instead he spent some time discussing what symptoms to look for if the baby didn't improve. She hung on his every word.

He left after profuse thanks from the woman.

Back in the car, he took a moment to study his blood test results. He still hadn't found time to see his own GP but he'd got his practice nurse to take blood from him. Geoff read it through again.

Normal glucose.

Normal cholesterol.

Normal testosterone.

All good. So his body wasn't crumbling. He folded the printout and put it back in his jacket. It was a puzzle why his dick was as limp as lettuce.

Laure

Perplexed, Laure turned her mobile off. The text said they had never met, yet he wanted her to come to his house.

Better get her head down and plough through the documents. It was hard to concentrate. One reason was utter boredom induced by the huge stack of papers on her desk. Although there were only two contracts, each had many addenda and appendices to be scrutinized as well. She was sure that someone more junior could have been delegated, but these were big deals.

It wasn't entirely what she had dreamed of doing, all those years ago when she'd decided to read law. What had she had in mind? She'd gone into the profession because she had an analytical brain and a good memory. She needed stretching, her teachers always said. As if she was a rubber band.

Her family had been supportive. Only Tante Lina, fretting about lines and wrinkles, was disappointed. She would have liked a plastic surgeon in the family.

Laure tried not to think of the brief call to her pay-as-you-go that morning, which was the other thing keeping her mind off those two contracts.

At lunchtime she turned on the cheapo Samsung again while waiting for the lights.

Thirteen missed calls. It wasn't Dan, she saw after she'd chosen a BLT and a packet of parsnip crisps. All the phone numbers were different. Not a single one recognizable.

There was a voicemail, from someone who left his number but no name. She didn't know the voice, and the hesitant message was mostly inaudible, apart from asking her to ring him back. Charlie Postie enjoyed practical jokes, but how would he have the PAYG number? Only those from the Jacaranda would know it, and only if she'd given them the number. Surely Dan wouldn't be messing her about. A couple of others had the number as well, but that still didn't add up to 13 people.

She pushed it out of her mind. When she left work, she turned her mobile back on. Half a dozen more calls. Weird.

There was another voicemail now. 'Hey, Lusty Laure, it's Barry here.' Apparently Barry had the hots for her and couldn't wait to feel her lips around him.

Ugh. She listened again. He'd definitely said 'Laure'. How many Laures could there be?

It was only a recording, she told herself, but it was creepy. She deleted the message and turned off the phone. All the same, she choose a different journey home and kept looking over her shoulder.

When she got in, she spent the evening with *The Feng Shui Bible*, a new book she'd picked up at Waterstone's. With luck, it would help her decorate her flat in a way that was pleasing to the eye and conducive to inner harmony. She wasn't convinced she could achieve harmony solely by having the right balance of wood, glass and metal in the northwest corner of the living room, but she would give it a try.

The PAYG sat on her glass coffee table, still powered off. Talking to Dan would have to wait.

That night she soaked in a warm bath and changed into a pink nightgown and pink fleece robe that was as soft as rabbit fur but a good deal more humane. After a cup of cocoa, she sprinkled a few drops of lavender oil on her pillow, had a brandy, popped in earplugs. Still she couldn't sleep.

Chapter Thirty-One

Sanjay

Mrs Shah pulled her dupatta across her shoulder. "It should have been cremation" she pointed out, but nobody listened.

Sanjay turned his mobile off and put it back in his pocket. He wiped his eyes on his sleeve. "Sita, why did you bring a tin of Felix?"

"It's for the after-life, innit."

The three of them were standing in the Shahs' back garden, with Sita in full-length white, as was customary for Hindu funerals. She was totally buying into the after-life thing.

"Besides," Sita added, "*Felix* means happy."

"I know" said Sanjay. "But Dainty preferred lobster."

"Iceland doesn't stock lobster."

Their mum peered into the ground. "Do you think it's too big?"

None of them was any good in the garden. Sanjay didn't have the strength, and the rest of the family wouldn't have known which end of a spade to hold, so the much-pierced teenager from next door, bless him, had come over.

In an open cardboard box that had once housed a pair of Sita's thigh-high boots from Russell & Bromley lay Dainty, wrapped in one of Sanjay's favourite shirts. It wasn't like he was going to get much more use from it.

"Also it is in wrong place" said Mum. "Look, *beta*, he dug up all the rhubarb."

True, nearly half the rhubarb patch had been sacrificed to make room for Dainty's grave, but Mum had not once picked any, as Sita reminded her, in the 25 years or more that they had lived at 32 Cornwall Gardens.

"But I could have used it if it was still there, *beti*." Mum did some over-the-top head-shaking to reinforce her logic.

Sanjay looked down at the parcel that was Dainty's body, smaller in death than in life. Sita and Mum were looking down too. Is this how they would gaze at him? When the time came, he too would lie inert just like this, though possibly without the salmon chunks in jelly.

Dainty had only been a little constipated. After forcing the syrup down her, Sanjay had even begun to think she was improving. Then, several nights later, when she was just padding across the kitchen floor to her bowl, she had stopped, had a kind of seizure and flopped down on the floor. Sanjay phoned the vet right away, but even before he got through to the emergency number he knew there was no hope.

Putting his hand on her chest, he felt no heartbeat, and her beautiful pea-green eyes had huge round unseeing pupils.

He had bent down and kissed her fur, the short fur on her head, the soft longer fur of her belly, the rough fur inside her ear, the tip of her tail (which still had that slight kink, even in death), and finally her little paws, with their delicate pink pads and the dense fur crammed in between them. Her fur was soon moist with his tears.

She was still warm when he found his shirt and wrapped her gently in it. He'd left her head visible for a while, but later that night, when she had grown cold, he covered it with a corner of shirt, after kissing the tabby patch on her head one last time.

Now it was time to put her in the ground. "Goodbye, friend" Sanjay whispered as he knelt down and put the lid on the box. Sita said a few words, none of which was in Hindi, and helped Sanjay fill in the earth with her hands.

He wiped his face with his sleeve again. Why did he have to lose everything that he valued and loved, he asked himself, getting up. Then Sita hugged him, and twined her muddy fingers into his, making him feel a little less shit.

Bollocks! He needed a drink now. When Dad came home, they opened a bottle of the first thing they laid their hands on. It was Jack Daniels. Dad had bought it years ago, when he'd decided he should become more modern and more British.

Tonight Dad didn't talk about import-export or what a bunch of bloody fucking numbskulls he worked with. He and Sanjay just sat and had what Dad called nearly bloody skin-full.

Sanjay wondered how he would die, and who would be there. Who, if anyone, would kiss him that last time. What they might bring him to get through the after-life, if such a thing existed, which seemed unlikely. Of course he didn't say any of this. He and Dad just sat in silence and downed JD.

Sanjay dreaded going back to his Dainty-less flat. What would he do there, except put on Janis and lose another little piece of his heart? Mum suggested that Sanjay should stay overnight in his old room. But he wasn't keen on that either, because if he feared never moving out again, except feet first.

Now that was one bollocking ridiculous expression. People always went everywhere feet first, reckoned Sanjay. Unless they had a serious stoop or an award-winning beer-belly.

In the end he stayed overnight, in the room that still had adolescent posters on the wall, a cricket bat in the corner, and a load of stupid cassettes, of which Kajagoogoo was a prime example. Ben had many of the same albums, posters and junk. That was because they'd bought loads of them together, way back when.

His legs ached worse than ever as he lay in the single bed that night, under the dark red duvet cover that Mum had always hated. It had to be washed separately or else the colour would run, as he'd heard a thousand times. As he drifted off to sleep, he thought of Harriet. It would have been good to have her here now, not specifically under the single duvet, though that could have been fun, but in his life. Would it have been a help? He didn't know. And he didn't know what to do next.

The truth was, he had no idea what he wanted. Bollocks, fucking bollocks! Surely he was supposed to realize by this stage in life exactly what he wanted to do.

Luckily there wasn't much deciding to do the next morning. He looked out of the window at the new patch in the garden, while Mum made him a huge and totally English breakfast of bacon, eggs and tomato, even though he'd told her he wasn't hungry.

She examined him critically as he sat at the table in front of the ginormous plate. "Your hair is all funny, *beta*."

"Yeah, I know." Did mothers ever stop commenting on how their offspring looked? They probably carried on till their kids were 70 or so. Not that it applied in his case, obviously. Sanjay patted the side of his head. Since it had grown back, his hair was like that pretty much every morning, plastered to one side of his face, on account of the relentless sweating every night. He wondered how many calories all that perspiring burned.

"I can lend you a comb" Mum offered. She probably didn't want to lend him a comb so much as to wield it herself, as if he were four years old.

"It's OK. I'll wash it in the shower later. I always sweat at night" he explained. "It's because of the chemo."

Of course, he regretted this before he'd finished saying it, because Mum looked shocked. "*Beta*, chemo was months and months ago."

"Yeah. Well."

"And when is your next appointment, har?"

It was exactly like being asked when you'd last changed your socks. Even though those interrogations were a long time ago, he remembered them well. "I think it's next week" Sanjay lied.

"Hah!" said Mum triumphantly. "Beginning of week or end of week?"

"Beginning. No, end. I don't know. I'm waiting to hear." To look nonchalant, Sanjay turned his mobile on. He couldn't really be arsed with texts and emails now, but fiddling with his BlackBerry made it easier to ignore his mum. He read a text which said *Please tell me when the funeral is. I'd like to attend. Harriet.* Fucking bollocks! How the hell did Harriet know Dainty had died? And why would she want to be at his cat's funeral after brushing him off?

Mum persisted. "What do you mean, waiting to hear? Appointments always sent long time in advance. I know from eye clinic."

He wasn't about to admit he'd missed two appointments. What was the point of wasting valuable time going for check-ups? It wasn't his job to keep the medical profession entertained.

Sita ambled into the kitchen wearing a yellow suede skirt that was so bright it made his eyes hurt. "Bro, you are so not waiting to hear from them."

"What are you talking about?"

Sita said there'd been this phone call while he was away. "And the letters."

This got Mum really interested and Sanjay really annoyed. "Oh, so in addition to making yourself at home in my bed" he said, making Sita wince, "you decide to check out my private correspondence. Nice. Why don't you get a job with Mossad or something?"

Looking as innocent as she knew how, Sita said nothing.

Best leave it, thought Sanjay. Mum appeared confused, which was never a good thing because it meant that any second now she would start firing more questions than he wanted to answer. To create a diversion, Sanjay dug into his breakfast and said "Lovely bacon, Mum." This pleased her. She told him it was from Morrison's.

Although he still had no appetite, he carried on manfully till the plate was nearly clean, then got up, his belly as tight as a drum-skin.

Sita grabbed him just outside the kitchen. "You've got to go" she hissed. "Suppose the doctors have a new treatment?"

He shrugged. "Whatever." The last letter had been from the consultant herself, the one that had supervised his chemo, and she said it was important. Even though a new treatment was about as likely as winning the lottery when you hadn't bought a ticket, he figured he owed it to his family to make the effort of attending once more.

Which was why, a few days later, he found himself waiting in the familiar surroundings of Clinic 5, watching the nurses go to and fro across the squeaky vinyl, and commiserating with the other miserable saps on their slippery plastic chairs. The familiar pageant of clinic life.

Sanjay installed himself under the sign that instructed all and sundry to switch off their mobile phones. Bollocks! As if anyone did that. Firstly, that tiny amount of radiation had no effect whatsoever on medical technology. Nor on any aircraft systems or petrol pumps, come to that. Secondly, you never saw doctors turning their mobiles off, the reason being that they considered themselves way too important. Couldn't other people and their time be important too? Sanjay compromised and set the BlackBerry to Vibrate.

Suppose this was his last day, he thought, inevitably. What a crap end, sitting watching everyone worry about their cancers, worry about their appointment times, worry about lapsed parking meters, worry about whether their husband or wife wanted a cup of tea from the League of Friends stall.

He was glad he'd persuaded Sita not to come with him. What was the point of dragging her here as well? The mention of shopping had had the desired effect. There was a world out there, he'd told her - clothes to buy, shoes to try on, hair to dye some ridiculous new colour that would probably clash painfully with the yellow skirt. In the end, she agreed to let him attend alone. "But promise you'll call me as soon as you're done, yeah?"

He promised.

Someone's name was called. The guy sitting next to Sanjay looked up momentarily then continued to cut out, with meticulous care, a coupon from a waiting-room mag. Sanjay wondered if he would live long enough to use the 20p savings or whatever it was.

The patient who got up to go into Consulting Room 3 had surely arrived after him, thought Sanjay. And he looked bloody healthy. Didn't the guy know that some people were dying? Sanjay wanted to kick the coffee table and send all those pathetic magazines and leaflets flying.

Instead he picked up a flyer about hepatitis C. Well, that was uplifting. It could give you fever and loss of appetite, and make you feel tired all the time. Sanjay had all the symptoms. He'd never injected drugs, which meant he must have caught it from reading the leaflet. Sanjay was just coming to the fun bit, all the other ways the virus spread, from dodgy tattoos to sex with men, when he heard someone call out "Sanjaykumar Shah?"

Inside Consulting Room 3 was the doctor he'd seen four months ago. She looked really glum. Maybe her cat had died too. She managed barely a thin smile as she asked him to take a seat.

"I have some very good news for you" she began.

"Oh?" Maybe the polar ice caps were going to be OK or the two Koreas were going to be best buddies. It seemed more likely than any good news about cancer.

"And it's rather unexpected," she went on. Well, that clinched it. Not that the doc looked deliriously happy about the polar bears. "But I do also owe you a profound apology."

He shrugged. "It's OK." What the bollocks did she mean? The wait in the clinic hadn't been at all long. Sometimes it was literally hours.

"Mr Shah, there's been a mistake on our part."

What sort of mistake? Mum was always reading bits out of the paper about the wrong leg being sawn off and dirty great swabs left to fester inside patients, so he didn't see how any medical mistakes could be good. His phone buzzed in his pocket. Probably Sita itching to hear from him.

Anyway, the consultant's explanation was long and involved, and delivered in measured tones. The gist, as Sanjay finally understood it, was that he didn't have cancer of the testicle, and had probably never had it.

The phone buzzed again. Sanjay didn't budge. He needed to absorb what the doctor had just said.

Chapter Thirty-Two

Laure

"You're mumbling" said Laure. "Did you say cockroaches?"

Dan opened his eyes. "Yeah. Killed a couple of them. In my room."

"And that would worry me?" Sweet, she thought, as a satisfied smile spread right across her face for the second time that morning.

"Well, it might. Couldn't be sure how you'll respond to stuff. For instance, killing small things that have a right to live."

"Small ugly things" she corrected.

"OK. Small ugly things."

She glanced sideways. "You think cockroaches have a right to move into your flat?"

"Not really. Anyway, I've put boric acid down now. I'll give it a while to work."

By the look of things, he was going to give it quite a long while. He hadn't gone home for three days, and, now that he was nestled under her duvet, he seemed in no rush to leave.

She liked his skin. Firm, with a sowing of tawny freckles across the shoulders. He had a scar near his ribs, and his shoulders were muscular. She fingered his upper arm. There was only one tattoo, a kind of dagger on one arm. She'd expected a lot more. Even his toes were surprisingly nice. Just recently she had learned a lot about his toes.

For a start, he loved having them massaged. Squatting on the front of his thighs, she began to rub oil onto his feet, then in between the toes, working each digit individually. Too bad about the noise. Anyway, if the neighbours heard his moans as they came and went with their Burberry bags and their baby-buggies, they'd be too polite to comment.

Nor did she care that Dan was getting a close-up of her bottom, which was probably huge from there.

Things had progressed fast. She'd phoned Dan from her iPhone in the end, and decided to see him just once more, to see how she felt. Yes, this was that once. And she definitely knew how she felt.

"I live in a dump" he'd said. "And I'm not good enough for you."

She told him she'd be the judge of that.

For the record, the sex really was good enough for her.

"Why did you hide your job from me?" he asked the first time they had been to bed.

"Because lawyers aren't sexy."

Dan leaned up on one elbow. "They are so! Don't you ever watch TV?"

"Maybe they're hot on the box. Not in real life." She didn't even want to think of Charlie Postie right now. "Besides, it scares guys off."

To his credit, Dan didn't look at all intimidated. She had also told him about the conversation with Charlie. "I spoke to a colleague. The bottom line is that your case could be reopened, if there's new evidence."

He thought for a bit before he shrugged. "The thing is I don't have any new evidence."

"Nobody who can make a new statement?"

"Nobody at all. I want to clear my name. But I can't see how to do that."

"That is sad."

"Yeah, well. I have to live with it. Hopefully the worst is over." His grin was wicked. "Actually, I think the best is yet to come."

So right now, as she worked him into a frenzy by massaging his toes, he was caressing her buttocks and back. He moved to her sides, and finally her breasts. She didn't get to finish his toes, because he pulled her up towards him and they rearranged themselves.

She went on top. Best way of all. It needn't even take much space. At a pinch the passenger seat would do.

Dan brushed playfully against her for a minute or so before she sat on him. Then that utterly delicious moment that felt the exact reverse of a champagne cork popping. As a bonus, she could look right into his face. He looked so dangerous, yet so totally familiar. She took in his increasing excitement, his closing eyes, his final open-mouthed cry.

"You're so smoking" Dan said afterwards.

Laure lifted her head to look.

He laughed. "Not there, silly!" Then he got up and went to bathroom with a tube of Fixodent to do something he refused to let her see.

After he made cups of tea, Dan said "Know what I really want to do?"

It turned out he really wanted anal sex. She really didn't. It sounded horrible. Even the name for it was horrible, though it wasn't the phrase he had used.

"You want to take me up the arse, as you put it" she repeated, trying to keep horror out of her voice. In all her life – and she had forgotten how many boyfriends there had been - not once had she wanted to find out what it was like.

It had happened a lot to him in jail, he admitted, his jaw set.

"Maxy?" she asked.

He nodded.

That was no real surprise. "The stories about dropping soap in the shower are all true, then?"

"Pretty much."

"What is it like?"

"I think you've got to find out for yourself."

She stared at him. "No."

"You might like it."

"Did you like it?"

"No."

"Well, then."

"It's different for women. You might like it" he said again.

It was turning into an argument. She had managed to like sex just fine without anything finding its way into her back passage, thank you. Yes, she did have one or two women friends who had tried it. But how could it be enjoyable? It was practically miles away from the clitoris. "And now you want to bugger someone like they buggered you." It wasn't a question.

"No. Well, yes. And no. Look, it's complicated".

She was sure he had lots of strange emotions after being in jail but, as she explained, she wasn't there for him to take it out on her.

"I'm not going to force you" he said. "Anyway. You might like it."

"That makes three times you've said it."

Now that he was out of prison, it made sense in a way. It was just that the prospect was so utterly unappealing. In the end it was curiosity that got to her. That, coupled with the realization that she had done everything a different way round with Dan. Plus there was a giant bottle of lotion on the bedside table. Well, what harm could it do?

It was best to be relaxed, he explained. He would fix her a drink.

She nearly changed her mind halfway through the killer gin and tonic, but the novelty factor won out.

Oh! How come she had never done this before, she thought an astonishing feeling grabbed her from behind and engulfed her pelvis. She was unable to move. At first she was afraid movement might cause serious damage, but then it was because she was pole-axed by the mind-blowing sensation.

The climax when it came was a wave, more intense than anything she had ever experienced. It shook her from top to toe. All she could do afterwards was lie sprawled out in sweat. She barely had strength to breathe.

He was talking again. She dragged her brain back from wherever it had gone. "What's that?"

"I said thank you."

"You don't need to thank me."

"But I do. You're amazing." He wiped a hand across one eye.

"You just mean you enjoyed that shag" she pointed out.

"Yes. You enjoyed it too. But that's not all I meant."

Men were so predictable. "Yeah, right."

"Seriously. For the man, it's not so different. Except on entry and then at the end." He grabbed a tissue from the box on the floor and blew his nose.

"OK" she said. "Whatever."

He threw the tissue on the floor and cuddled up to her, one arm across her chest, his cheek on hers.

Her face was getting hot and wet. Sweat, she thought. Then he sniffed. Evidently his nose was blocked. When she turned towards him, she saw he was actually weeping.

"I can't believe how wonderful you are" he said, his eyes red. Then it came out, all of it. All the things that made up the parallel universe he had lived in. The fights, the claustrophobia, the desperation, but most of all the naked fear.

Laure really felt for him. It must have hurt all over again to tell his tale. She kissed his cheek, tasting the salt. No man she knew had ever cried like him. She wiped the side of his face with a finger and licked it. It was impossible to pinpoint exactly how she felt, let alone say it aloud, but she knew Dan was taking her all kinds of places she'd never been before.

So much for predictable.

After a while, they got up and showered. She let him loose in the kitchen and he made lunch, a chicken arrabiata. They ate at the dining table, him in boxers, she in a T-shirt. Surprisingly, the chicken was every bit as good as the lunches with Tante Lina and Tante Victorine.

"I thought you said you couldn't cook. Or was that another one of your whoppers?"

"Nope, it was absolutely true. I couldn't cook." He twisted linguine onto his fork. "But here's a lesson from the big encyclopaedia of life. If you don't know something, go and learn."

"You must have practised this recipe."

"Yep, and some others. I've watched a lot of cookery programmes. And I cook at work. At the garden centre."

She put a hand on his arm. "Dan, you're not meant to help yourself to veg and herbs off the display."

"Ha, ha, very funny. No, Big Ted the boss has a small flat there with a kitchen and when he's argued with his missus, which is quite often, he stays over. I asked if I could cook there sometimes and he agreed."

"That's brilliant." She really meant it.

"I've made a good few chicken recipes, and a kind of moussaka thing. And I'm learning a cod dish but Big Ted doesn't like the smell. He finds it recondite."

"Recondite?"

"Yeah." He glanced at her doubtfully. "As in hard to deal with. Why, is there something wrong with that?"

"No, not at all. I just never associated the word 'recondite' with cod. Or any kind of fish really."

He paused while he stacked their plates together. "I got the word out of a book. That's how I'm improving my use of language. Snag is, it's not always clear how to use a word."

"Don't let it worry you. You're doing great."

While Dan carried on clearing up, Laure gazed out of the window. The Japanese woman from the flats navigated her push-chair up the road. She was tiny, no match for the massive sports-type buggy that looked more suitable for a golf-course than the streets of west London. The woman was coaxing the contraption up the kerb, leaning on it with all her weight. Now Laure got a side view and saw a huge bump. So she was pregnant again, and surely only weeks away from pushing out another perfectly petite baby that looked like a doll and behaved almost as well.

She must have been showing for months. How could Laure have failed to notice?

Dan intercepted her thoughts. "Have you thought of moving the dining table to the opposite corner? Then there'd be more room for that massive sofa."

She hadn't considered it. Probably because it would open up a huge gap on the north side of the room, which, if she recalled correctly, was a Feng Shui catastrophe.

"Do you want me to move it for you? Then see if you like it." Yesterday afternoon he'd shifted pots on her balcony, so that the evergreens were on the far side where they helped keep out the wind. It meant one could sit out there now without being in a gale.

"That's not a bad idea. But it would make the table a lot further from the kitchen."

"Well" he said slowly. "If you let me cook for you more often, that might not be a problem."

She paused because she genuinely wasn't sure. Did she want him rearranging her furniture, literal and metaphorical? "I guess. You know, if I didn't know any better, I'd suspect you of being a closet gay."

"Oh, I'm not gay" he said unnecessarily. "Now don't do anything. Just sit there looking decorative."

This was a novelty. Nobody had ever thought her decorative in an old T-shirt with blobs of red sauce down the front. Dan moved everything off the table, including the piles of work that Laure never intended to bring home but still found their way into her flat regardless. He then pushed the chairs aside.

She enjoyed watching him move. He had no trouble lifting the glass table on his own and carrying it across the room, navigating the narrow gap between television and bookcase. A lot of men would have knocked into something by now, blaming their clumsiness on the furniture, the flat-owner, the architect or anyone but themselves. Dan was graceful as well as muscular. On the right below his ribcage she caught sight of the long pale scar she'd vaguely registered before.

Dan was right. The table really was better placed now, and the sofa no longer looked shoe-horned into a gap that was much too small. "Thanks" said Laure. "I like it."

"No problem."

"What's that scar?"

He appraised the position of the table for a couple of seconds and moved it by a few inches. "Nothing much" he said finally.

"It looks like it was probably something much at the time" she said gently.

"Yeah. Well. This guy Maxy took a swing at me with a chair."

"Vicious."

"Yep. But I'm not going to get too fussed about stuff like that. One lesson I've learned is not to get worked up about things you can't change."

She made a non-committal noise as she took this in.

Having finished shifting furniture, Dan bent down in front of a bookcase. "You've got a lot of books."

"I guess." Those were just her law books, history, biographies and novels. He didn't need to know about the self-help library hidden away in the spare-room.

"*Arsehole.*" Dan laughed as he picked out a book. "What's it about?"

She frowned. "I don't think I've got anything called *Arsehole.*"

"Hold on, it's the author's name. R- S- O- L- E" he spelled out. "You'd think he'd change it instead of risking it being pronounced 'arsehole'."

Taking the book from him, Laure said "That's by R Solé. See, there's an accent on the E. Robert Solé. And he's not at all an arsehole."

"Oh, yeah. I see. What's it about?"

"This one is a historical novel set in Egypt in the early 20th century."

"Wow. I could learn a whole lot from that. If I knew French. *Le Tarbouche*" mused Dan as he opened it. "It's a kind of shoe, right?"

Laure smiled. "Almost right. It's a hat. What most people call a fez."

"What's it about, then? Just a history of a hat?"

"It's a family saga, about Syrian people trying to fit in after they move to Egypt. It's a terrific book."

Dan looked up. "How does it all work out in the end?"

"I think the Syrian family just learns to live with not feeling at home. One foot here, one foot there." The story had a lot in common with some real lives.

He grinned wickedly as he put the book down. "I bet you identify with some femme fatale in the book. Am I right?"

"No, though there is in fact a femme fatale in the book. She's called – ".

"I don't give a flying fuck what she's called. Mine is called Laure Dimmock."

To Laure Dimmock's great surprise, Dan lifted her up and carried her back towards the bedroom.

"I suppose you want to take me up the arse?" she said hopefully.

He placed her gently on the bed. "No. You're going to have to wait for that."

"Sadist."

Later, when the sun was setting behind the row of plants Dan had rearranged on the balcony, he said something else that came from the big book of life of his.

"Dan" she said gently. "I'm not knocking books, but there isn't a big book of life. Sometimes you just have to write it yourself."

Dorottya

In the large brass bed, Dorottya was not at all enjoying being with Roger. Unfortunately, it looked as if it might be a while until she managed to escape.

Trying to pass the time somehow, she closed her eyes and thought back once again to the best summer ever.

Lake Balaton had been perfect. Dipping in and out of the still deep waters was a balm for everything, even the mosquito bites she got every evening. "Your skin is too sweet" Rita had said, rubbing calamine onto her thigh. "That's why they love you so much."

Rita's skin was sweet too, a nut-brown shade that merged beautifully with the shimmering lake. The wooden house Dorottya's parents had rented had a deck around it, with a secret area underneath. Rita had stroked Dorottya and said "I know you will forget me." But Dorottya never had.

Her plan was simple. The list was already in her head, not on her mobile phone. Dorottya had already chosen a case for the sleek jeans and tight T-shirts she liked best, and of course the fur coat she had wheedled out of Roger. She hated it, but it was, as the English said, worth a bomb. There were lots of elegant outfits, many of them silk. When she wore them, men became putty in her hands – another good English idiom – but they weren't her at all.

Then the paperwork. She needed a few documents, and, crucially, credit cards. They were on Roger's account, but wasn't that what marriage was for? She sighed. It was also for sex, of course. The trouble was that she was getting very tired of sex with Roger. She felt stirrings of real empathy for his first wife.

How long did men need to sleep? "Dahlink, I need a wee" said Dorottya. She nudged a still-sleeping Roger, making the handcuffs clank against the brass bedstead.

Chapter Thirty-Three

Sanjay

The sound was ear-piercingly loud. Sanjay had never heard anything like it from any musician, living or dead. He would have liked to ask whoever was making the din to turn it down, but his body was no longer under his control. Blood coursed through it, carrying oxygen round his limbs. His arms were outstretched but couldn't move them. Every single bit of him felt warm and pain-free, and it was all effortless.

He didn't even need to breathe. He was at exactly the same temperature as the air around him, and contained exactly the same elements in exactly the right proportions. All of this he knew because he had somehow floated up out of his body, and was now looking down at himself from the ceiling.

The room was a brighter white than anything on a paint chart, and it was flooded with light. You couldn't actually see the walls. Even they were pure light.

Surely it was impossible for this place to get any brighter, Sanjay thought, when a light approached.

As it got closer, Sanjay realized that it had actually been there all the time, away in the distance. He just hadn't spotted it before.

He was approaching the light very fast, or maybe it was getting closer to him. It was probably a star which had been knocking around for a billion years or so. Suddenly he felt at one with everything in the universe, with everything he had ever experienced. It made complete sense. He must have died. After all, it had been a long while coming. Either that or Ben had finally got some decent weed.

Then Sanjay felt himself open out like a flower. As a rule he didn't know jack about flowers, but he knew all about this one. His flesh turned to petals, his muscles and bones too. He was a white flower, which was odd, what with him not actually being white, but all the same it seemed totally logical.

If he'd had to pin it down, he'd have said honeysuckle. This one had huge trumpet-shaped blooms that were making a noise as well as a smell. The light got closer, the sound got louder, and the scent was overpowering.

"Bro, you OK?"

"Yeah." His voice was surprisingly normal. Everything was fine. The flowers assaulted his nose as Sita hugged him. She never did that, which proved he must have died. How long he'd been dead, he had no idea.

He moved his arms. They worked OK, given that he had a drip in his left hand which hadn't been there before. Now he could see that he was lying in a hospital bed, and Sita was perched on a chair next to him, looking over him intently. He remembered peering over at a boxful of kittens in that exact same curious way when he was 10 or so, watching them for hours. Sita had never looked at him with this much interest.

"You were in x-ray, bro. Do you remember what happened?"

Bits were coming back now. He'd had a chest x-ray, then sat on a bench outside the room with a red light over the door. If it was on, you weren't allowed to enter under pain of death. Next to him there'd been a laundry bin for dumping your hospital gown after your x-ray. As if anyone would want to take it home with them, unless they had a really lame fancy dress party to go to.

It had been an age since the x-ray chick had told him to wait while she checked the picture. Bollocks! Didn't hospitals have digital photography? Then he felt himself getting light-headed before it all went blank.

"Did you buy shoes?" he asked Sita now.

"No. I got perfume."

He wrinkled his nose. That accounted for the pong.

Sita filled in the gaps for him. When he'd hit the deck, they'd summoned the crash team. After resuscitating him, someone rang Sita, her number being the first one in his mobile (*A* for *Annoying Sis*).

Now he remembered some more. He'd been put on a trolley and there was an incredible level of activity. Loads of people milling round like extras in *Holby City*.

Sita's version of events was solemn, and she hadn't once said *innit* or *like*. It must have been pretty serious then.

"Did you tell Mum?" asked Sanjay.

"Sort of. I told her you could have visitors soon but you were in semi-isolation at the moment. But why were you in x-ray? And what's this about seeing a different specialist?"

Ah, that was it! "I've got TB."

"Bro, I'm really sorry to hear that" she said.

"I'm not. I'm ECSTATIC!" This was obviously louder than necessary because the old man in the next bed moaned and a couple of other patients pricked up their ears. The poor suckers probably had cancer instead of TB. What shit luck.

In the clinic, his consultant had been embarrassed and apologetic.

She'd steepled her fingers and the tips, Sanjay noticed, had gone white. He had seen a lot of doctors behind a lot of desks, and most of them joined their fingers like this at some point. He wondered if they taught them special doctor body language at medical school. "If you recall," she began, "we'd said about 18 months ago that the histology wasn't typical."

Apparently, as she explained to Sanjay, seminoma of the testicle could have giant cells.

I never knew mine were that big, he'd thought fleetingly.

She actually meant in the lab under the microscope. The histology, as she called it. Anyway, TB could have giant cells too, which was where the confusion began. You'd have thought doctors could tell the difference after centuries of medical advances. There were breakthroughs every other day, according to the papers. So what the bollocks were they breaking through?

Anyway, the histology wasn't typical. That was her mantra. At the time they had talked between them, the various specialists, at their MDT meeting, whatever that was, and following their discussions they'd decided it must be cancer of the testicle. That was after all a lot more common than TB of the goolies. So, even though the histology wasn't typical, they'd treated him for the Big C, lopping off his left testicle in the process.

That was where the real trouble had started. The chemo he had afterwards knocked off his immune system some more. It had almost certainly made his TB worse, the consultant admitted, accounting for the fatigue, weight loss and night sweats. When lymph nodes had enlarged all over the place, they'd thought it was the cancer spreading.

"But that was really the TB" she said triumphantly, becoming unnaturally cheerful for a moment.

Doctors were weird. They looked sad when they were giving good news, and were unremittingly jolly if they thought you had only weeks to live. Not only was their body language odd. It was also their choice of words. One newbie doctor had asked Sanjay what he was most worried about. Sanjay said it was impotence, and the newbie replied 'Cool.'

Anyway the consultant then arranged an urgent appointment for him with a TB specialist. Of course, she said again, she and her team were all very sorry indeed. He had every right to be angry, she continued. It would be understandable if he preferred to be treated at a different hospital now. She didn't say anything about him suing the hospital, but she was probably thinking it.

As he explained all this to Sita now, she sat clutching the edge of the hospital sheet, her eyes glistening.

He'd only fainted because his blood sugar dropped too low, they told him. Even so, that hadn't stopped more doctors wanting to do tests on his adrenal glands, just in case, as TB could affect those too. TB was a real goer by the sound of it.

One of the doctors had been again to explain the treatment, a cocktail of four different drugs. Sanjay liked that idea. Was it going to have a dinky little umbrella in it? Then the doc spoiled it by saying the drugs might make him feel very sick. Also his urine could turn orange and he might go colourblind as well.

Now how the fuck you were meant to know what colour your piss was if you'd gone colour-blind? And why would you fucking care if you were puking your guts up anyway?

A nurse had just been round with the first lot of drugs, not a cocktail at all but some orange pills and a couple of white ones big enough for a cart-horse, and then another nurse came to check his pulse and stuff. Sanjay smiled at her. She didn't seem to be smiling back, but it was hard to tell behind her paper mask.

"Am I contagious?" he asked her.

She didn't answer.

None of the nurses knew anything. The only person who knew stuff was that one doctor, and he was more interested in explaining jolly things like the side-effects of his treatment. He did ask Sanjay if there was anything else worrying him.

"Am I contagious?"

The doctor said almost certainly not, but added that Sanjay needed a brain scan and a few other things besides, just in case the TB had gone there too. At least he didn't say 'Cool.'

Sanjay thought his brain was working just fine. Everything around him was hyper-real, like the red jumper on the back of the chair over there, and the dazzling yellow poster on the far wall that warned you to use the hand rub every five seconds if you didn't want to catch bubonic plague. Sounds were extra loud too. Sanjay feasted his senses.

Odours were just as strong. Sanjay had told the doctor about his sense of smell becoming more sensitive after chemo. The doctor nodded. That was the TB, he explained, not the chemo.

Now Sita let go of the sheet and smoothed it down. She said she would have to go home and see Mum soon, and explain what was happening, tell her the news about his TB and everything. Dad would of course go into a rant about incompetent doctors, while Mum would be thrilled and probably want to throw a party.

"Is there anything you want me to bring you?"

Nothing, unless you counted Dainty. Bollocks, he bloody missed that cat. In the end he said "Kiwi fruit. And a pen and some paper. Lots of paper." He intended to make a list, a long list of things he would actually have time to get through.

At the moment he was in a state of suspended animation. That was the way when you were in hospital. He was also exhausted even though he had done nothing and gone nowhere.

While Sita was gone, Sanjay checked his palms to see if his sweat was turning orange or red. Then he looked under the bedclothes for joint swelling or the urticarial rash the doctor had warned about. He wasn't sure how an urticarial rash differed from any other rash, but he had bugger all else to do. He was pretty certain he didn't have blurred vision, numbness, tingling or shortness of breath, so that was all good.

"What are you smiling about?" said the umpteenth nurse who came to check his vital signs.

"Everything."

The old boy in the next bed moaned again, this time trying out "Help me" in a different octave. Sanjay wondered why nobody came to his aid.

The nurse who was writing in Sanjay's chart looked up. "He doesn't recognize his wife. She comes every day, but he complains she never visits. He says he'll divorce her when he gets out."

That was so sad. Sanjay didn't ever want to be that senile, yet that too was one of the infinite possibilities that lay ahead of him.

He would stay in the flat, even if it was crap coming home these days. Sometimes he thought Dainty was still there, in the corner of his eye. It could be on the sofa, in the hall. Anywhere really.

After washing her bowls, he had put them away in a kitchen cupboard. She hadn't touched the tuna chunks in delicious gravy. The food smelled so rank that he'd tipped it down the loo rather than put it in the bin. Though he put out clean water for her every day, she never used it. She preferred drinking from a tap. The one in the kitchen was her absolute favourite. She would wait patiently for Sanjay to turn it on to a slow trickle. Then she'd tilt her head just so, and glug happily. Afterwards, the fur on one side of her face would be all wet.

He found her hairs everywhere. A couple of whiskers too. Those were longer and coarser. There were a couple of claws too, by-products of her manicures on the Ikea sofa. In reality they were just the outer parts of the claw, of course, but they contained DNA, for sure. Sanjay had thought he'd have gladly stumped up ten grand or whatever it was to clone her.

He'd sat in the dark, listening to the Carpenters, thinking about his cat. No matter what they said, it was never going to be yesterday once more.

Later, much later, when the bowl of kiwis Sita had brought was nearly empty, and the pages of the notebook she'd brought were half full, and his drip had been removed, and he had managed to charge up his mobile, Sanjay began to think about the future.

This wasn't easy because Mum and Dad had arrived.

"*Beta*!" shrieked Mum, grabbing his face. "Are you all right, ha?"

Dad was pretty excited too. "God, Sanjay, the doctor says you have TB. Well, better than bloody cancer, yar. But these doctors. They are so bloody fucking useless, they really need good bollocking." Now he was threatening to sort out the entire medical profession. Of course it was an idle threat, because Dad's speciality was swearing and waving his finger, and then being as nice as pie to the person he'd just insulted.

Mum was more worried about Sanjay's stomach. "You should have had breakfast before clinic, *beta*. Then you would have been OK."

All that was happening just outside Sanjay's head. Inside was a tangle of urgent thoughts and feelings. And long lists of things to do and savour.

He would be home soon. Just now a doctor had said it might be tomorrow. Sanjay felt much better now, ready to resume the rhythm of life. A real life. Including women to shag.

He'd better call Ben too.

For the first time in days, Sanjay turned on his BlackBerry. There were loads of missed calls from

Sita two days ago, a message from Ben, and that weird text from Harriet about Dainty. He should have answered before, but he'd been too upset.

He pressed Reply now.

Chapter Thirty-Four

Geoff

Where's my fucking patient, went Geoff, though what he actually said was "Where's my patient?" He'd got into enough trouble already.

"Maybe she's gone to the toilet?" suggested Alexa the receptionist.

"Hrmph" said Geoff. Alexa was sweet and patients loved her. She gave them the benefit of the doubt, even when they nicked prescriptions from the desk and mugs from the kitchen. If half as many patients went to the surgery loo as Alexa claimed, the Guinness Book of Records people would have called round.

"Perhaps she popped out for a smoke" said Mina, who'd been a receptionist far longer.

The *No Smoking* sign outside didn't stop people. Some of them stubbed their ciggies on the sign itself, like Craig, who used its concrete post for support while coughing his guts out. In the consulting-room today, Geoff had doled out the usual treatment, but Craig held the prescription with nicotine-stained fingers and said he had no money left. Couldn't the doc do nuffiink else?

There was a scream from the toilet followed by the words "Oh my fucking God!"

"Is that my patient?" asked Geoff.

"I said she'd be in there" said Alexa.

Nobody heard what Mina said because there was another long scream then "Help me, for God's sake!"

"Well unlock the door then" said Geoff.

Another groan or two followed but the door wouldn't open no matter how hard Geoff pushed. He went to fetch the tool-kit used for odd jobs around the surgery, jobs that his partners, professing abject ignorance, always left to him.

"Are you in there, Kristyna?" Mina asked.

By way of reply there was another scream, just as Geoff prised open the door with a straight-blade screwdriver.

Kristyna was crouched over the loo, her hands between her legs as if she was trying to push back a blood-red grapefruit. Here, in this tiny room with its notices exhorting you to leave the room as you wished to find it, and to have a chlamydia test because you never knew, Kristyna's baby had chosen to make its entry into the world.

"No need to panic" said Geoff as convincingly as he could. Should he ask for the obstetric flying squad or just a regular ambulance? "Call an ambulance, Mina. Tell them it's a premature birth." Looking shocked, Mina left to phone. "Don't worry,

Kristyna. It will be fine." If forced to give a prognosis, Geoff would not have picked the word 'fine', but he had to reassure this young woman with blood streaming down her thighs. "We need to move you out of here." He appraised Kristyna and wondered which bit to pick up.

The practice nurse arrived with a dressing pack.

"Shall I boil a kettle?" asked Alexa.

Laymen always thought boiling lots of water was a must when birth was imminent. In reality it just kept busybodies occupied making tea. "Good idea" said Geoff.

"I couldn't find a cord clamp" said the nurse.

"Artery forceps will do." The important thing was getting Kristyna out. As long as she stayed in the toilet, he had no way of checking that the cord wasn't around the baby's neck, and no way to stop its head plopping into the toilet bowl either.

Kristyna looked at him desperately. "OK, hang onto my neck" he said, lifting her off the loo.

"I can't" she wailed.

"You have to" said the nurse, who had already put on latex gloves. "Don't worry, I'll be at the baby end."

Geoff dragged her off the toilet and carried her to the treatment room. As he negotiated the corridor, with the nurse shuffling alongside like a crab, Kristyna opened her eyes wide in alarm and pain. Heterochromia iridis, thought Geoff. He had never before noticed that her eyes were of two different colours. And she had blood on her nose. There was also blood on the corridor wall and the door-frame. Hell, the stuff was everywhere. Unlike his nurse, Geoff was wearing neither gloves nor plastic apron. But what did it matter as long as nobody died?

To vacate the treatment room, some old biddy with ear wax had to be bundled out.

Geoff placed Kristyna on the couch. "Not to worry, the ambulance won't be long" he said breathlessly as he gently checked the baby's neck. Kristyna screamed. Luckily the cord wasn't around the neck, but the baby looked horribly puce. Didn't they all look a bit like that when only their heads were out? If the placenta was still attached, and there was no reason it shouldn't be, then the baby would still be getting oxygen via the cord. He hoped so, anyway. Shit! It had been over 15 years since he'd delivered a baby.

"They said 10 minutes for the ambulance" reported Mina.

That was a hell of a long time, especially with another contraction coming. Nurse wheeled out a canister of Entonox and put a mask over Kristyna's face, telling her "Could be a lot worse, love. Once a patient had her baby in the carpark. In a VW Beetle, no less." They all laughed nervously, except for Kristyna, who gave a muffled cry through the gas mask.

This contraction was huge. And the shoulders seemed very broad for such a pre-term baby. Had Kristyna got jiggy with a prop forward? But he didn't have to worry about shoulder dystocia for long, because suddenly the whole body came flopping out like a huge fish on the bank.

"It's a boy. Isn't that marvellous?" said Geoff.

The marvellous thing was that the baby was alive. It was a very bloody vernix-covered boy, not very big, but troublesome nonetheless. Geoff recalled Davey's birth. The Lindo Wing with its tasteful décor, adjustable beds and, most vital of all, specialists on tap, couldn't have been more different to the surgery treatment room.

Kristyna was crying. The baby wasn't. "Come on, come on" muttered Geoff, willing him to breathe. And there was a load of blood. "Have we got Syntometrine, anyone?" he asked.

The nurse went and rummaged at length in a cupboard.

Geoff grabbed a rough hand towel that was draped over the radiator. God only knew where it had been. Rubbed with the towel, the baby began to stir. He breathed in deeply once then gave a cry.

Geoff let out that sigh. Kristyna sobbed. The staff held her hand.

"Here" said Geoff, offering up the baby in the towel. "Look at him."

Kristyna cried. "Oh my God, he's beautiful" she declared, even though he looked like a prune and his hair could have been a loo brush.

Something behind Geoff's eyeballs began to smart. Silly, really. All those births. Even more deaths, of course, because doctors ushered out more people than they ushered in. He fixated instead on the walking stick in the corner, left behind by the old biddy whose ears still needed syringing.

Kristyna was tugging at his arm. "What is your son's name, doctor?" she whispered.

"It's David."

"David" she repeated. "Yes. I will call my baby David."

As he held an oxygen mask over little baby David and watched him breathe, Geoff dabbed his eyes surreptitiously. He felt good, bloody good. It would be sad to leave the practice, but all the same the elation and the fear he had felt today only reinforced his decision.

Finally the ambulance turned up, then a midwife and later Kristyna's boyfriend in a paint-splattered beanie hat. By now there was quite a crowd of patients waiting to be seen. Time for him to get back to his consulting-room. Geoff strode through the waiting-room, feeling 10 feet tall.

Then a middle-aged woman stopped him midstride and tapped her wrist for emphasis. "My appointment was half past three, you know."

Karen

She stood as still as a mannequin while Geoff undressed her without haste. Her breathing almost stopped when he threw her bra aside and licked each nipple in turn.

This evening there was no hurry to rip each other's clothes off as soon as they got through the door. No racing upstairs. No rush at all, since Rose was staying the night with the kids.

Over a glass of wine, Geoff had told Karen about the birth in the surgery.

"You lead an exciting life" she said.

"It was more hair-raising than usual. But I enjoyed the adrenaline surge."

Karen felt a stab of envy. Geoff had a job that kept him busy, lately even at weekends. She hadn't realised GPs still had to work weekends.

Her own life had never been that eventful, probably never would be. A lot of it was down to having kids, of course. You couldn't go places if you were buried up to your neck in the sand, but that's what children did to you, and it was fun in its way.

There were times while the kids were small when she'd wonder when things were going to get better. The bottom line is that the good times were right here, right now.

That was especially true tonight. They had drained their glasses and gone up to bed. Geoff kissed her neck, then ran his tongue all the way down with exquisite slowness. She returned the favour.

"What do I taste like?"

"Salty."

There was just this. Just now. Karen had enough brainpower left to know why. It was passion rather than lust. And she was in a trance. Lips, ears, nipples, shoulders, buttocks, toes, fingertips, neck, ankles, belly. Every touch was heady. She breathed in the moment, letting it draw her deeper.

Tonight Geoff was harder, much harder, yet there was no urgency. Finally she crouched over him, savouring every second. By the time he found his way in, a shiver ran through her core and practically sent her into orbit.

Open-eyed, they moved together, giving and taking with each giant wave. She loved watching him right now, relished his sensuous mouth, his intense brown eyes, the lost look on his face. Had she ever felt this close to anyone before? As if to prove it, they erupted simultaneously, closing their eyes as their climax went on and on.

"See how happy you made me?" he said as they cuddled afterwards.

She nodded. "I feel the same. It was amazing." It seemed a bit inadequate to convey that all-over glow, but it was the only word she could find.

"It certainly was." He paused. "I didn't even take a tablet."

"What tablet?" They said medics were all junkies, prescribing themselves everything.

"Viagra. I've been needing them recently. Anyway, I ran out, so tonight I did without."

At least it wasn't coke or heroin. "Well, maybe you don't need Viagra. Do you know why you had trouble?" she asked as lightly as she knew how.

"I'm not sure. ED is really complex. Which is what medics always say when they don't have a clue."

"Well, I'm pleased." She smiled in the darkness. So she really meant something to him too.

The alarm clock, when it went off at silly o'clock, tore into her dreams. She removed his arm from across her chest.

"I've got to get home before the kids get up. Can't stay here for long" she said.

"I know." He brushed her shoulder with his lips as she dragged herself out of bed. "None of us is here for long."

That was so odd. Karen couldn't think what he meant. Then came the bombshell.

"I've got something to tell you. You know all those weekends I've been busy lately?"

Chapter Thirty-Five

Sanjay

In companionable silence, the two of them sat on the patio late into the night, until Dad suddenly burst out "Oh God! I have to do bloody washing-up now." But he didn't move just yet.

Sanjay was feeling so much more energetic. The night sweats had almost vanished. He enjoyed evenings again, even staying up late. The pain and fatigue that used to take over his body were no longer there either. Once, there had been dirty great piano wire threaded up and down his limbs. When had it gone? He wasn't sure.

"Well, I am going to kitchen" Dad said, finally heaving himself up. "To see what bloody mess is there, yar."

In a bit, Sanjay would get up to help too, even though Mum had said there was no need, *beta*. It was a party to celebrate her son's recovery, she insisted, not make him tired all over again.

Tonight there'd been a load of people that his parents couldn't have done without, which obviously included every single cousin, auntie and uncle. One of the uncles had shocked everyone and married a Chinese girl. The family was pretty cool about that. That was the thing about them. They had been in the UK long enough to be broad-minded, not long enough to turn into bigots.

There was also the disgraceful auntie that had been teaching Sanjay to dance cheek-to-cheek since he was about nine. She always reminded him that she had a beautiful daughter just right for him. But she still acted as if she wanted him for herself.

Mum had made all the usual things, like her special samosas and pakora, and then she'd really pushed the boat out with hundreds, or so it seemed, of sickly sweet desserts which all tasted exactly the same, the only difference being that some had chopped pistachios on top. She urged Sanjay to eat them, reminding him what happened to him when he hadn't eaten before his hospital appointment.

There had been booze, of course, because that's what British people served. For over six hours, everyone acted completely hammered even though barely two bottles of wine had gone.

They'd had some background music, but nobody could hear it above the din of at least a dozen simultaneous conversations. In Sanjay's view, this was just as well. Dad had chosen a very English CD, without realising that Diana Krall was Canadian and a gay icon.

Sita pranced around in some new get-up that gave Lady Gaga a run for her money. "That's a most unusual hat" guests kept saying about the purple and red thing perched on Sita's head like a diseased parrot.

"It's not a hat" explained Sita. "It's a fascinator."

And the aunties and uncles nodded and wobbled their heads, and agreed it was most fascinating, isn't it.

It would have been great had Harriet been here too, but she'd told Sanjay she wasn't ready yet. At least things were progressing. He looked forward to her finally moving out of the flat she shared with Simon, although she still hadn't decided where to go. He wasn't going to ask her to move in. There were things he wasn't ready for either.

Obviously she'd been shocked to hear from him. He had phoned to assure her he wasn't texting from beyond the grave. "I know that!" Harriet had said. "But still."

"Besides, I bet there's no signal in hell. And the bollocking BlackBerry would melt in the flames" Sanjay added.

She had been really sorry to hear about Dainty. "I never met her. She sounded really sweet."

True, she was sweet. And a bit icky, like those inedible desserts, thought Sanjay. "Yeah. I really loved that cat. She could be cantankerous and she threw up, but she was very affectionate." Sometimes she still had a little smear of sick around her chops when she'd come over and purr on Sanjay's neck. But he didn't tell people that, not even Harriet.

It was a relief to be getting better. Bollocks! The word 'relief' barely covered it. Sanjay found that his new diagnosis took a lot of explaining. How could the medics have got it so badly wrong? And what had made the doctors review his case? Apparently one of the research fellows had started going through all the cases diagnosed in the last three years, Sanjay had been told. He guessed that made sense.

"But that is what doctors want you to believe, *beta*!" Dad had cried.

He'd had to talk Dad out of suing the hospital, the doctors, the NHS itself. "Dad, I've had an explanation, I've had a personal apology, and a written one too. And I've got my life back. Why would I want to spend it making lawyers rich?"

Other family members thought he should sue too, and pressed on him the names of various brilliant lawyers they knew, to whom they were all distantly related. Randy Auntie's husband took him aside in the kitchen to whisper urgently. "You can get £20,000 for cock-up like this, Sanjay."

For now, Sanjay had no intention of pursuing anything through the courts. Just this minute, he was revelling in having his life back.

Getting your life back. That was what it was about.

Ben had been there tonight, scrubbed and shaved, not looking bad at all. Standing up, he looked as tall as ever. The infection was under control, he told Sanjay, and he was going to get more rehab.

"Have you got your pulling pants on then?" Sanjay had asked.

Ben leaned confidentially towards Sanjay and gave his trademark lop-sided smile. "Mate" he said, patting his camo trousers. "My C95s are so my pulling trousers now."

This evening, two young sons of one of the aunties were hanging on Ben's every word.

Bollocks, thought Sanjay. He hoped to God that Kiran and Pradeep wouldn't enlist. He'd have to have a word with them later. And if that didn't work, he'd talk to their parents. At least Ben had changed his tune a bit lately. He'd stopped fantasizing about going back to Afghan and said he'd quite like a desk job after all. Grinning, he explained that he'd meet more women in an office.

Sanjay picked up a tray and circulated with another batch of miniature bhajis, eating five of them on his way round the room. His appetite was back, big-time. As he paused by the window, Randy Auntie pinched his cheek again. Thank God it was the cheek on his face this time.

Escaping neatly from her with his tray, Sanjay noticed one of his cousins standing about two feet from Ben. She was one of the south London contingent, born when Sanjay was about eight. He couldn't remember her name just now, but she had dead straight hair down to her waist and a sparkly little stud in one nostril. Now she was smiling shyly in Ben's direction. She was too young for him. But hey, maybe those really were his pulling trousers.

Chapter Thirty-Six

A few months later

Dorottya

Finally the Malév plane was taxiing towards the stand. Passengers champed at the bit, fiddling with the seatbelts that had to stay on till the aircraft came to a complete stop outside the terminal building but rarely did. While some turned on their mobiles or adjusted their watches, Dorottya got out a small mirror and reapplied her trademark red lipstick. She turned to smile at the passenger next to her even though she did not remotely fancy the sad and slightly sweaty man who had occupied the seat for nearly three hours. He was probably already imagining her horizontal. No doubt his pathetic little penis was upright, dribbling in anticipation of what he would never have.

Men – ha! Still, she knew she looked good. It had been a smart idea to max out Roger's credit card on the expensive short hair-do that required no more than a flick of her head to keep at its best. Not to mention all the other things that cost money and were needed for her get-away.

Behind her she'd left no note, no hints at all. Just a book by Baroness Emmuska Orczy for Roger's oldest daughter, the nice one. Dorottya hoped she would enjoy reading the exploits of the Scarlet Pimpernel, even if *I Will Repay* was perhaps not the most appropriate volume in the circumstances.

Dorottya's mobile had had to be left behind. People could trace you on that.

Only in the arrivals hall at Ferihegy did she get the faintest attack of tremor. It was just the effect of the flight, she told herself, plus the lack of decent food, and the mind-blowing banality of the in-flight magazine.

She headed for the phone boxes on wobbly legs. It had been a turbulent flight, that was all. Her hands shook as she got out the worn piece of paper, wrapped around that other most precious belonging, Roger's Visa card. Was it too much to ask that Rita would be the same after all this time?

Michael

Michael had identified another speed-dating evening. A fresh start. This time he would not make the same mistakes as last, though, truth be told, it was hard to break the routines he had built up. Where would he be without routine?

He turned off the skin-flick in time to print off his forms and then to despatch a Granny Smith and a hunk of cheddar before going out.

He cut the cheese into little yellow cubes of almost exactly the same size. It was easy now, since he had been doing this for so long. Unfortunately one of the cubes was not quite even. He lopped off one corner angrily and tossed it into the bin.

Then he cut the apple into segments, again making sure they were as identical as could be. There were now the same number of pieces of apple as there were cheese. This pleased him more than anything else he had achieved all week. He undid his flies to celebrate.

Dan

Deep within the steam and noise, Dan stirred the stockpot while adding chopped fennel. Perfect with hake. He added a little more, telling himself there was no need to be so parsimonious.

Cool word, parsimonious. Even though it had nothing to do with parsley.

Already it had been three weeks and he felt at one with the kitchen. The equipment. The routines. Even the other staff.

Fuck! He'd burnt his thumb on the side of the pan. As he ran cold water over it, he realized he had not thought of Maxy in a long while. Maybe he didn't need counselling after all. Laure had offered to fund it, but Dan intended to pay for it himself, if he needed it, however long it took. The last thing he wanted to do was shaft her. Well, not in that way.

He wasn't a cadger or a thief, he told himself. Except for that time he'd nicked a leather belt when he first came out of clink. Would he have pulled someone as classy as Laure had he been badly dressed that night at the Jacaranda? He had no idea. Meeting people was so stochastic (his word of the day). Just showed what could happen in three minutes.

Of course, what Dan really wanted was probably impossible. A family would be amazing but it was probably too much to ask. Laure was such a career-person. Anyway, Dan had had more second chances than most. Best not be greedy.

Christ, chef was throwing another wobbly. Came with the territory, thought Dan. He wasn't a bad bugger, was chef. You learned a fuck of a lot from him.

Dan turned off the tap. Perhaps one day he would have his own restaurant. For now, it was good to be free. To have work. And the love of a good woman.

Scrap that. Not a good woman, but a woman so amazing that he could not have even dreamed her up.

Yet for all her elegance and education (and his own lack of both), they were very similar. In some ways, anyway. He dried his hands and examined his thumb, wondering if he needed a plaster.

Fuck it, everyone was the same under the skin. All of us.

Except Maxy, obviously.

Laure

In the sandwich shop, Laure bypassed her usual chicken, bacon and avocado. Today she could barely stand the thought of it. She chose egg and cress instead.

Thanks to Dan's cooking, she ate pretty well these days. Now she rarely had sandwiches for both lunch and dinner.

It was bizarre letting him into her life. After their first few days together, Laure wondered if she was supposed to say 'That was nice. Bye now.' Leaving the party early was often a good idea, in her experience. It saved a lot of awkwardness.

She was glad she hadn't said that this time. Instead she had gently mentioned something about taking things one step at a time. Dan had nodded sagely and replied that Athens hadn't been built in a day.

Now she'd talked to most of her friends about him. "So what's he like?" they'd asked.

"Tall. Slim. Bald."

"What does he do?"

"He works in a garden centre." Cue explosions of mirth. Or, on occasion, a shocked silence followed by the predictable "Oh well. As long as he makes you happy."

Yes, he made her happy. And those friends that had actually met him thought him charming, especially when they heard he now worked in a good restaurant.

She carried her little paper bag with the egg and cress sandwich and an apple juice back out of the shop. There was one thing she had to do on the way back to the office.

Approaching Soho Square, Laure saw a grating in the road. She dropped the PAYG SIM into it and watched the little gold chip as it disappeared.

In the lift she felt a bit nauseous. She would take care to hide her sicky headache and her bloating. Nothing would have annoyed her more than to give her colleagues ammunition to make a personal remark, especially not a sexist one about premenstrual tension. Perversely, this was exactly the type of remark favoured by all the lawyers she knew.

She had already taken two paracetamol before leaving her desk. So far they had done nothing. Usually she drank coffee with it, to make the painkiller work more quickly, but she had gone right off coffee and tea.

Karen

Karen took a couple of pegs out of the peg-bag that Ashley made her last Christmas out of a wonky hanger and a T-shirt. She began to hang out the teatowels on the line, then changed her mind because it was a waste of time. Most domesticity was.

Even so, she thought as she heaved the washing-basket back inside, these were not wasted years. She only had to look at the kids when they were asleep, ideally before they wet the bed or got up for a snack, to see that. But it was still curious the way things had worked out, like taking an unintended turning in the Hampton Court maze.

Motherhood changed you beyond belief. The other day Karen had caught herself smiling at a dog outside Argos. A dog, for God's sake! She didn't even like dogs. It just showed that mothers could empathize with anything.

As Karen dumped the washing on the chaos of the kitchen table, Rose popped in for a cup of tea, swearing that she'd never been this parched. "When do you start?" she asked, plopping in a Canderel into her mug.

"September" said Karen. "Not long now."

"Lucky you. But won't you get sick of being with kids all the time?"

Karen put down her mug on the sticky table. "For a few hours a day I can easily put up with other people's, especially with 12 weeks holiday a year. Want another cup?"

Rose did. "You know, I'd consider doing an education degree too if there were more good-looking male teachers. Anyway. What about your doctor chap?"

Karen shrugged as casually as she knew how. When Geoff came back in a few months, maybe they could hook up again. That might be nice. If he was still the same person, which wasn't a foregone conclusion. Everyone knew what war did to people. "I don't know. I really don't."

"Trust you to find another man who needs to go off to find himself." Rose stirred her tea. "I thought you two had been getting on really well."

"I did too. But you can't always tell, can you?" At this point Karen wasn't sure she would date for a while. But yes, she would miss the sex.

"Well" Rose finally said, scraping back the kitchen chair, "if you haven't got anything juicy to tell me, I suppose I'd better get back to the ironing."

"Enjoy."

Rose pulled a face. "Chance would be a fine thing."

Karen shoved all the washing into the dryer and turned the dial to 50 minutes. That would cook the lot.

In the living-room Edward was playing with a doll that used to be Charlotte's, while Ashley and Damon argued about the correct names for plastic dinosaurs. From the dining-room there were muffled thuds. Charlotte's music practice was going a lot better now that she had a mini electronic drum kit. With headphones, so the noise wouldn't send Karen crazy or drive out the neighbours.

There were just the five of them again. Thomas finally went back to his floozy, though he still swore that Karen was his best friend ever. That was because she was the mother of his children. It was also because he'd need a bed for the night when his woman turfed him out again.

Karen wondered if she should do more washing. But the tunic she had on had a forgiving print, and she could hardly see a trace of Bolognese sauce. So she sat down and went back to her Sudoku. In many ways it was better than a one-night stand because you didn't need a baby-sitter.

Suddenly Ashley shouted "I am so not a dick-head!"

There was enough time for Karen to enter another line before Ashley came in and said "Damon just called me a dick-head! Mummy, what's a dick-head?"

Geoff

The cabin lights were dimming as Geoff strapped his helmet on. This was it. You lived and died by your choices. As did your patients, of course.

He had learned how to breathe and run inside full body-armour, how to triage and how to set up an intra-osseous drip, but if he was going to fix people there was still much more to learn. Names, however, wouldn't be a problem for a while. Everyone had their name on their right breast, as well as on the front of their helmet. And ultimately on their dog-tags.

In the cabin black-out, which was essential on approach in case a ground-to-air got lucky, Geoff could barely see the lad next to him. The kid had stopped talking now. For at least half the flight from Brize, he had bored the arse off everyone with descriptions of the ways in which he was going to give the Taliban serious grief. Now that they were nearing Kandahar, the squaddie's fear was as pungent as his bravado had been earlier.

Strange to think that Davey had flown over this hostile land on his way to Australia. Once on the ground, Geoff's own view of the country was going to be completely different. But already his view of the world had changed since joining up. The army had shaken up his synapses.

Of course, some things did not change. Geoff shut his eyes and offered up a silent promise to be back for Davey before long.

Please God.

Insha'Allah.

Harriet

Harriet installed herself at her favourite table, which was perfectly positioned within reach of an electrical socket and a cappuccino. It would be ages before the coffee was cool enough to drink. By then she'd have done at least 1,000 words, half her target for the day. Get it all down, she told herself. Critical editing would come later. Harriet re-read her latest para with growing satisfaction, and thought that yes, Starbucks was definitely her workplace of the year. Well, this year, anyway.

She liked Starbucks and, as Simon would have put it, everything it stood for. To Harriet it stood for a space of her own.

When all was said and done, there hadn't been much to pack up. Harriet left with two suitcases, a couple of boxes of books and her laptop. The folders full of press releases and drawers crammed with free samples all went in the bin. She saw no need to hang onto umpteen bottles of cleanser, canisters of fake tan and bottles of various head-lice treatments. All along, Simon had been right about the mountains of freebies and brochures. No doubt he also knew all there was to know about viola construction in 18th century Austria. It was just that he was wrong about practically everything else.

Harriet had signed a letter agreeing on how much she needed to pay Simon back. On the day, she left the key on the glass table as promised. It made hardly a sound.

Was this all she had to show for eight years with Simon, she wondered as she lugged her things down to the waiting car. But, she reassured herself, there were benefits to travelling light.

Harriet would never forget the jolt of hearing from Sanjay. As his name appeared on her mobile, she prepared herself for an agonizing conversation with a bereaved relative. Maybe even his mother. What the hell could one say to someone who'd lost their child?

"Hey, Harriet. It's me, Sanjay."

Her heart did a somersault.

"Are you there? Bollocks, don't blow me off. You're the one who got in touch with me, remember."

This was impossible. "I thought you were dead" she blurted out. It sounded dreadful.

"Yeah, well, that's not going to happen for a while now. If you want to hear the news, I think you'd better sit down."

Now Harriet glanced out of the window. Outside Starbucks there was a traffic warden, keeping a predatory eye on the van that was about to be there fractionally longer than loading ought to take. Outside Tesco Metro, a lad sold the *Big Issue*. Harriet wondered where he was sleeping that night.

She felt lucky. Already she had been at Virginia's several weeks, paying token rent for the spare room. A work contact, Virginia was generous in every way, but Harriet didn't want to impose.

Sanjay kept asking if she would move in with him. He was much better now. Gaining weight, now handsome as well as funny. An irresistible combination, thought Harriet, but she told him it was far too soon for a huge step like that.

His flat, with its catalogued CDs by dead musicians, its 40" flat-screen TV, the occasional cat-hairs still on the sofa, and the plants doing their best to die in the corner, was his home, not hers, even if she did spend a lot of time there. Moving in might come one day, but she wasn't going to make the same mistakes she had made with Simon.

"Instead of settling down right away," she told Sanjay, "maybe you should see other people. What with being cured now and everything." She hadn't specifically mentioned Shelley Ritchie, though she was still on Harriet's mind. When she'd said this,

Sanjay had nodded, apparently taking it on board, but she hoped that he wouldn't act on the suggestion.

Today Harriet had brought her own mug. Starbucks charged less if you used your own. She sipped the rest of the cappuccino and let her fingers trace the embossed slogan on the side: *A home is not a home without a cat.* Sighing, because it was true, she put down the mug and bashed out another 155 words of her novel.

The Jacaranda had the longest zinc bar in Marylebone. Occupying the lower two floors of a Georgian building, the restaurant was surrounded by upmarket grocers, specialist bookshops, funky gadget stores, designer boutiques and a couple of charity shops which took in a lot of designer cast-offs. Despite there being more cafés, patisseries and restaurants than anyone could possibly need, they were always full of customers lured by the aroma of warm bread and freshly ground coffee. Marylebone was very much the place to be, especially if you had nothing very much to do.

Using the outside stairwell, she went straight down to the bar on the lower ground floor. Inside, the walls were wood-panelled, and the famous bar would have caught her eye even without the pink fluorescent sign above it that said, elegantly yet superfluously, BAR.

A young woman in a flapper dress and pearls busied herself ticking people's names off a list.

Now that Harriet was free of Simon, she knew that she would not delete the whole page later. The title was as yet undecided, but the dedication was certain.

For Sanjay.

Sanjay

Bollocks! The flat was a complete tip, Sanjay saw as soon as he opened the door. He had some mega tidying to do.

In the living-room, it looked like Shelley had barely moved all day. The lazy-bones had probably spent it on the sofa, eyes closed, blissfully unaware of the mess around her.

Even now that Sanjay was home from work, she was still dozing.

"Come on" Sanjay wheedled. "Are you going to lie there till Harriet turns up?" By way of response, Shelley stretched out one leg, exhaling slowly with the sheer pleasure of being alive. Hard to believe looking at her now that she was utterly wild last night.

He bent down to kiss Shelley gently on the top of her head. Then he tickled her right in the middle of her furry tummy, where the patches of ginger and black blended to form the most perfect tortoiseshell pattern he had ever seen.

THE END

A MESSAGE FROM THE AUTHOR:

If you enjoyed reading ONE NIGHT AT THE JACARANDA, please would you take just a moment to leave a review on Amazon or your favourite book-reading site? I'd really appreciate it. Thank you.

You can keep in touch with more of my writing on my blog pillsandpillowtalk.com.

Acknowledgments:

My thanks go to all the wonderful people who've helped or encouraged to write this book, among them Tara Gladden, Catriona Graham, Ian Jacklin, Sally Mason, Martel Maxwell, Pixie McKenna, Gill Pountain, Chris Webber, Amy Waite and Catherine Clarke at Felicity Bryan Agency, and of course my husband Jeremy Grundy. It's usual to describe the spouse as long-suffering, but we only married in 2013.

About the author:

Carol Cooper has written for a long time, starting in childhood with stories about witches who shouldn't have smoked in bed. Her literary career was interrupted by her medical studies. She graduated from Cambridge University and is now a doctor and writer living in London. Her three sons inspired most of her health and parenting books. She is also a columnist for *The Sun* newspaper.

Printed in Great Britain
by Amazon.co.uk, Ltd.,
Marston Gate.